Song of the Selkie is an intensely experienced novel with a compelling narrative. Erica Yeoman has consummate ability to tell a great story in the tradition of Sir Walter Scott who plays a part in the novel.

The tender singing of the seals adds a surreal mystery to the tough realities of the story.

Wendy Robertson – Best-selling author.

This is a novel of two opposing songs, the chilling call of smugglers whose livelihood depends on the sea's angry mood and the song of the selkie and lighthouse builders who cry their warning in the fog.

Avril Joy – Prize-winning author.

To Jan
Best Wishes
Erica Yeoman.

Song of the Selkie

by

Erica Yeoman

Book cover from an original painting by the author.

COPYRIGHT © Erica Yeoman 2014.

All rights reserved. Erica Yeoman has asserted her right under the Copyright, Designs and Patent Act 1988 to be identified as the author of this work.

This book may not be reproduced in whole or in part, stored in a retrieval system, or transmitted in any form or by any means electronic, mechanical or other, without written permission from the publisher, except by a reviewer, who may quote brief passages in a review.

Certain characters in this book do exist in history. Though I have imagined their actions and reactions within this novel I have stayed as close as possible to the known facts.

The Selkie's Song.

I am a man upon the land
I am a selkie in the sea.

Traditional Orkney song.

From The Iliad

So to night wandering sailors
Pale with fears
Wide 'oer the watery wastes
A light appears,
Which on the far-seen
Mountain blazing high,
Streams from some lovely
Watch-tower to the sky.

(Translation by POPE 1720)

FOR MIKE.

THANKS
to

Pippa and Catie for their expertise.
Audrey, Elspeth and Lynne for Edinburgh.
Tommy for East Coast tales.

About the author

Erica Yeoman draws inspiration for her writing and painting from the wind-swept beaches and rugged Cheviot Hills of Northumberland.

As an historical geographer, she is fascinated by Man's influence on the land. For Erica, time and place produce their own characters and it is of little wonder that her favourite author is Thomas Hardy. Folklore and fact, people real and imaginary, interweave her historical romances with deeply believable characters.

Erica taught in Edinburgh before moving to Northumberland where she lives with her husband and cocker spaniel.

Her first, novel, 'DEVIL'S DROVE' was published in 2010 by Roomtowrite - www.roomtowrite.co.uk

Her second novel, 'SHADES of INNOCENCE' was published in 2012.

Her latest novel, 'SONG of the SELKIE', written in 2014, continues the adventures of **Kitty Macnab** first seen in 'DEVIL'S DROVE'.

Part one

One

'What am I doing here? Why on earth did I come back? Questions without answer spike her sleepless state.

How can she sleep when she knows he will come? She lies rigid, the night hours suspended like the rhythm of her breath. Wide-awake eyes scan the dark line beneath the bedroom door. She's alert for the warning light as a lone sailor fearing shipwreck on a hostile shore.

And there it is. Just as Kitty had expected; under the sill a candle flickers in an uncertain draught. Her breath is a sudden gust as though to blow it out, but the yellow flame beams again its menace. And then it is gone, a lighthouse flash in the country dark made intense by the night chill. There one minute, gone the next as feet continue on beyond her door.

No lift of the sneck on the door, no figure beside her bed. Once more the dark is blanket-thick… where is the light of dawn? It cannot be far off. She'd left the curtains undrawn to catch the first glimpse. Kitty sighed, drapes at the window! They'll be a luxury to be paid for sooner or later! Wasn't everything in life added-up and written on a slate?

She swung her legs over the side of the bed and made for the window,

'But there are my hills! Surely here I can be happy again?'

Pre-dawn frost patterned the panes in fanciful shapes. She rubbed the cold glass but -inside and out- it clung on defiantly. She could see nothing, but she had no need, out there lay the Cheviot Hills in their familiar outline. She breathed in deeply, straining for the old moorland smell; but John

Armstrong *glassed* his windows! There was no clinging aroma of early morning grass and heather smeared by the smell and feel of frost.

In the past she would have lifted the latch of her father's cottage door and in a few steps would have been out on the hillside. Now a staircase and corridor hindered escape from this large and unfamiliar house. How could she be thinking of that already?'

Shivering, she retreated back to the comfort of the blankets. John Armstrong provided a good bed, luxury indeed to have a sheet as bedfellow! What had she expected? Certainly not her own space alone in a double bed!

Beyond her door on the other side of the passage, baby Katharine slept alone. The busy breathing that had interrupted Kitty's slumbers for the past year did so no longer. She strained to hear the sound of peevish cries through the thick walls. There was silence. Then surely little Katherine slumbered untroubled, accepting her new home with innocence and trust. She was too young to know anything about bills on slates. And in yet another room John Armstrong's head lay on his own pillow!

Of course he'd be tired after the journey. Wasn't he just a few year's short of her father's age? And their journey had been ponderous, slowed by her worldly possessions- one year old child, a sack with their change of clothes and a wooden replica of one of his Majesty's Men of War. All that had been salvaged from the wreck of her previous life.

She stretched again knowing that there would be no answering grope of a man's hungry hands. What bliss. She sighed and closed her eyes- time for another few hours of sleep- something she had learned to savour in her years of ill-use.

In the morning, relieved to find the house empty, she trod the stone-flags to the front door and stood gazing out at the scene before her. A rock- coloured grouse shot into the air in startled protest. Her eyes followed its flustered flight and then its effortless glide to a new refuge. 'How easy it is for you... if only I had wings.' she murmured.

Her eyes levelled to the distant hills of this northern corner of England shadowed by Scotland. A few steps and she could be out in the pale, winter -dry grass. Instead she turned back into the house and slammed the door behind her. The year away had been a long one.

Two

'What yer deein' here, Kitty?' The question was from the lips of the man who had brought her back to Barraburn.

Mid-morning, and benefactor Armstrong came striding into the kitchen, outer garments and boots mud-spattered, black hair dishevelled, his ruddy face pinched by the perfidy of April. House-bound Kitty, looking pale and tired in contrast, sought to tidy her hair, but it lay in neat coils about her oval face. She bent and smoothed the hair from her little daughter's face and got a shriek of protest. Kitty flashed her most arresting smile at the newcomer she had combed her stray locks for his return... it would be his expectation.

'What yer deein in the kitchen, Kitty?'

The newcomer's voice was brusque, his wrinkled forehead concertinered into a deep frown. He was a large crag of a man, etched by the winds and storms of the wild landscape he called home. Large hands and feet spoke of sheep-farmer and peasant stock but his uncultured appearance was softened by the cut of his clothes. They were the best that money could buy, jerkin and breeches, purchased in the city of Newcastle fifty miles to the south and befitting this local Magistrate of Coquetdale.

'Why yer lurkin' here?' His piercing look had her back in his courtroom.

Kitty arched her dark eyebrows and the exaggerated gesture made her look innocent. Kitty Macnab knew only too well the benefit of hiding her rebellious streak with a coating of incomprehension.

'I thought to make myself busy... the child needs attention.' Though half his size, she looked up to meet his gaze. No one overawed Kitty Macnab for long, whatever their status, and she frowned at the temper of the man. Only two days before, he had offered her a home. Whatever his reasons, whatever hers, she'd had little choice but to take the offer. Was he already regretting his words as much as she regretted the accepting?

Yet she had known there could be no permanent place for her and her baby in the bachelor manse of Pastor Gregory, stifled by his pious morality after their illicit love-making. He had not been father to her child. Perhaps that would have been more acceptable than the hateful truth. Even if the paternity had been Magistrate Armstrong's it would have been greeted with a shrug of the shoulders by his fellow farmers!

Impulse had returned her here to the hill country where she belonged and where *surely* her child would be accepted. It was wild and remote and she'd grown up with Newcastle bastards and their snivelling poverty. She had been forced to stand on her own two feet since the age of fourteen; she had made choices and stuck by them. Now with the child to consider she was as irresolute as the month of April; for in this upland place it was neither winter nor summer.

'Yer place is not in the kitchen.'

'So where *is* my place?' she looked him straight in the eye. Only a few hours ago, she'd been relieved to see his light go beyond her bedroom door.

His silence was long, her words peevish, 'I am in the kitchen for the child is in need of milk and there is none to be had.' She bent to her daughter clinging at her skirts, but the child struggled against her embrace and let out a piercing cry.

Kitty grimaced, 'Hush, what a racket,' she knew well enough small children and bachelors did not go well together. Even being the mother tried the patience.

'This is na place for the bairn.' Magistrate Armstrong gesticulated at the bare stone walls and the stone flags whose chill rose to ankle height. A desultory fire hovered in the fireplace, lit earlier by some unknown hand. Now it made little impact on heat or light in the large, gloomy room.

'Yer're expected in the parlour, Kitty.' He turned to the door and his voice sharpened, 'But without the child this time. Where is the woman when she is needed?' His voice boomed as on open moorland and the startled child wailed again.

'Whist, baby, no need for tears,' Kitty swooped up her daughter and began to rock backwards and forwards in a desperate attempt to divert the little girl. But the screaming continued. Reluctantly, she put the child down on the floor and left, closing the door on the indignation and followed Armstrong.

The wails of protest were lost behind two stout doors. Hill farmhouses relied on solid oak to seal against draught and unwanted noise. Kitty closed the parlour door behind her, straightened her back and leant against the reassurance of the wood. Two men had risen to their feet and the elder man held out his hand in greeting.

'Sir Walter,' John Armstrong put out his hand toward Kitty, but he did not touch her, 'May I introduce my ward, Miss Kitty Macnab.' He had lost his Northumbrian burr!

'Ward!' Kitty noted the introduction. Whatever her role at Barraburn, it was not to be revealed to the present company.

'Please excuse Kitty that she was not here to greet you. Her head was deep in a book and she did not hear our arrival.' Armstrong's put-on voice was city-correct. The shorter, stouter of their two visitors let out an exclamation of pleasure and Kitty smiled, her responsive brown eyes warming to the stranger. He was grey-headed but his facial hair had a reddish tinge still, his weather-beaten face told of country living though more refined than that of his host. But it was the speckled pupils of his eyes that held her gaze. They were kindly and bursting with curiosity.

'So you are a bookworm, young lady? Farmer Armstrong, I would see your library!'

Kitty's smile became broader. She guessed countryman Armstrong had no need for such a room, his long nights spent in the illicit drinking den that was Slymefoot half a mile up the Coquet valley. It was there she'd come to know and fear the man who was now her so-called 'guardian'.

The stranger advanced toward her, 'Miss Macnab, there is no better pastime. When I was but a young lad I read the great novels of Smollet and Fielding, I even forgot dinner one day I was so deep in a book.'

As he spoke, their visitor glanced down at her hands and it was there for all to see, they did not belong to a novel-reading lady. Interest and amusement creased his face as he shot her a shy sidelong glance. Kitty made no reply; her lack of education for ever a regret, her ignorance something to hide if she possibly could.

'There - there is surely no better place to get lost, would you not agree Miss Macnab than in a book.' The man's soft Scottish burr was more pronounced as he sought to place her at her ease.

Kitty grinned. 'I dare to disagree, Sir.'

The silent Armstrong beside her stiffened, 'Kitty, perhaps you...' but the girl interrupted, her eyes returning the enthusiasm of their visitor, her sallow cheeks flushed.

'I believe the best place on earth is a valley, deep in these hills, lying in the grass, hearing nothing but the wind and the skylark, and seeing no person but a boggle from the past.' She was laughing now in her returning passion for her homeland, slipping easily into the local word for a ghost. Yes this was the landscape she had always loved... only events had made her see it differently.

The enthusiastic stranger laughed. 'Aye boggles haunt both sides of the border.' So he also knew the word. Yet though his stature spoke of country life, there was an aura of sophistication not seen in these parts. Perhaps, Kitty surmised he was some land owner from over the border that Armstrong sought to impress.

'I cannot argue with your sentiments, young lady, when I was a laddie my Aunt Janet used to read stories to me seated at our parlour window. It began my love of the Borders, both in Scotland and England.' He spread his large hands in an inclusive gesture, 'But might I suggest that my book of border tales and ballads would make an admirable companion and would not upset your ghosts.'

Kitty laughed, 'I have no need of such tales I can hear such stories on the breeze.'

'Indeed.' The exclamation of delight from her interrogator was heart-felt and Kitty sensed the tension in Armstrong subsiding as he gestured to Sir Walter.

'Kitty, enough, we have stood too long. You must be tired after your travels, Sir Walter, may I offer refreshment.' He motioned to his guest to be seated and the older man turned to the hearth and subsided with a satisfied sigh beside the roaring fire. Kitty noted that their visitor was lame and that he moved stiffly. Rheumatism frequented houses both north and south of the border.

'So, Armstrong, I thought you to be a man of discernment and now I find you have a ward of equal merit.'

If only he knew! But she'd long kept up a facade and now was not the time for uneasy truths. A canny tongue could see Magistrate Armstrong and his friends open up a new world for her and her bastard daughter. From the general atmosphere of the room she knew she had passed the first test.

'And Barraburn- do you have stories of hereabouts Miss Kitty?' Their visitor stretched out his lame leg before the parlour fire and Kitty was amused to see his polished boots had traces of mud whilst one was badly worn.

'The Wedders leap, have you heard of that, sir? Just a mile away on the Coquet, I...'

'Kitty, it is Sir Walter Scott who is the renowned story teller.' Armstrong interrupted and Kitty's cheeks flamed.

'Did you say, Sir Walter Scott?'

'Aye, lass... have you read my work?'

'Ivanhoe is my favourite!' She remembered the only book she had ever possessed. 'Rebecca is *my* idea of a heroine!'

Scott looked gratified. 'What would you say, Olaf, is she your idea of a heroine?'

They all turned to Scott's companion and Armstrong looked concerned. 'My apologies, Mr Magson, I have been remiss in my welcome of you.'

Kitty noted the silent young man, he'd not expressed a single word since she'd entered the room and had stood first on one foot then the other. Tall and willowy, he was like a caged animal.

His hair was sandy brown, thick and wavy with an untidy tuft at the crown but it was his startling blue eyes that dominated his face. Now they looked blank and Kitty thought he's bored, anxious to be gone and felt her ready feeling of pique as he thrust out his hand, a sardonic smile on his lips. Who did he think he was? But his handshake was firm in spite of his reluctance, the palm of his hand smooth in contrast to a jagged white scar that ran from thumb to wrist. She thought he's as unsure as I am in such company.

Sir Walter smiled indulgently as he indicated his companion. 'My friend Olaf here would take issue with you about the most perfect place on earth, Miss Macnab. I would wager his would be no hidden hill cleft. Am I right, Olaf?' His voice was at once easy and friendly.

The young man nodded without hesitation. 'Hills obscure, one cannot see beyond the next spur.'

'So!' Kitty raised her eyebrows in elaborate surprise, 'Where would be your choice?'

'Out over the sea, where only the horizon stops the eye.' There was a glint of pleasure on his face.

'But in a sea of grass you can go on forever.'

'Have you no heard of ships, Miss Macnab? They do go beyond and over the horizon.' Olaf Magson's tone was contemptuous, his Scot's brogue thick in his disdain.

'Perhaps, I should explain Olaf comes from the Orkney Isles and therefore has the sea in his veins.' Scott chuckled. 'There is salt in his very pores. I swear if he took off his boots he would reveal webbed feet.'

'Aye,' the young man had the grace to laugh at his companion's words. 'Its aye for all Orcadians, we live where it is neither land nor sea; rocks at our front door, the tide at our back.'

Scott nodded his approval, 'Olaf above anyone knows the challenge of the sea.'

'Aye fishermen read the weather better than do farmers; don't their very lives depend on it?' The young man's eyes flashed, his words rose and fell in the rhythm of the northern isles that were his home. And again Scott's upper lip extended into a benevolent smile at the Orcadian's zeal.

'Tell them the story about the Mester ship, lad.' The arch storyteller beat his stick on the floor in encouragement, hitting his lame foot before it bounced off; and Kitty could see how the writer's shoe had become scuffed. 'Go on lad.'

The young man shrugged his shoulders and looking directly at Kitty, said, 'There was a great ship that sailed between our islands. The biggest you've ever seen. The skipper ordered a young man to go forrard, to tell the men to weigh anchor.' He paused for effect, 'When he returned he was a decrepit elderly creature.'

Olaf Magson's voice held no emotion and his words hung in the silence. Scott had a strange far away expression on his face and seemed elsewhere than in the Cheviot farmhouse. Kitty's amused laugh rang through the room. And Scott frowned.

'Young lady, the mester ship was so tall that when a sailor up in the crow's nest dropped his knife, it was rusty when it hit the deck.' The older man's words continued the myth.

Kitty looked from Scott to the young man, both were unsmiling as though they believed every word of the Orkney legend. And then Olaf gave her a slow, knowing wink.

'Enough,' Scott's eyes twinkled. 'Of sea or hills, what better place than my birth place Edinburgh? There can be no finer view than to stand on Calton Hill and see on one hand the Old Town and on the other the fine mansions of the New. Soon we shall be known as the Athens of the North and rightly so.'

'Aye, Sir Walter, I would agree with you there.' Armstrong had returned to the room with a tray filled with glasses and a bottle of whisky.' He seemed strangely at ease with the famous man.

'Miss Kitty, have you been to Edinburgh?'

'Sadly no, sir I've not had the pleasure.' Kitty smiled at the enquiry, now wholly captivated by the eminent writer. She could hardly believe that she sat at the feet of the best-known storyteller either side of the border and he waited on her words; besides his young companion had had more than enough of the attention with his taller than tall stories. Her adventures if dared tell could top his any day!

'I have not been to Edinburgh.' She said lamely.

'Then that should be rectified.' Walter Scott turned to his host and wagged his finger at him. 'John, you must promise to bring your ward to Scotland.'

Kitty interrupted, 'Oh, if it's Scotland you mean, I've been there many times.'

The famous Scot beamed, 'I'm glad to hear it, lassie. Where might I ask?'

Kitty looked at the man's thin, slightly bent legs. 'I think, sir on paths you will not have taken...'

Scott raised his eyebrows.

'...on the high smuggler routes that cross the border.'

Her words fell into the room and Scott half rose from his chair in surprise, 'How come, lassie?'

Armstrong interrupted, 'Kitty likes to tease.' His voice was disapproving

But Scott narrowed his eyes, studying the slight but well-made girl before him. 'Are your shoulders broad enough to carry the kegs of whisky on such paths?' He pursed his lips, 'Indeed Barraburn lies very close to the border.'

'Indeed. What better disguise for a smuggler than living in the home of the local magistrate?' Kitty lowered her eyes and looked demurely into her lap.

Scott exploded into a roar of approval, whilst Kitty could hear Armstrong swallowing his chagrin in an intake of breath.

'So then, lassie your next trip must be to Edinburgh. I have never had whisky delivered to my door by such an unlikely hand.' He turned to Armstrong, frowning at his host. 'Make sure you come with your ward, whisky smuggled by pretty girl and prominent magistrate would make a memorable tipple to swallow. Promise to come, young lady. It is something my wife and I shall anticipate.'

Kitty smiled. 'I cannot think of anything I would like better,' pleasure was written all over her face, 'b-but...' in the harmless fun she'd forgotten her daughter abandoned in the kitchen. A mother now, she was no longer free to roam as she pleased.

'Little Katharine?' Guilt flooded over her as farmer Armstrong shook his head.

'Your small sister is with the girl in the kitchen and is enjoying her crowdie. She comes to no harm I do assure you.'

He turned to Scott. 'Kitty and I shall visit Edinburgh at the first opportunity.' He paused, and then attempting to sound as flippant as his ward,

'Rest assured it will be on a dark moonless night.'

'Champion, man. Now then, Olaf we should not tally, we must return to Abbotsford, my new house nears completion but there is still much to do.' He rose stiffly and righted his footing before attempting the door. His limp was pronounced.

'Olaf, you have not answered my question. What do you think of her?'

'Whom do you mean, sir?'

'Why young Kitty, here, is she not your idea of a heroine?' Scott took hold of Kitty's hand in a show of warmth, 'Is she not a Diana Vernon?'

The young man laughed scornfully, 'It is well known that Rob Roy's heroine is your favourite female character and she is every reader's idea of goodness, beauty and brains. But…' Olaf's voice reflected his doubt. 'It is a likeness yet to be seen in Miss Macnab.'

Three

'I've got to get out...this house already feels my prison.' Kitty closed the door behind her and went to the river that thundered feet from the farmhouse. Here the Barra Burn downstream from Windy-guile joined the wide Coquet in a cacophony of noise. The turbulent water tumbled about the rocks in a discussion as playful as the one Kitty and story-teller Scott had just shared. She closed her eyes, jumped and landed midstream. Her thin boots took in the water, and she wriggled her toes in appreciation. She jumped again and achieved the bank.

The climb was steep out of the valley and at once there was the familiar mantle of the hills, wind in her hair, and the soft drizzle of rain. She raised her face so that she could feel the droplets explore her eyes, her cheeks her chin before dripping down on to her shawl. She was wet in minutes, and she was happy. Her morning reluctance to seek the hills was a million miles away.

Kitty's breathlessness revealed her year's exile in noisy gasps, and the sudden stitch in her side made her stop. The view she had but recently boasted of was only to be imagined in the encroaching mist that swirled about the hilltops. No matter, she knew the scene eyes open or shut. Smooth rounded tops cut by turbulent streams in steep narrow valleys, lay in every direction. They were blocked by spurs of land, but her feet like the water knew every escape route. Surely, Armstrong had brought her back to tread once more the high secret routes of this border country?

Was Walter Scott even now laughing at her preposterous boast of whisky-smuggling; this demure novel-reading lady resident in the comfortable home of Magistrate Armstrong? He had looked at her hands and his storyteller's insight had seen that here there was a story. But, surely not the one she told. Kitty laughed aloud, and the mist threw the laughter back at her. Her indiscretion had been worth it just for the look on Armstrong's face. If Scott had studied his host's expression at that moment he would have seen there was something worth the ferreting!

The mist swirled. There was no expansive view. Here, in the shrouding gloom, she was not likely to convince the young Orcadian of upland superiority when his need had been the wide horizons of the sea.

Olaf Magson...an intriguing young man. She peered into the mist as though, besides its echoing sound, it could mirror back Scott's companion. Beyond the sardonic smile and the ruddy-hued impatience there had been soft, blue eyes and a mouth that turned up at the corners in spite of his open contempt. That contempt had been saved for her; for the famous man there was respect, even affection. And Scott had returned it, the two men easy in their banter together.

The younger man's eyes on her had been a searchlight and she'd felt exposed. Could he really see her for what she was, that her teasing words were no jest? Yes, she thought petulantly, he knew I wasn't lying. He'd listened to her stories spun in an act of bravado and no doubt at this very moment he'd decided to laugh them to scorn in an attempt not to be trumped. That young Scot had also been out to impress!

If he could see through her then equally she could read him. An uncultured islander from Orkney with but a veneer of sophistication, how hard wrung she could only guess. He was a strange mixture of man of the world and a childlike love of his homeland myths.

She had set out to annoy Armstrong and she'd seen the throbbing-pulse in his neck as she'd teased his guests. The tough countryman had not been amused by her words, keen to maintain his border gentleman status. She should have known better. But she'd always loved to mock, even when there was little to laugh about and the young Orcadian had been pompous; now Sir Walter, had had a definite twinkle in his eye. He would not think her childish!

Childish…she thought of the sleeping child in her cot back in the farmstead dependant on the wits of her lone parent. What had she done to deserve such a mother? The unlooked-for product of a perverted union, poor child, Kitty's cheeks were moist though the rain had stopped. The mist was clearing so that landscape and unhappy reality stared her full in the face. What chance was there for either of them? Whore with bastard meant but one pre-ordained path to take.

For others, life was clear-cut from the outset. It was obvious Sir Walter came from a privileged home, and Olaf Magson, however humble his origins, they would not be of a scandalous nature she felt sure of that. What of John Armstrong? She knew nothing of his back- ground. Why had he offered a home to old friend, Jock Macnab's smuggler daughter encumbered now with child? Surely a backward step to return to the scene of her shame!

How the drinkers of Slymefoot must have sniggered into their dram's about the Macnabs and what went on behind the closed door of Wholehope illicit whisky still. It was not just illegal production of their favourite tipple and the outwitting of His Majesty's excise men. Oh no, it was what a father had done to his daughter. What had John Armstrong called the bairn… her sister? His words stated the cold hard facts. Kitty was both Mother *and* sister to the tainted child.

She walked blindly, like Cheviot sheep on well-trod path, so that she was not surprised when she saw the building lying below her. Where two streams met, the valley opened out in enough flat land to hold the alehouse.

'Coquet and Rowhope,' she said aloud, 'Slymefoot, where else would my footsteps lead? A den of iniquity is where

I belong. I should never have left.' An involuntary smile crossed her face. What fun she'd had here. It had made her life bearable in the times when she could escape the attentions of her groping father.

Smoke spiralled upward, thick and mist grey. She breathed in and caught the tell-tale aroma of peat. Only inside would she smell the whisky.

Silence met her. She could neither hear nor see anything in the unlit gloom. And then she saw them, the figures seated about the room, huddled black shapes that suddenly towered above her as to a man they rose to their feet.

'Still ever the gentlemen! Glad to see you get up when a lady enters the room.'

A snigger broke the silence, head high she faced them. Rob Shiel, Jed Dodds, Jo Robson, they were all there, shepherds, farmers, hill men; hard and uncouth, their natural reaction to a newcomer had brought them to their feet, no inbred courtesy.

'So if it ain't Kitty Macnab.' Rob Shiel echoed their surprise, and with her naming they resumed their seats, all except the speaker.

'You're back man!' He raised his eyebrows.

Kitty nodded, 'Why aye Rob, I couldn't keep away.'

He smirked, 'What a delightful surprise but Slymefoot's no vicarage drawing room,' he aped a posh accent, 'then that is for ladies.'

'So with good reason you'd agree why I didn't fit in,' Kitty kept the smile on her face. She was a match for any in this room. That had been her salvation.

'Come to the fire man, you're soaked to the skin.' Shiel's fingers twisted a dripping ringlet as he leered at her sodden blouse rounding her breasts.

'I've been plodging.' She pulled away from him; they had all seen her soaked at the end of her border forays. She was still the same old Kitty, but now she hated their ogling eyes. A blush crept from neck up to her forehead. And they stamped their simple delight.

A young man at the back of the room got to his feet and pushed his way to the front, intrigued by the girl with cascading black hair, wide-set eyes dark as peat and a provocative smile.

'Who's the lass, Shiel?' His brogue was broad Northumbrian, but she'd no difficulty in understanding his words or his interest. She jerked away from his rough hand on her bare arm and Shiel stepped between them.

'Leave her!' He barked his words and the lad retreated. 'Kitty, pet it's good to see you.' Rob Shiel, now master of his surprise, smiled, but his eyes were still wary. 'Good to see you can still get clarty boots. Have a dram with the lads?'

'Ta, Rob. It's good to be b-back.' She tossed her head and grinned back at him. She'd always liked him; the crack between them a harmless game. Still the same old Rob, straight forward, no nonsense hill-man, who feared nothing except for his wife. Kitty had always known how far to go when she flirted with the local shepherd.

Those days were over. She had changed. In the past she would have pushed past Shiel to the new young man, with a come-on quip to start the evening entertainment; it was obvious there was only one thing he wanted. Not that he would have got it, but she'd have enjoyed the pursuit. If Rob had to watch wife, she had to answer to her father. All knew Jock Macnab had a temper. Did they ever guess he'd wanted no other man's attention for his daughter because already, he violated his own flesh and blood?

She took the whisky from Shiel and nodded her thanks, it had always brought a deadening forgetfulness, and a bravado for the high paths, turning the excise men into a game of chance on the rock-strewn goat trails. Now as she sipped the moonshine she saw that there was a wariness about the room, eyes did not meet hers. How dare they? She drank a deep draught and choked at the well-remembered odour. It had ruined her life.

Jed Dodds shouted from the back of the room. 'Come on, pet can't you down it like you used tee? You were as good as any man here, better than some, eh Shiel?' All knew wife Jean also rationed his drink!

Rob Shiel grinned sheepishly and raised the clay hen full of their favourite tipple looking to give her more. The smooth outline of such a jug had been her constant companion over the border paths from Scotland to England and at hidden Wholehope she and her father had filled them. Daughter Katharine would never know the jug or what it carried.

She shook her head and placed her hand over her drink and there was a snigger of derision.

'Yer ain't living up to be Jock's daughter, the old sod.' Jed Dodds sneered. '*He* never said ner to drink…then he never said ner to owt!'

A roar of laughter shook the wattle walls and someone stamped their feet. She should never have come back.

'So we hear Magistrate Armstrong has taken the place of your faither?' There was a burst of ribald mirth.

Rob Shiel's eyes flamed. 'How dare yer, Dodds, yer bloody hypocrite! Everybody knars your missus has to sober you up of a Sunday morning to get yer to church in Rothbury, an' that's after she's turfed the maid from yer bed1' Shiel raised his fists to support his words. A table overturned in the stampede as men cleared space for the impromptu fight. They'd have a ringside seat for the entertainment.

The old Kitty would have stayed to see the outcome.

The new one sought the door.

The mist had cleared and a hazy sun polished the backs of the cuddies tethered outside awaiting their mounts. A faint steam rose from their coats, as patiently they pawed the ground, later they would find their own path home whatever the state of their rider. Here in this remote land the needs of life were basic, just a hidden drinking den and a steed who knew the way back to the family farmstead. Yes, Jean Shiel has more sense than most.

Back to Barraburn, Kitty took the path that clung to the river, her eyes fixed on the way ahead as it meandered this way and that beside the fast-flowing water. The Coquet had cut out the valley floor so that the path dropped gradually down to the sea. The going was easy, unlike her earlier hill climb and she walked briskly. By the end she was almost running. How long had she been away? It felt like forever. What of the bairn? How could she have left her so long?

Guilt kept pace beside her. Since feeding the child and putting her to her morning rest she'd given little thought to her daughter. But at Slymefoot she'd come face to face with reality and reality was bitter medicine, for inwardly she suffered an incurable guilt. She'd stumbled out of the drinking den addled by the unhappy truth that if pushed she would have denied her own daughter. How hard it was to face her shame.

When she reached the farmhouse she turned her back on the river leaving it to fall freely down to the sea and Olaf Magson's utopia. Here, in the hillside home of Magistrate Armstrong, lay her fettered duty.

The kitchen door was ajar so that she could hear the child, followed by the deep tones of a man's voice. She burst into the room frantic now at the time she had been away. How *could* she?

John Armstrong was on his knees shaking a rattle at the little girl in her cot who was shrieking with laughter. When her mother appeared her face puckered and she began to cry. Kitty laughed her relief and scooped up the child and the large man still on his knees looked disconcerted. He staggered to his feet righting his shirt cuffs as he did so and smoothing away the thin shock of grey that had fallen across his thick-set face.

'Thank you, John.' Kitty gasped her thanks- she'd not waste breath on apologies for her absence. By the look of it no harm had come by it.

Instead she mocked, 'I promise not to tell the Slymefoot drinkers I saw the power in the land down to the level of a child.'

'Slymefoot... so that's where you've been?' Armstrong raised his eyebrows and his face darkened. 'It's not taken you long to run back there.'

Kitty shrugged her shoulders. 'It was a mistake. It's just a hovel with mindless drinking- men seeking oblivion. No, it's not the place for me.'

But she knew Armstrong had been there only last night, she had heard him go out, heard him come home and had smelt the drink on his breath in the morning. One rule for men and quite another for her sex, but one she'd always blatantly contravened. Now would be no different. She would appear to do the man's bidding but her Slymefoot reception had stiffened her resolve to return at the first possible chance and then she would give as good as she got!

'It's no place for a lady.'

'Lady?' Kitty laughed as she buried her face in the warm bundle of her daughter.

'Yes, your time in the care of school mistress Cecilia and Pastor Gregory has been well spent. You are an intelligent girl and hopefully you should be able to put your past behind you.' He sounded magnanimous and Kitty smothered a retort. Again anger threatened to surface but, mention of her good friends down in the Tyne Valley should bring only a rush of gratitude; if it were not for them and for the man in whose parlour she now stood she would be in prison or even worse.

'From wild hill-girl, you've achieved the veneer of a lady.' Armstrong nodded thoughtfully. 'Even Sir Walter Scott equated you with his favourite heroine. Only his companion doubted.' Now John Armstrong shook his head. 'Who was that young Orcadian to think he could look down on you?'

She smoothed a stray curl from her forehead. Little wonder Olaf Magson had laughed at her, his feet were planted firmly on the ground whilst the master of Abbotsford was a romancer. A highly successful one at that, but reality was not his chosen venue.

Armstrong was still annoyed. 'Together we'll make that young man realise that you have, 'goodness, beauty and brains to match any character in a book.'

Kitty looked down at the work-worn hands that held her child. They told her past to any who cared to look. But dig deeper and there was more to find and even Armstrong had acknowledged her intelligence. Could there be even more?

Armstrong was in expansive mood. 'I too am a mixture, Cheviot farmer, local dignitary and some might say, opportunist.' Armstrong nodded thoughtfully, warming to his subject. 'I hobnob with the likes of Sir Walter Scott, and yet at Slymefoot I down the whisky that I've smuggled across the Scottish border; your father and I were long time rivals in trade.'

Kitty stared at the many-faced man relaxed beside his fireside. He had offered her a home at Barraburn. If she knew Armstrong there must be a strong element of self-interest. It had been no act of kindness.

Katharine was cooing, looking up at the giant figure leaning just inches from her, a coy smile about her face.

As if he could read her mother's thoughts, Armstrong said, 'You should know, Kitty that there isn't one of us who hasn't relied on good fortune sometime or other. Sometimes self-preservation needs a helping hand from some local magis-.'

'I know I owe you-.'

He shrugged his shoulders dismissively. 'There's never any harm in charity for want of a better word.'

At last! She was about to hear what he expected in return, why she and her child were resident with a man not yet fifty, greedy in his appetites and pursuits. She breathed in quickly and clasped her hands together. In the past he'd openly admired the wild daughter of Macnab making it obvious on many a Slymefoot drinking session; good reason then, why she'd lain in the night hours alert listening to the man's feet outside her unlocked door.

Armstrong took a step towards her and stopped. She waited, nerving herself not to move away from him. His face was flushed.

'Old Farmer Armstrong of Barrowburn went to Berwick to buy a ram and came home with a foundling child he'd almost trodden on in the gutter. I have him to thank for everything.' He waved his arm about the room.

Kitty stared in disbelief. So Magistrate Armstrong was repaying history. He wanted nothing more than to honour his good fortune by helping her and her fatherless daughter.

Four

There was a figure at the sink.
'Pleasance, is it you? Oh it is!' Kitty gasped her surprise. 'It's so good to see you!'
'And you too, pet.'
Kitty could hardly believe her luck, a known face and one that was friendly. The woman methodically dried her hands on her apron and then Kitty's arms were about her in a heartfelt hug. When at last they broke loose, Kitty beamed at the barmaid. Pleasance was the same old Pleasance. Hazel eyes sparkled mischievously so that one did not see the woman's other features combining to make a less than perfect whole. Pleasance was ugly by *any* comparison. In the gloom of the kitchen *or* in the dark recess of Slymefoot where Kitty had last set eyes on her, Pleasance was made for the shadows. Yellowing skin, blotched and wrinkled, spoke of age beyond her fifty or so years. She was slight of frame, with a pronounced hump-back, though she lifted a barrel with the best!
'Ah hinney, it's good to see yer.' Kitty added her childhood endearment, overcome to see the Slymefoot barmaid standing in the Magistrate's kitchen. So she no longer dispensed whisky at the inn. It had been more than a year since the Black Grouse lek at the drinking den and Kitty's last drunken evening.
The baby struggled in Kitty's grasp, holding out her arms to the stranger and shrieking with laughter as Pleasance engulfed her in a bony embrace; the next few minutes were spent pulling at her new friend's straggly hair and from the loud peals of laughter it would seem those arms were as comforting

as the flesh and luxuriant locks of her mother. Kitty watched the easy natural rapport between the two as Pleasance bent her head and began to sing a soft lilting tune -
Early one morning
Just as the sun was rising
I saw a pretty maiden
In the valley below-
Oh don't deceive me
Oh never leave me...

Her voice was a young stream issuing from a granite landscape. Over and over again the patient woman moved gently with the baby to the old folk song until, satisfied, she handed back the pacified child saying,

'Now the bairn will be wanting a shive of ma barley - dick and some warm milk.'

The earthy words rooted in hill country brought a smile to Kitty's face and she sighed- how good it was to hear the well-remembered Coquet dialect. She sat and watched as the woman went about her task, shaving a slice from the stick of new-baked bread. And only when the child's needs were met did Pleasance delve her hands back into the flour in the mixing-bowl sifting it high in the air. She added water and lard, a yellow handled-knife completing the pastry. Now the pie is something to look forward to, thought Kitty, craving comfort herself.

There was reassurance in Pleasance's repeated movements. Kitty could feel her shoulders relaxing and the tight headache that had pulsed her forehead since early morning seemed to be fading away. The Lullaby had had similar effect on daughter *and* mother!

'She's bonny.' Pleasance nodded in the direction of the baby. 'Then she takes after her mam.' She eyed Kitty's thick dark tresses as she brushed back her spindly hair, so thin that it patterned mousy brown with her pink scalp. But her face creased into an appreciative smile.

'John said she was a little beauty...didn't yer?' There was a nod of welcome as Armstrong came into the kitchen bringing with him a cold burst of the outside.

'Close the door, the bairn does nee want to be in a draught.' Cook scolded master and Armstrong did as he was told.

'Aye it's a raw day, the wind is getting up. The sheep are moving down from the tops, we could be in for some snow.' He blew on his hands and moved to stir the fire into activity.

'So pet, you've met our small distraction?' as Armstrong spoke he seized a biscuit just new from the oven, blew on it, broke it and handed half to the child. There quickly followed the other half.

'Enough of that, we'll no spoil the bairn,' Pleasance remonstrated and the large man retreated from the figure before him.

Pet? He was free with his endearments. Had he addressed the child or Pleasance? Warmth from the open oven surged into the room and Kitty felt a rush of well-being. The woman's presence in the house made everything seem suddenly different. She was seeing yet another side of Armstrong, one that she had not seen before; the gruff, hill farmer tamed by his domestic help. She found herself hoping that Pleasance was a live-in maid, how much better to have another woman in the house. Her unspoken fears were fast disappearing.

The pie appeared at supper, after a happy afternoon wrapped up against the winter cold and scrambling about the hillside, her unsteady daughter ever more confident as her feet became accustomed to the springy turf. Tumbles and spills were cushioned by the soft cover. Here was a safe nursery! Kitty lifted her eyes to the hills, in time her daughter would climb to the wide horizons she had extolled just the day before, until the descending mist had returned her fears and doubts. She'd thought of moving on? 'Where to?' had never had an answer.

Once Katherine was fed and bedded, rabbit pie was served in the kitchen, the crust crisp and melting, the meat tasting of the open air and natural grass. A hungry Kitty savoured the last crumb and smiled across the table at the cook of the household. 'That was delicious, Pleasance...as good as my Nana's.' The woman nodded her thanks.

Cook seated with master and guest...! Magistrate Armstrong was not conventional in any aspect of his life!

Silence, and their stomachs filled, Armstrong emptied his glass of ale, belched loudly and then belched again before his words began to flow. He was in expansive mood.

'What do you think of my home, Kitty? It is built from the stones of the old Pele tower from more troublesome times but now it is a substantial house.' He sounded the prosperous landowner...

'Yes, indeed.'

'I think Sir Walter cannot have been unimpressed?' he questioned, clearly eager to hear the girl's reply.

'It does you proud, Magistrate Armstrong.' Her voice mocked but her face showed she knew its worth.

He nodded then frowned, 'We dine- nay, I should say 'eat' in the kitchen. Perhaps that is something to be changed now you and the child are here. The dining-room has not been used for many a long year. But it has an ancient carved table, Pleasance, perhaps it is time to get out the beeswax.' He looked in the servant's direction but his words were for Kitty,

'Tell me, did Rector Gregory in Tynedale provide a fine table?'

'Good wholesome food from a locally-crafted oak table. But it was not fine. A poor country parson cannot compete with a successful business man.' Kitty looked to flatter him and he nodded abstractedly as though it went without saying. His face was smug. It annoyed her.

'But John, I look forward to seeing the library. That will be something to show Sir Walter on his next visit.' She taunted, but already she knew her host would feel no hint of chagrin. He was not a man who harboured doubt for long. Gregory Felton had been riddled with it and it was her uneasy night fear that dear Gregory thought her now to be an opportunist? She hoped not. Only time and events had brought them together, and it was never meant to be for long, she had known that in her bones.

'Ah, yes, th-the library *and* the dining room will need some attention. I shall see to it. It must be a fine home for little Katherine.' He belched loudly and spat into the fire.

'It's warm in the kitchen. The dining-room would mean another room to heat.' Pleasance added her measured voice to the discussion and Armstrong frowned.

Kitty laughed up at her host. 'Then your peat kyles will have to be the height of an old gadgie.' She raised her hand indicating a man-high heap of fuel that would be needed to keep the fires burning thinking as she did, 'so he plans nothing but the best for little Katharine!' She felt a surge of well-being; life had taught her to seize the chance; if not, the *fox* would grab the dead rabbit whilst you were still eyeing it. The magistrate was obviously intrigued with the child, if their future lay here with their wealthy benefactor, well so be it!

And Armstrong had aspirations for his home; it mattered little where his money came from. The Macnabs had not been the only ones who knew the back ways into Scotland, but Armstrong had influential connections along both the hidden paths and the more accepted routes and the latter led to people like Sir Walter Scott! Farmer Armstrong mixed in a higher society than she and her father had ever done.

She stole a glance at Pleasance seated opposite her host. She had eaten delicately, her hand lightly clasping her knife as though she had always done so. But Kitty knew she came from one of the poorest families in the neighbourhood. Was she another of Armstrong's kindly acts? Kitty frowned to herself. She had never associated such motivation to the man before.

But it *couldn't* be just philanthropy that gave Pleasance a place in the farmhouse. Long hours in the back of the house would be spent on the laundry, an ancient press with roller mangle filled a recess; a cheese press and chesfit for the curd stood waiting for the cow's milk, and all needed her guiding hand. The peat fire burned twenty four hours, the live ashes being kept during the night in a peat hole beneath the fire grate. A woman's work...and Pleasance's labour was endless. And when it was done, she sat opposite Armstrong at his table. Kitty glanced at her placid face, and then down to Pleasance's gnarled hands that showed early signs of arthritis. She worked hard for her living.

Pleasance, apron now removed, merged comfortably into the background. She wore a plain brown skirt and blouse in white homespun cloth that sat uneasily against her yellow skin. Kitty had remembered likening her to a used candle. In contrast, Kitty had changed from her travel-stained clothes into those carried here in her bag. A cream calico was fresh and starched, setting off flushed cheeks warmed by the ale and the fire halfway up the chimney.

There was silence. Armstrong's head fell to his chest; Kitty wanted nothing better than to tumble her endless questions in the direction of her host. Host...guardian...rescuer? Or perhaps she *too* would be working the mangle or cheese press any day soon?

But Armstrong had called her his 'ward', did he mean to improve *her* along with the unused rooms in his house? He was watching her now from veiled lids and she sat straight-backed, her hands in her lap. Was his intention to raise her to a distant horizon above those who assembled nightly at Slymefoot? *Her life could be changed forever if only she played her cards right.*

Another world beckoned. She looked about the stark kitchen. She must see to it that Armstrong's plans materialised. Sooner rather than later she could be seated in a fine dining room and then perhaps the *cook* would keep to the kitchen. Nothing but the best for her and her daughter!

Armstrong and Kitty moved from kitchen table to seats either side of the hearth as Pleasance washed and stacked the dishes. Kitty wondered if Pleasance sat in the seat she occupied on a normal evening when no guest frequented their table? Why not? It was a comfortable arrangement, master and servant around the one source of heat. It amused her to think of the two of them similar in years, but separated by every other comparison; well-known local Magistrate and farmer-benefactor, his greying temples just feet away from a work-worn servant with little of life's endowments. A sliver of her barley-dick must be worth a lot! Kitty stifled a giggle.

There was no more peat to bank the fire. Kitty could feel the chill of the stone walls wrap around her. Armstrong was snoring. She rose to her feet and smiled across at the woman at the sink.

She whispered, 'I must check to see the baby sleeps. Thank you, Pleasance, for that delicious pie.'

Kitty sought her candle and its light flickered as she moved out into the dark, draughty corridor. She could already imagine snow about the farmhouse walls. A hill winter lasted long. She had seen snow here in June.

The child was crying, a dismal wail hidden in the depths of the walls, but rising on the opening of the door. How long would it take *this* time to pacify her? Kitty was no Pleasance. She lifted the struggling child and tried to snuggle her to herself, but Katherine was having none of it and her cries reached a new crescendo. Kitty felt her inadequacy painfully. She was no natural mother. Then it had been no natural birth. Her milk had dried almost immediately, there had been little bonding at *her* breast. She put the red-faced child back into the cradle and the wails followed her as she closed the door behind her.

Flustered, Kitty reached her own room as a light flickered on the stairs. Armstrong and Pleasance lit their way past her door and along the passage in a swish of the woman's skirts. They stopped and Armstrong opened the last door. Pleasance went into the room and Armstrong followed shutting the door behind them.

Kitty threw herself onto the bed and buried her relief and laughter into the depth of the mattress.

Five

Snow! As surely as it covers the land it blankets life. Normal life suspended.

The morning was beautiful; crisp and untouched. The scene from the farmhouse was a picture waiting to be spoilt as Kitty pulled on woollen hat and scarf and did the same for the child. They ran and slithered into the suddenness of nature and left their mark in the sullied, scurried footmarks that quickly ruined the perfection. In turn they were soon wet and shivering from their act of violation. The child's shrieks of delight turned into wails, small fingers aching with sudden pain.

Kitty clasped them between her own chilled hands and rubbed briskly against the resistance. She remembered her own childhood hot-ache as though it were only yesterday. Life's first awareness of an unkind nature that ruined what should be perfect.

'Oh little one.... let me make you better!' She smothered the huge tears that welled and slithered down her daughter's purple cheeks. There was no consolation, just a greater volume of noise that could be heard in the next valley.

The warmth of the house and the obvious refuge of the kitchen beckoned. Pleasance, on her knees at the fire, rose stiffly and the child held out her arms to the woman. A grateful Kitty handed over her burden and removed the wet clothes from a wriggling child who was soon pacified with a biscuit.

'You have the right touch.' Kitty sounded her pique.
'How *is* that?'

'Ah was the eldest of a big family, so no a bairn for long. Ah become the mother.'

'So it was other peoples' tingling hot-ache you suffered, not your own,' Kitty grinned at Pleasance. She was learning very quickly the woman's worth. Like the beautiful unspoilt snow outside not everything should be taken at face value. John Armstrong was to be counted amongst the discerning. Pleasance was a dark horse. Kitty turned away to hide her amusement.

Next day, their footprint scars in the snow became permanent in the unforgiving frost. Little Katharine clung to Pleasance so Kitty went out alone. She walked aimlessly and with difficulty in the ice-painted landscape. She had turned in the opposite direction to Slymefoot drinking-house, and followed the path of the river. The Coquet was muted. She turned back the way she had come.

Armstrong's house huddled in the encircling hills as though frozen into the landscape. Pleasance's kitchen was the obvious haven but she, Kitty, would bring outside chill to the homely scene for she felt a growing childish resentment of the barmaid, cum- cook, cum-everything else.

Instead, she sought the part of the house she hadn't seen. As expected there was no library and the dining room was empty but for the old solid table and sideboard. Antique, Armstrong had called it, but that only hid the rough nature of the wood and the stains of everyday life left by the once-family home. She shuddered, the marks had taken years to make whilst her two days here had already seemed a lifetime.

Kitty stared unseeing out of the window... there was nothing but a cold white land; no movement, no sound. The river was silent. By tomorrow it too might even be frozen? Her father had talked of such things. Did the sea freeze? She did not know. Did Olaf Magson have a winter story for his mester ship? Surely so in the long winter that was the Orkneys?

The dining room was as bleak as the landscape. It needed decoration. She climbed the stairs to her room and took from the empty cupboard the one ornament that she owned; Pastor Gregory had spent hours in his church crypt fashioning the replica of his wartime ship and it had been his farewell gift to her. She carried it down to the dining room and placed it in the centre of the table and stood back to admire the effect.

She felt a lump in her throat. Gregory Felton had fashioned every minute plank and mast and she, with her good friend Cecelia, had watched the delicate task over the months of her own pregnancy. She relived the scene when she'd found him putting the finishing touches to his labour of love. He'd listened silently to her decision to go back to the border hills and then had thrust the ship into her hands; an inappropriate toy for a little girl but one who would grow to be a tomboy like her mother. Kitty hadn't bothered to say that her upland rivers were not the place for such a craft.

The sight of the model Royal Sovereign brought a mixture of emotions; the sea-faring Padre, now in the remote parish of north Tynedale, had come to accept his lot. Could that ever be true of her? She sighed deeply. Life for her was not the passive making of a toy ship to appease unquiet thoughts. The model might be perfect in every detail, but it needed a heaving sea and foreign shores!

She relived her spur-of-the moment decision to leave Tynedale; she and her child were cuckoos in the nest; and what cuckoos! Whore and bastard taking charity from good upright people, too good! And that she was not and never could be.

'Pleasance, we shall dine in the front room tonight.' She strode in to the kitchen and seizing the cutlery from the cupboard drawer returned to the dining room and laid three places. It was a large house and there to be used!

The ship sat between them, its large masts obscuring the view of her host so that she could only guess at his annoyance at being moved from the warm kitchen. The ornate grate smoked its protest into the chill room and the rabbit stew was thin and tough. Pleasance had accepted the extra work without comment but Kitty had watched her struggle with the fire with a growing feeling of guilt. Her selfishness had upset them all.

Armstrong and his shepherd had been out in the snow all the light hours. Kitty watching her host thought, 'before winter is done there might be less than a thin rabbit stew on the dining room table. The high paths to Scottish whisky would be treacherous and besides, rumour already reaching the Thorneyburn Rectory was that whisky smuggling across the borders was no longer so profitable. Stocking Armstrong's fictitious library shelves might very well be a fanciful dream. What then for her daughter and all that Armstrong had promised for her?

They ate in silence, the only sound cutlery on plate. The coarse green ware was chipped and as ill-used as the table. Kitty fixed her eyes on the wooden ship. It had been lovingly made. The candle light shimmered on the decks and in the flickering light it was not hard to imagine the vessel moving upon high seas. She said flippantly,

'Do you not think my ship enhances the room?' There was no reply.

'It hides the dark stain at the centre of the table,' Kitty added.

Again Armstrong said nothing and Kitty frowned.

'It hints of brave deeds when surely, here, we're marooned on a desert island!'

'Desert island...' Armstrong's tone was of the Arctic. 'Young lady, I cannot remember if your *father's* cottage even had a table? Or perhaps it was of the finest mahogany? *Do* tell us!' He smirked at her across his table, moving the model to one side so that she could fully see his displeasure.

Kitty flushed a deep crimson. She had gone too far and she knew it. Pleasance rose to clear and her arthritic hands fumbled to hold the dishes.

'Stay. Kitty's legs are younger than yours.' Armstrong thumped the table and it wobbled. 'Perhaps you should begin to earn your keep, young lady! Sit down Pleasance it's time *she* took your place.' His face was expressionless as he watched a furious Kitty seize the dirty plates in the woman's stead and remove them to the back of the house. Washing-up would be her next task. Anger boiled in her humiliation. How long could she accept the future that Armstrong was deciding for her minute by minute? To sit night after night, the three of them, with her reversing the role of Pleasance, constantly being reminded of what she owed to Armstrong? All for a roof over her and her daughter's head?....so that one day, her hair would have turned grey and her hands arthritic and Katharine would be the accepted young lady seated on the other side of The Royal Sovereign?

'It is time Pleasance, that Kitty *took your place*.' That night as she laid in bed his words rang in her ears so that his step upon the stairs brought a spasm of disgust. Could it be in *other* places than just at the sink that Armstrong would expect change?

It could never be. She dragged her chest of drawers in front of her bedroom door and finally fell into a deep sleep, though it was far from untroubled, in her dream, pirates attacked her ship and in front of the crew she was ravished and humiliated. She had jumped overboard to save her honour.

In the morning Armstrong was nowhere to be seen. Pleasance reported he was gone from home and would be away for several days though there was no mention of destination. Of more immediate concern was the bairn. She had a cold and was feverish. Kitty looked at the restless child and felt a stab of guilt; she had not been the best of mothers, restlessly dragging the small tot… legs not high enough to rise above the drifts- out into snow!

It was Pleasance who dosed the child with honey and glycerine, kept her warm before the fire and made it her routine for the next four days. No one interrupted the women's regime and Kitty accepted the respite of Armstrong's absence gratefully. With her child in good hands she was free to wander ever further into her childhood hills.

But it was with increasingly heavy feet she trod the bleak paths alone. The stark hills had become barren and unfriendly and she purposely skirted the hidey-holes that had hidden the young Kitty from the sprites of the hills. Now she felt the unseen pressing about her and they were alien.

Indoors, the house was chill and dark. The late cold snap entered her bones nipping with hostile fingers. The child's cold had gone on to her chest and little painful coughs broke the silence with fretful cries. The women's supper-time returned to the kitchen, the only source of heat, and where little Katherine had the greatest chance of avoiding the pneumonia that was the dread of any childhood. The fire was their primeval focus and their lives reduced to its limited red glow. Beyond the room was numbing darkness and in it The Royal Sovereign sailed unheeded on the empty ocean of the dining room table.

On the fifth night Kitty laid the usual two knives and forks on the kitchen table and, when sudden noise in the hall told of Armstrong's return, she set another place with sinking heart. He had come back a day too soon. The snow would be gone by tomorrow and she had schemed escape from the prison that was Barraburn; her child was at last improving, the cough infrequent and the rasping of her wooden rattle toy had replaced the noise of congested lungs. Her daughter had the stamina of her mother. Surely she was fit enough to travel? Now the unwelcome return of Armstrong threatened to upset her plans. What matter, tonight would see the chest of drawers wedged in front of her door for the very last time.

Armstrong burst into the room, his large frame scattering the narrow female huddle about the grate. Ignoring the two women he made straight for the baby, his weather-beaten face wreathed in a foolish smile. He gazed down at the cradle retrieved from the attic on their arrival, large enough for two, for then babies came one a year. His large red hands stark against the white blanket fumbled for the coarse wooden rattle in the child's grasp and there was an immediate wail of anguish.

John Armstrong laughed as from his pocket he produced a replacement toy with the flourish of a magician.

A silver rattle to take the place of the wooden one! The peevish crying subsided in a last sob of anger and there was a squeal of delight as grasping hands seized the new plaything. Like mother, like daughter. No wonder! Kitty raised her eyebrows. Armstrong's gift to the baby was of solid silver. It gleamed in the burst of firelight as the burning log subsided into glowing ash and the sighing fire was echoed by the contented child. Neither Kitty nor Pleasance said anything, but Kitty noted with relief that her host's good temper had returned along with the trinket.

'The little lass will join us tonight in the dining room. There is a high chair in the attic.' Armstrong nodded at the two women and left the kitchen taking with him the peasant toy. The child clasped its replacement as though her fingers would never let go.

Four round the dining table. Kitty's wooden ship was not to be seen. She felt an irrational irritation at its removal- it surely reflected her position in this household- her one solitary possession not deemed to be good enough!

'What has become of my ship?' She emphasised her ownership; Gregory's ship would be going with her when she and the child left early next morning; the handmade replica held intrinsic value that she could never explain to Armstrong. But the silver rattle was valuable and could be hidden in her baggage.

'Where is my ship?' Her repeated question was met by silence.

'It covered up the unsightly mark on the table,' Kitty said peevishly, 'and there are spelks that will tear my dress!' Her fingers brushed the uneven wood. Armstrong's so-called antique was nothing but a pile of firewood awaiting a match.

Armstrong said mildly, 'It is returned to your room. Your daughter deserves only the very best.'

'But-' Kitty stuttered her annoyance.

'Your man of war is made of wood, it will give you spelks like the table you complain of.' Armstrong uttered the local word with contempt, 'just an artisan piece, homemade by a *country parson*.' Armstrong smirked at her, the triumph bright in his eyes.

'I have brought Katharine something of much greater quality from my travels.' Again he stated his wealth and Kitty bit her lip not to rise to the bait.

She thought, 'we're like children scoring points in a game, *my silver is better than your wood!*' She scowled into her lap as Armstrong rose from the table, surely the man hadn't wasted his money on yet another expensive trifle?

A wooden box, larger than Armstrong's two great hands together, lay on the sideboard. With a satisfied smile on his face he placed it in the middle of the table over the blemished wood. With theatrical flourish he opened the lid and lifted out the contents. The two women could only murmur in amazement.

Kitty stared transfixed. 'It's the most *beautiful* thing I've *ever* seen!' she breathed.

'So you like it?' Armstrong nodded with satisfaction.

'Why aye!' Kitty was stunned.

A new ship stood in place of the wooden man-of-war. It had made them all gasp, and little wonder. The baby gurgled her delight leaning forward trying to grab it with her left hand. Kitty caught hold of her fingers; didn't everyone say the left hand was unlucky? She wanted this luck to last. The child wailed, knowing nothing of the superstition, but she thrust out her right hand instead and Kitty smiled at the youngster's quick thinking. Armstrong banged the table with satisfaction.

'Sensible child you know its worth. And you, Kitty should learn to *had yer gat,* or in the words you now use, *keep quiet!*'

Armstrong sneered. 'You learnt to be a lady in the time you spent with your friends in the Tyne Valley and this is no time to forget it. So I want to hear no more *why aye's or spelks.*'

Kitty said nothing, Armstrong looked at her coldly, 'it is time for not only your mouth to forget the local dialect, but for your hands to become used to the finer possessions of life.' He pointed to his new purchase.

The replacement centre-piece was solid silver! Thin masts rose from the deck in a delicate tracery of sails. Its prow boasted a figurehead, beautiful and seductive, every small porthole and fixture had been lovingly replicated in the expensive metal. Both Kitty and Prudence stared aghast at Armstrong's purchase.

'So, what do you think of the Silver Neff I have bought for your daughter, Kitty? Is it not fine?'

'Tr-truly.' Kitty stuttered. The ship must have cost her host a fortune, the hull was at least half a foot long.

'Yes the neff is the best money can buy.' He rose to his feet, scraping his chair against the bare wooden floor boards and towering over Kitty,

'Not only is it exquisite, my dear Kitty, it is also functional. It has purpose. Can you guess what it is?'

Kitty shook her head, she'd had enough of games. He gazed down at his acquisition with undisguised triumph, 'Look at the main mast.'

She focused reluctantly on the silver ship and saw nestling within the intricate crow's nest a small cup filled with salt. In the arms of the figurehead was piled dark pepper and in a small dinghy, lay a gleam of yellow mustard.

Slowly and deliberately Armstrong deposited a sample of each on to the plate in front of her as though she was a starving waif, desperate for any last morsel she could get.

'So the neff is not only beautiful but functional as well...' he smiled at her. '...which must surely be a winning combination?'

Kitty made no reply and Armstrong laughed. It was not a pleasant sound. 'My dear you are beautiful, now you can also be *useful*.'

Kitty drew in her breath and clenched her hands.

'You spoke longingly of desert islands, my dear. I cannot produce one of those, but I have the next best thing for you.'

He banged the table and echoed a loud guffaw.

'What say you Kitty, to, not a *desert* island, but a *Holy* Island? Would it not better answer your needs?' His belly laugh shook the table and with it its silver ornament as though caught in a sudden squall.

She stared back at him defiantly; his eyes were slits but everything else about him showed his gloating. Whatever future he had mapped out for her lay behind this blackmail of silver, *look what I will give your daughter in return for-*.

'Your destination is such an island. Men call it Holy Island.' He paused for effect- so after all she and her child were not to languish in this remote valley.

'Of course, you go alone, you leave the child here.'

'But that I cannot do!'

'You have no choice. Pleasance will be mother in your stead.' His words sank into the silence as she struggled to take in his words. The child left behind, as hostage? She shuddered and stole a glance at Pleasance. The woman smiled.

'I'll love her as my ain. I promise no harm will come to her.'

Armstrong smirked, 'Just think of it as one last time for you to feel the luxury of freedom. No child trailing your skirts.'

Kitty flushed guiltily.

'And I do assure you, my dear, it is Holy Island only in name, so I'm sure you will not feel out of place. Some call it Lindisfarne, but whatever its name you'll discover it's a place of *dark deeds* kept hidden from the world by a confining sea!'

Six

Kitty stood by the sea her mouth wide enough to catch a haul of sprats. The ocean spread before her away to the dark straight line half way up the sky. With a gasp of delight she sank to her knees scooping up the water like a delirious child. It was icy cold and tasted of salt. She gasped and spat it out, wiping the sleeve of her dress against the bitter intrusion. It had looked *so* beautiful. She'd been tricked just as easily as little Katharine in the snow. It looked benign and yet...

So this was Olaf's sea. It lay flat calm lapping at her feet like a purring kitten drinking a saucer of milk, sky-reflected clouds in the water white and creamy. The movement of the waves was hypnotic, backwards, forwards in a never ceasing murmur of content. Kitty delved, and sifted high the myriad ochre grains of sand, vivid against the blue sea. She laughed aloud, scooping... sprinkling... piling... scooping... sprinkling... piling. Destruction... building... destruction. It was a game that could last forever!

She gazed across the water to the island lying just out of reach, as though a careless hand had let it float away to be grounded in isolation. So near and yet so far! A drifting mist made it transitory land like a siren beckoning to her. She turned and stared back at the mainland. Now it was the hills, pale and remote, that looked unreal. Somewhere back there, she had left a small bairn.

Water surged about her boots, slithering and slipping and then retreating in a change of mind. It was as unpredictable as she herself and again she laughed. She was a ten-year old playing truant. The bread in her pocket bulged out her skirt and hungrily she devoured the hard, stale crust. The kind hand that had wrapped it in the cloth was at this moment cradling her abandoned child. She had not felt so free in years! For the first time in her life she answered to no-one... and the strange Holy Island lay waiting for her.

She said out loud.

'All I need is Olaf Magson's mester ship and then I could walk over to the island on it dry shod!' She laughed happily, how useful his make-believe ship would be to span the gap between mainland and isle. She thought of the Orcadian. Here she was sitting beside his beloved sea looking out to the thin blue line that he had called his horizon.

Patience was not her greatest virtue but she'd been told to wait. When a carrier cart appeared it would be time for her to cross to the island. It was hard to believe. Water still lapped about her boots. How could it be? Wait for a miracle, that's what Pleasance had told her.

She was breathless in excitement. Pleasance had laughed at her disbelief that there was no need for a boat to carry her over the sea. When the tide heeded the moon, the sea would disappear and the cart would carry her across untouched in shallow water- it was unbelievable that *twice* a day the island became part of the mainland. 'No wonder they called it Holy Island, it's as good as Moses and the parting of the Red Sea', Kitty mused. Could Holy Island be her Promised Land?

The water receded before her gaze, drifting back down the beach and leaving frothy lines like scum about a bowl. Mesmerised, she watched its going, unaware of the horseman until he had reigned in beside her and the hot breath of his mount was on her neck. She jumped to her feet.

'Oh you made me jump... I swear the sea has me bewitched.'

But already the horseman was fording the water and if he could do it so could she. There was still no sign of the cart, lifting her skirts Kitty followed him out into the retreating sea.

Her boots hung dry about her neck. The going was easy, the sand firm, her destination swam in a haze of sunlight and mist a half mile away, her path marked by a line of wooden stakes like erect sentries. All she had to do was follow the ordained route to reach the fabled isle.

Her strides were confident as sea birds paddled in the shallows and there was a soft twittering and calling of welcome. The eastern sun shone on her face and dazzled. A gull swooped low and startled her and suddenly she was in feet of water and floundering up to her knees in the out-going tide. She let out a shriek of alarm and immediately the horseman was back beside her.

'My mount has longer legs than either of us. Up you get.' The rider bent down and with ease lifted Kitty up to sit before him. She could see and smell the gentleman, fine leather jacket, the thoroughbred flesh of his horse, no ordinary cuddy, as her soaked skirt dripped over her, the rider and their mount.

It was like no journey she had ever taken in her life; the high steps of the horse splashing up the stranded pools about her ankles, the steady rhythm of its body like a gently rolling boat and the light touch of her rescuer as he held the reigns loosely about her waist.

The island rose out of the sea like a giant saucer. A great sweep of sandy hillocks topped by high waving grass and then they were descending along a cobbled way and there were houses.

'Oh... a village in the middle of the sea?' she laughed her disbelief. 'I think I must be dreaming.'

'So would it help if I pinched you?' amused eyes looked down into hers and Kitty tossed her head.

'Hadaway, you've already done more than enough.' She eyed the damp patch she had left on his tailored clothes. Then more fool him to wear expensive breeks in such a place.

'I swear I was dying of impatience back there, but I never thought the tide would decide to turn and come back when I was half way across.' Her careless reading of the current had been foolish. 'The sea is treacherous!'

'It's still going out I can assure you, you might have got a soaking but there was no fear of drowning. Still, you're right to treat it with respect. I've known my horse forced to swim when the tide is unusually high. So be careful, for you'll find the sea can be fickle. Drowning is an unpleasant end.'

'Dr-drowning?'

Her rescuer laughed, 'I've rescued a landlubber to be sure.' His eyes showed his disbelief.

'Aye, solid earth under my feet is what I'm used to, not untrustworthy water.' Kitty scrambled down from the horse and the man's grasp to reach the reassurance of terra firma and gazed up at her rescuer.

That he was a gentleman was obvious but his appearance brought a quickening of interest. If she had been asked to describe her idea of a fictional pirate it would be her rescuer. Thick black hair crowded his face on head and chin, tough brown skin was cut by a dark red weal across his cheek and his eyes reflected a wariness that an innocent man would not merit. He stared down at her, suspicion etched in his very nature. Kitty bent to her skirt that clung to her legs and squeezed out a puddle. What did she look like?

He said, 'I've picked up a sea urchin from the shore.'

She narrowed her eyes and said. 'Might I be addressing Mister Henry Smythe?'

'You are indeed, young lady. But how did you -?'

Young lady indeed, their ages were not that different but his height and obvious assurance gave him the advantage over her. That he was disconcerted at her pronouncing his name gave her a stab of satisfaction. 'Yes', she thought, 'inborn suspicion keeps his back ramrod straight!'

She grinned up at him. 'Your kinsman, John Armstrong, painted an accurate portrait.'

Henry Smythe laughed though the easy explanation made no difference to the look in his eye.

'So he told you what a handsome chap I am?'

'No.'

'You come from Barraburn?' He stared down at her- a host of unasked questions crowding his face. He said,

'What is your name?'

'Kitty Macnab.'

'So then, Kitty, what news is there of John? Come climb back up on the horse, you must come home and meet my sisters. They'll welcome the diversion and we would all hear of Cousin John.'

The horse clambered up the few feet that kept land from sea, and traversed the village street. Mean houses huddled together, low, thatched with white painted walls, broken by door and one window. The street- for want of a better word- was strewn with drying nets and lobster pots, and a smell of fish hung about the eaves. It invaded her nostrils and she thought of the fresh air of the hills with a twinge of regret. The sea *stank* for all of its daily changing!

Eyes, as suspicious as those in the hills, watched their progress and Kitty kept hers lowered. From the mainland the island had appeared a floating, hazy refuge. In reality it was like any land untidily peopled and strewn by every-day living. The only difference it was surrounded by sea.

'Welcome to Pilgrim House.'

Henry Smythe lowered her to the ground and jumped down beside her. Their destination was a fine sandstone house that dwarfed its neighbours. Three stories and a collection of windows spoke its worth. They had entered a stone-flagged courtyard surrounded by outhouses and a young lad was soon on the scene to lead the mount away. Henry led her through a fine high-mantled door and shouted their arrival. There was instant answer and Kitty found herself engulfed in a flurry of skirts.

'Oh, Henry, you've been fishing and look what you've caught!' A peal of laughter echoed the girl's words as she eyed Kitty's wet clothing.

'Didn't I tell you, Marion, I would bring something back for supper and here she is, Miss Kitty Macnab,' her brother announced their visitor with a flourish and the girl seized hold of Kitty's hand in a warm gesture of welcome.

'Your best find yet, I do declare, brother.' The girl a little older than herself kept hold of Kitty's hand and beamed.

Kitty grinned back at her. 'It doesn't have to be fish that comes in on the tide.'

'Well you don't look like or smell like one.' Marion breathed in deeply. 'Though can't quite place your perfume. What do you think, Louise?' She turned to a younger, version of herself, a forced frown across her brow. 'Where do you think she comes from?'

The deep concentration was repeated as Louise Smythe studied the new arrival, 'Not from these parts or she would not be wet. I think I was six the last time my skirt hem touched the water!'

Marion wagged her finger at Kitty, 'There, Miss Kitty that's you told off.'

'Personally, I think she comes from Mars. Do you know… she has never seen the sea?' Their brother sounded his amazement.

'So you tried to walk on water did you, you poor thing, you might have drowned.' Mock horror covered her face but Marion was wiping her eyes, tears of merriment staining her cheeks.

'But, you've missed the point, sister,' Louise interrupted. 'Just think… our brother has brought home an alien. I've never met anyone who hasn't seen the sea. Is it true, Kitty the moon is made of cheese?'

At this both girls dissolved into open laughter and Kitty joined in. They were waves playfully tossing her backwards and forwards on the incoming tide. She hadn't had such *fun* in a long time.

'Enough, sisters mine, you must attend to our guest. Find her some human garb that she can change into and then we may all begin to question the invader.'

A pair of hands seized her and, with a giggling Louise behind her, Kitty ascended the stairs. Half an hour later and their visitor had been transformed.

'Why, you are human after all!' Henry Smythe greeted their return with unconcealed admiration. 'Mother may I introduce Kitty Macnab.'

Kitty smiled at the small grey haired woman seated by the parlour fire as she extended her hand to their visitor.

'You even *feel* human, Miss Macnab. That is quite a relief. We never know what Henry will bring home next, do we Marion?'

Her elder daughter gazed up adoringly at her brother, 'Henry is a magician.' She pointed to a carved bronze figure on the mantelpiece. 'Do you know he found that on the north shore last year?' She took it down for Kitty to hold and admire. It was a fine miniature statue of a young girl. *Anyone could see it was valuable.*

'Put in your order, Miss Macnab, whatever you want, Henry will find... a pair of pearl ear-rings perhaps?' Louise Smythe smirked.

'Louise!' Her mother chastised. 'You always manage to sound disproving. Your observations are hardly worth the utterance. Why do you always disparage your brother's efforts?'

The younger daughter shrugged her shoulders. Kitty looked from her to her sister. On first sight she had thought the two girls similar to look at; fair hair and fair complexion- unlike their brother, they would *never* be taken for pirates. Their noses were straight and well- proportioned and their cheeks were fresh, pink and healthy. The sisters' greatest difference was in their eyes. Marion's were pale-blue and wide, whereas the eyes of Louise Smythe held the same deep suspicion as her brother's eyes. And that suspicion, Kitty could already see, was first derived from their mother.

Mrs Smythe turned her gaze on Kitty and smiled thinly.

'Cousin John sends a letter of introduction. How fortunate that Henry met with you even without knowing that your destination was Pilgrim House. There now, Louise, as always your brother manages to be one step ahead.'

The woman turned triumphantly on Louise who, again, shrugged her shoulders. Mrs Smythe nodded her satisfaction that she'd made the point and turned once more to Kitty.

'What brings you to Lindisfarne, young lady?'

'It's a long story.' Kitty smiled as she took the proffered chair rehearsing over in her mind the exact explanation that John Armstrong had told her to tell. She had been word perfect before she left Barraburn!

'I'm an orphan, daughter of a good friend of Mister Armstrong.'

'In his letter he says your father died recently in a flash flood in the hills above Barraburn. That is truly a misfortune.'

The Smythe daughters unisoned their agreement, pretty Marion turning her wide eyes on Kitty in open concern, Louise looking down at her fingers and beginning to fiddle with her dress and Kitty noted that the younger girl was large boned and with coarser features than her sister.

'Do stop fidgeting, Louise. Come, you will read Cousin John's letter aloud, then we shall all know why it is he has seen wont to send Miss Macnab to us.' Her mother handed over the page and closed her eyes. Without a word Louise handed the sheet on to her sister.

Marion laughed and passed it back. 'You know, our Louise you are a better scholar than I.'

Brother Henry tutted his annoyance grabbed the epistle and began to read and Kitty smiled her relief. The family aggravations grated.

She looked about the room. Of good proportions, it was filled with furniture, heavy brocade chairs, a large chaise-longue, dozens of ornaments and potted-plants all dwarfed by an ornate fireplace. The effect was overpowering; Kitty guessed it was just like the stifling effect of living on an island. Already it was obvious that petty niggles surfaced readily in the enclosing waters. Still what was that to her...she had come for other reasons!

Henry's voice droned on above her thoughts, she must heed Armstrong's words- all that mattered was that she told the same story.

'Kitty has been ill, she needs the good ozone of the island to restore her to her former health.' Henry paused looking concerned.

'What has been your ailment?'

Kitty pursed her lips there could be no hint of child-bearing.

'I was caught in the same storm as my father, developed pneumonia and lay for many weeks between life and death.' *That* should get their sympathy.

'Oh you poor thing!' Marion looked horrified. 'Already I know it was God's will to save you so that we can love you as our very own sister.'

Louise said. 'I wouldn't wish that fate on anyone,' and laughed scornfully.

'Enough, brats! Little birds in their nest agree.' Henry glowered.

'Not these.' Louise scorned. 'The nest is too small and the birds should have fledged long ago.'

Kitty looked at her and felt a stab of understanding for the girl. She could sympathise with such sentiments. How old were the Smythe girls? Marion must be all of twenty two or so, her sister about two years younger, maybe her own age. That they still idly kicked their heels in the family home belied her experience of life. She had entered the adult stage at fourteen, the year her father had stopped treating her as a daughter. And as for Mrs Smythe...*all* parents had a lot to answer for!

Her bedroom looked down the main street and when Kitty opened the window she could smell the herring. It was so strong she could almost taste the fish. She coughed, struggling with the pungent aroma, it was all consuming but underneath the patina Armstrong had said there were hidden island secrets for her to discover. Surely there would be enough to earn the Silver neff and other such riches for her daughter, as long as she did as bidden. She pushed from her mind the niggling fear that her daughter was an innocent pawn left in Armstrong's controlling hand.

Nothing, he'd muttered, *can be just beautiful but must be useful as well,* and his eyes had moved from the silver condiment ship to Kitty.

'You will repay my hospitality, by making a trip to Holy Island.' His voice had threatened as he said, 'The Scottish border paths are no longer as fruitful, sea- routes hold the better profit now.' He'd banged the table as he spoke and the silver boat had shuddered.

'And someone on Holy Island is sabotaging my business. You must discover the culprit.' His flushed cheeks showed his anger. 'But also the Smythes are society and a family to emulate.'

Kitty stared down into the deserted street. *Why* had she accepted...a sense of adventure when already Barraburn imprisoned ...a need to prove her worth? Or was it her fear that already she and her daughter owed more than was seemly to the local magistrate...or maybe it was the chance to escape the thrall of motherhood?

Reasons aplenty and they were all true! Excitement throbbed at her temples. Holy Island was an interlude with the tide in. When it went out she would return to Barraburn- task accomplished! She would pick up her daughter and with her the Silver neff. With its value, mother and child could walk away to a new life, leaving behind the worthless, wooden man-of-war and all vestiges of her former shame.

Seven

The sea was calling. Immediately she was wide awake, above the dawn chatter of birds she could hear the lapping of the waves on the shore. Early morning light streamed through the window.

Which way to go? The island was surrounded by water, whichever direction she took she would come to the sea. All she had to do was follow her nose. Again she felt the breathless excitement of yesterday.

Narrow lanes pointed in all directions, rows of stone-built houses with blue-slated roofs crowded cheek by jowl with red-tiled cottages. She turned eastward toward the morning sun still low in the sky and hazy. She was not the only one, villagers were abroad already, but she knew no one in the Smythe family house would miss her. They had retired late and she guessed they were not early risers.

Along the cobbled road she followed a flurry of women coming from the squat dwelling houses carrying with them the odour of fish. Pulling their shawls tight about their shoulders, their uniform pinafores told they were making for the beach and their daily work of gutting and cleaning.

Minutes from the village was an arc of flat land, where the sea lapped the shore. Piles of shellfish nets, drying on the foreshore and barrels stacked ready to take the herring, spoke of the day's work ahead. Noisy activity rose from the jetty with moored boats nestling under a giant crag of rock on which towered a castle. Stark and impressive, piercing the clouds, that phallic symbol was entering the low hanging mist in a gesture of control. She turned her back on the confusion and made for the open sea, her feet flying over the short, fine sward.

The grass was as soft as down on a baby's cheek. Now beyond her first birthday, baby Katharine had unblemished cheeks. Till then long nails had scratched angry red wheals. Local custom left them uncut in the first year so the child would not grow up a thief. Some would have said 'just like her mother'? Perhaps her own mother had ignored the old superstition so that when Kitty saw beautiful things she had to own them? She thought of the silver ship gracing Armstrong's table.

Birds wheeled and called above her head, swooping almost to land on her shoulder. But they knew better, hovering and squawking just out of reach. The noise was deafening as she watched them turn seaward and with a final swoop fly out into the mist, mocking loudly because she could not follow.

'A pity we've nar got wings.'

Kitty jumped. She'd been thinking the same. An old woman was sitting on the beach, her clothes the colour of the shore, her weather-beaten cheeks rounded and etched with wrinkles of erosion like the aged rocks. Slowly, with the help of a crooked piece of wood, the figure straightened, tall, angular, her head bent forward like the handle of her stick.

'Where're yer off to, lassie, yer look to be heading out into the Ooze?' She wheezed, rheumy eyes narrow and intent.

Kitty shivered, 'Not this time of morning.'

'It's never warm enough. Ah've lived on the island seventy years and I've never been in the water beyond my shoulders.'

'I'd call that swimming.' Kitty smiled.

'Almost, but not quite, an' that's what matters. Me feet've niver left land, even when we women were forced to wade out and launch the boat for those fool fishermen caught in the storm.'

Kitty looked at the woman. Loose garments could not hide her lack of flesh- making her the tough coil of rope that would not break whatever the test!

'The March just gone and the men floundering off Emmanuel Head in a sudden storm and only the sexton, vicar, two sick old men and we women to launch the rescue boat!'

The old woman began to sing
'*A lonely sail is whitely shining*
In the mist of the endless sea.
Yet only storms are her pleasure,
Her peace is when the tempests blow.'

Theatrically, the old islander raised her hand in warning and without thinking Kitty shrank back out of her reach, but the crone only pointed at the girl, a strange look on her face.

'Old Jennet says divint gan to the Head.'

'Head..?' Kitty frowned.

'Aye, Emmanuel Head. It's yon way.' She pointed in the direction Kitty was going.

'But why not…how far is it?'

'Too far!' The old woman turned back toward the village.

Kitty watched Old Janet go. What had all that nonsense meant? Unperturbed she continued northward along the shore, wanting nothing but to be beside the empty ocean.

She had passed the lofty castle, deserted now except for gulls manning the ramparts. A wide, smooth path tracked the coast, boulders and pebbles skirting the waves. The sea was at work pummelling the land in a harsh continuous grating. Constant noise, constant pounding never letting up for a minute; awesome in its power! It wasn't hard to imagine that one day- in place of the island would be just a *heap of sand*!

She was alone, just the German Sea between her and the continent of Europe. The sense of isolation made her catch her breath. Here only the eyes of the sea would watch the sea-borne trade along this rocky coast, legal *or* illicit. No wonder Armstrong blessed this secluded isle. But someone was stealing his profit. She was here to discover who it was and she relished the task.

The headland jutted out into the sea. The old woman had called it *Emmanuel Point* and had told her not to go there. Was it because unknown feet were not welcome on the smugglers path? She looked about her. There was nothing to see but a few retarded hawthorns, like bent old- Janet- against the salt winds! The only sound was the distant roar of rolling surf and the faint echo of sea-birds.

Now the land turned westward into a series of sandy bays and intersecting headlands. 'The Garden of Eden must surely have had a coastline,' thought Kitty as she sank down onto the flat grassy platform with an uninterrupted view in every direction, 'and in the garden a resident serpent?'

Her head sank onto her raised knees. She wanted this moment to last forever. Here was solitude that reminded her of her beloved hills. She closed her eyes. Soon she must return to reality and Pilgrim House, where her hosts would be wondering where she was. How long could she stay with the Smythe family? On this first day she wanted to stay forever.

Armstrong had said they'd be glad of the diversion her visit would bring. Yes even heaven must eventually get boring. She thought of her new friends, Marion and Louise; impelled to contradict every word that the other said, in sport or deadly earnest she was yet to discover. And their brother, who was casual as though nothing mattered, only it did. Hopefully, all three would see her as a welcome intrusion into their narrow lives. She was not so sure about their mother, head of the household when Sea-Captain husband was away from home!

Kitty was lost in reverie, a relaxed tiredness sweeping over her body after what had seemed days of travel. Barraburn was a million miles away back across the sea. There in the farmhouse they would have already eaten, Prudence would have seen to that. She need not worry, but she did. Every day since the little girl had come into the world there was the constant fear and guilt. Wasn't *Wednesday's child full of woe,* an old-wives' tale to be forgotten...that baby-Katharine carried with her that unlucky rhyme was *not* to be dwelt on.

Too much solitude! Breakfast called, it was many hours since she had last eaten and it would take at least twenty minutes to return to the village. Kitty opened her eyes, blinked and blinked again. She could see nothing. She held her hand up in front of her face but all she could see was the mist, thick, white and choking.

Alarmed, Kitty scrambled to her feet that were somewhere at the end of her legs but she could not see them! She took a step forward and stopped, *that* was not the way to go, the sea was pounding the shore just inches away, louder and more menacing in the opaque gloom.

The fog swirled, clutching at her hair and bare arms, and she breathed in deeply to calm her rising panic. She remembered the old woman's words - *Do not go to Emmanuel Head*. And now she knew why. The sea and old crone were in collusion, summoning the blinding fog. She should have heeded the warning!

Stop! The sea was like the hills- it liked to tease. Often she'd been tested on the Cheviot paths, where one minute you knew which way you were going, the next you'd lost your bearings in sudden engulfing mist. Stop, take stock... listen. The sea had been her companion and it would be on her return, only now it would change from being on the right to sounding on her left- that way she would get back safely to the village.

Kitty turned as her common sense dictated and the sea thundered just as she had reasoned -on her left. She took a step forward and then another. The noise of the waves was getting louder. How could that be? She stopped and breathed in deeply. And then came a different sound, and it was like nothing she'd ever heard before. Out of the mist came a shrill crying that chilled her blood, a keening, wailing sound that was not of human kind. Silence! She must have dreamt it...then there it was again- a shrieking, loud and urgent taken up in an unearthly echo just feet below her, in the dense, consuming fog.

'Who's there?' she shouted. And again came the ghostly sound.

Trembling she turned, her desperate feet seeking the familiarity of solid land. She stumbled across the unseen grass, tripped in a rut and fell headlong. Putting out her hand to save herself she grasped flesh and blood, her scream was as loud as the uncanny noise rising from the sea and there was a rueful laugh just inches from her.

'Whist, lassie, dinna fear. I'm as lost as you.'

The voice was soft, not the harsh Northumbrian but a lilting Scots that instantly calmed. She stood in the embrace of a perfect stranger savouring the warmth of a fellow human being after the unearthly noises that had come unbidden from the sea.

She shivered. 'What in heaven's name is that sound? It's like the cries of the dead!'

'No don't say that.' The voice sounded concerned. 'The very opposite, ye ken. It's the selkies or seals crying their warning in the fog so that sailors listen out for them- knowing that they will be lying on the very rocks that would endanger their boats.'

'Oh! Is that all it is?' an embarrassed Kitty stepped away from her protector, though still relieved to be close to another human being. The stranger spoke words of reason, how *foolish* to be so disturbed by an unknown noise, surely the penetrating fog had crept into her brain! The weird crying of the seals was an alien sound but she'd heard the man's soft brogue before. What nonsense, other Orcadians than Olaf Magson would come to this island off the east coast of England!

'Both they and you sound unearthly.' Kitty could smell his presence though she could no longer feel him. She could not see the colour of his hair, but already she knew that her companion was tall, broad shouldered with untidy tufting hair. His gaunt, sharp features were hidden, his pale blue eyes as misted as the sea but it was Olaf Magson that stood just inches from her.

'I can assure you both the seals and I are flesh and blood.' He laughed good-naturedly. 'There's a logical answer to all things, you know.'

'Of course, but I'm glad you're here. They had me scared. Well...when I first heard them.' Kitty reflected her returning confidence.

'I've grown up with selkies. There are as many grey seals on the Orkney Islands as there are here, two a penny in fact. They're part of our everyday life, in fact, *we* believe that seals unify land with sea.'

Kitty smiled to herself, how logical was that belief? But she only said, 'they sound very strange, what do they look like?'

'Have you no seen one?' He gasped his incredulity out into the fog, 'Come on,' and again he fumbled for her hand. His was warm and reassuring and she felt a surge of liking for the thoughtful young Scotsman. How different was he from the prickly visitor who had accompanied Sir Walter to Barraburn!

Kitty said. 'Tell me about the seals,' as they began to walk back along the way she had come, the mist still floating as white sheets pegged out along the coastline.

'They are really just big blobs of blubber or fat, the bulls can be up to ten feet long with hind limbs that propel them in water but are useless on land, though their front flippers can help manoeuvre them onto rocks. The cows are smaller.'

'Oh, you don't make them sound very attractive. I do wish this mist would clear, I would love to see one.'

The young man squeezed her hand, 'Let's be quiet.' He stopped. Then he whispered, 'the mist is beginning to thin...you could be lucky!'

As he spoke, the sea swam back into vision, flat calm, unruffled; nothing broke the surface. There was not even a seabird in view. They stood expectantly, her companion peering at the empty scene with a boyish eagerness. Kitty willed the animals to appear, if only for him!

The incoming tide rippled like lines of eels, in contrast, Olaf was perfectly still, restrained and patient. Kitty found herself savouring his quality of peace. How long before he would tire of this childish pursuit?

'Where *are* they!' the disappointed child was not far away in Olaf's exclamation and then came an urgent whisper, 'Can you sing, lass?'

'Why?' Kitty sounded her surprise

'Seals love music. Come on join in, the louder the better...' and he broke into song.

I am a man upon the land
I am a selkie in the sea
And when I'm far from every strand
My home it is in Skule Sheery.

Silence, and he repeated the verse, his voice louder this time; and Kitty, entranced by the words, slowly began to sing- following his melody, her soprano joining his baritone as the music drifted in unison out over the waves.

Together they sang the song and then when still nothing broke the flat sea, it was Kitty's turn to sound her impatience.

'They *must* be somewhere close, one more time!' and they began again in even louder voice. '*I am a man upon----*'

And then suddenly there were the animals, straight in front of them.

'Oh, look!' Two domed heads bobbed in the water and Kitty could see inquisitive black eyes and hairy nostrils. Their singing had summoned the seals! She watched spell-bound as the sea-creatures acted out their partnered ballet just feet away; moving together then drifting apart like two furry balls floating in the water. And then as if suddenly bored they both dived back below the surface leaving hardly a ripple. It was as though they had never been.

'Oh, thank you for showing me them.' She imagined a young boy on his lonely Orkney shore conjuring up hidden playmates from beneath the surf. No wonder he loved the sea. And here he was on Holy Island!

Without turning to face her he said dismissively, 'But surely, you must know all this if you live on the island.' The Orcadian's feet were back on dry land with a logical answer for everything and voicing his doubts of her.

'No I'm a visitor, Olaf just like you. I arrived but yesterday.' His name was out before she could check it.

'You know my name?' He let go of her hand in an exclamation of surprise.

'Yes, I'm Kitty. We met a few weeks ago, do you remember?'

Heightened colour flamed his face as recognition dawned. The man who'd thought nothing of singing to seals instantly mortified that he'd been so foolish in front of a woman. *And* one he knew. His eyes showed his chagrin.

'Miss Macnab..? I'll detain you no longer… I'm sure you are able to find your own way… now that the mist has cleared.'

Eight

Two fair heads bobbed into view as she approached Pilgrim House and Kitty waved her greeting.

'You look like two seals come to the surface, and I didn't even have to sing!'

Both girls frowned and Marion Smythe questioned. 'How do singing and seals go together?'

'No matter,' Kitty laughed, already she felt a conspiratorial link with the man she'd just left. Olaf Magson had a hidden, playful side to his nature and because of him, she knew seals liked music - a fact her new-made friends obviously did not. The girls had never bothered to discover the finer points of their island home!

'If you sing, Kitty, you can entertain our guests tonight.' Marion nodded her satisfaction, ignoring their visitor's shake of the head.

'Sorry, I'm no soloist.'

'More important is that you can hold a hand of Whist.' Louise had a pleading note in her voice and her expression said clearly that this time they would not take no for an answer.

'Oh I don't mind trying my hand at cards.' Kitty smiled. The suggested entertainment for the evening could not have been better. Card-holding sessions at Slymefoot drinking den had been long and competitive and she had more than held her own. Tonight the players might be from more sophisticated society, but the cards would hold the same value and she savoured the chance to show her skill!

Marion linked her arm through Kitty's. 'Where have you been?' She was smiling but her eyes questioned. 'Not one day in the house and you are forsaking us. Could you not sleep? Was the mattress not to your liking?'

'Everything is perfect and I slept the sleep that knows no waking.' Their guest sought to annul any suspicion of discomfort.

'Oh, do not say that even in jest. It is full water now but the tide is on the turn and that is when the last breath is wrung.' Louise, looking stricken, crossed herself, and Kitty thought, *so she at least knows something about local lore.*

Marion Smythe laughed, seizing hold of Kitty, 'nyway hopefully not, my dear Kitty, before we've had the chance of beating you at cards. I hope you come laden with shillings!'

'I didn't realise it's an island pastime.' So the card-playing was *serious* stuff. Kitty sought to keep her voice non-committal. She dismissed Marion as a serious challenge but Louise could prove worthy opposition; unlike her sister, she appeared to have the concentration needed for a meaningful contest.

Louise took hold of Kitty's free arm, 'In the meantime it's our intent to show you the island. That is if you haven't seen it already? What have you been doing whilst we lay sleeping?'

'Oh, nothing I do assure you. How could I in such a fog, it was as though I was in blindfold?'

'Oh, good,' Louise skipped beside her. 'It's not often we are able to be guides.'

Marion lifted her eyes in disdain, 'There's not an awful lot to see, only sea and more sea and the smell that goes with it.' She wrinkled her nose in disgust, 'I swear it clings even to us, the passers-by!' She waved towards the fisher-women Kitty had seen earlier down on the shore.

Louise wagged her finger at her sister, 'Shame on you, those women are baiting the summer lines with lugworm. It's a horrible job. They say it takes three hours to do a line and their hands get horribly stained.' The more down to earth Miss Smythe bent towards Kitty and laughed. 'I do *declare*, you've already acquired the perfume; 'Eau de peche' is its name. Have you been helping to gather mussels down on the beach with the women? They must be skyent by now'

'Louise, how do you know such words and what on earth does it mean?' Marion shook her head, exasperated at her younger sister.

'Shelled of course, what else do you do with mussels?'

'So is that really a word you need in *your* vocabulary?' Marion sneered her contempt sounding just like her mother.

'Don't listen to her', Louise smirked. 'If you are looking for a big handsome fisherman you are halfway there, Kitty. Not that I am saying you reek of fish.'

'Louise what would Mama say if she heard you speaking so?'

'Well she can't, and I wouldn't say no to one of them, and neither would you, Marion. Chance would be a fine thing.'

So saying, the girl came to a halt beside two island men, down on their knees, engrossed in the task in hand; neither looked up to acknowledge their audience. A large sail, pale from the winter gales was spread flat on the cropped grass. Marion seized Kitty's hand to move them on but Kitty stood her ground, intrigued to watch the sail-cloth changing to a rich brown hue. The men worked in rhythm, dipping long poles with brush heads into a liquid that bubbled above a fire then transferring the new colour in wide arching sweeps.

'It's called barking or tanning the cloth.' Louise pointed out.

'It's a beautiful colour,' murmured Kitty. The men made no reply and Louise giggled appreciatively as they caught up with Marion who strode on ahead.

'That Dougal Patterson is canny. Don't you think so, Marion?'

Her sister tossed her head and Kitty smiled to herself; the two young men were to be noticed; weather-beaten with black beards, tough out-door types in their gansies and high boots. Though neither had heeded the three girls, it was obvious the men had been aware of them. Louise inhaled loudly as she said,

    'Do you know sister- the sweat of a working man is my favourite perfume? Perhaps you could get me a bottle for my birthday. I think you know a source.' Louise smiled innocently at Marion who looked daggers.

    'So th'lier yeedee is nowt.' The island patois tumbled again from Louise's lips. Her listeners gazed at her in amazement.

    'Louise, where on *earth* do you hear these things?' Marion flounced away from her sister and Kitty laughed. 'I do declare I've come to a foreign land!'

    To distract the arguing girls she pointed to the ruin lying behind the harbour that dominated the skyline.

    'What is that?' Her guides followed her finger to the once-magnificent building arching into the sky, fragile in its great age.

    'That's the Priory.' Marion was dismissive. 'You know - monks and things, hardly anything to see now but just a few grassy mounds and a jumble of stones lying about the place.'

    Louise smirked. 'But it gave the island its name. *Holy*! Island… *was ever a place more wrongly named?* Now it's as though everyone tries to prove it untrue. You'll discover Kitty, how well we succeed…'

    'By now you'll have learnt not to believe a word my sister says.' Marion turned away from the ruined monastery, 'anyway it's not worth a visit' as she eyed her smart ankle boots and the wide expanse of grass to be crossed with a coating of rime glistening in the sun.

    'The ruin was ideal for hide and seek when we were children,' Louise, in stouter footwear stepped in to the field without such hesitation as though she still would play the game.

    'Look at it! The Monastery can be seen for miles around, built by men too trusting of their fellow human beings. The even earlier Abbey brought invaders in long boats bringing with them death and destruction!'

Kitty stared up at pink stone warm in the morning light, the ruin a beautiful reminder of the island's turbulent history.

Louise bowed her head and put her hands together, her voice mocking, 'The monks' prayers weren't loud enough. Take heed Kitty, best to be on your guard than uttering futile prayers. In fact you should have eyes in the back of your head on this island.' She stopped and they watched an approaching horseman.

'Halt, friend or foe!'

'An invader with intent!' Henry Smythe reigned in his mount and grinned down at the girls his good humour belying his words. He turned to Kitty,

'I hope you're going to come quietly, or I shall have to throw you over my saddle, my boat awaits in the harbour.'

He pointed to a vessel drawn up under the ridge of high ground that backed the bay.

'Oh, Henry...!' Kitty raised her hands in mock subjection and gathered her skirts as if to run.

'Might has right.' Henry grabbed at her, 'But you're supposed to put up more of a struggle.' He sounded disappointed and Kitty shrugged her shoulders.

'I know better than to resist a dominant male come from the sea.'

Louise interrupted, 'Easy conquest brother mine, but just remember tonight it will be female dominance at the cards.'

Marion turned in the direction of the village, 'Come on Louise, we were on our way to see old Janet *if* you remember.'

Louise grinned, 'Off you go, Kitty. When a Viking longboat sailed into harbour you never knew which handsome man was going to ravish you.'

In the evening Kitty took care with her toilette. Within her carpet, bag her blue muslin had suffered hardly a crease and it fell softly about her slim form. Her cheeks were healthily pink and her eyes surveyed the assembled company with unconcealed interest. Fresh air and new excitements had brought back her old sparkle. It was a long time since she had felt so good!

Henry was immediately attentive as she entered the room, openly showing his admiration as he took her arm and guided her to a group of unknown faces.

'Let me introduce you, Kitty, to our fellow card players.' Names followed handshakes, but the curtseys were accompanied by quickened interest or frowns of speculation, depending on whether they were male or female. Kitty smiled demurely at them all, eyes lowered, handshake fleeting, she was a guest in the Smythe household hardly to be noticed. She knew already she'd made one enemy on the island!

That morning Henry had led her away from his sisters just in time. Already she resented being used as a dartboard on which the Smythe girls fought out their sisterly antipthy. Unused to female company, Kitty found their quarrelling irksome. Brother Henry was different - flippant, sardonic, intriguing, and *very* attentive!

Long, purposeful strides had brought them to the jetty and she'd no difficulty in keeping up with him, her journeys on high tracks over the border had quickened her pace to that of any male. It pleased her that there was no lessening because of skirts.

'Thought you might like to see what gets me away from island introspection.' Henry turned and gestured toward the village and the retreating figures of Marion and Louise. 'The sea is a lifeline- always has been.'

'Not always, judging from the ravening hordes that came across the water intent on *plunder*.' Kitty grinned remembering Louise's words.

'...another name for trade.' Henry laughed.

'It was a man's world. According to your sisters no woman was safe.'

'I think they would have been,' Henry grinned down at her, 'now you would have been different.'

Kitty frowned at him, her good humour gone in an instant.

'So do you *really* think I would have welcomed such a fate?' She turned away to hide her anger. Did all men look at her and see her as easy meat? At that moment she cursed her black curls and the banter that came easily and unguarded. Together, they gave an impression she had no wish to convey. She thought of Olaf Magson. How obviously he disapproved of her!

Henry came to a halt and stared down at her. 'Forgive me, I spoke in jest. Well, concerning you. For my sisters… it's the truth. They would have been standing on the shore hailing the boats in a loud descant, their eager hands beckoning like frenzied windmills.'

Kitty laughed in spite of herself. His words rang true; the sisters were caged lions as she had been in those snowy days at Barraburn. Yet what did they seek, children clinging about their skirts..? Marion perhaps…but Louise must have other ambitions. And what of her own bairn, clinging now to another woman's skirts?

'Ahoy there Dougal!'

They had stopped beside a boat large enough to be seagoing, drawn up now at the end of the jetty under a rocky ridge of high ground that shielded the on-shore winds. It was a natural harbour that served the island well. Beyond the bay, waves were beginning to rise and fall in a gathering breeze.

'Welcome to *The Sea Plunder*. She is my escape!' Pride of ownership cut across Henry's usual mask.

Kitty grinned, 'She's well named. The first time I saw you I thought you could be taken for a pirate.'

'Really..?' Her companion was amused.

'Well not everyone has a scar like that...' she eyed the prominent mark on his cheek,

'…my badge of office!' He fingered the blemish with a fondness that was as deep etched.

'Hey, Dougal, where are you, man?' Henry called across the bows as a head appeared from below deck. 'Oh, there you are. Kitty, let me introduce you to my Captain.'

The tall, swarthy seaman who earlier had been the focused attention of both sisters looked down at them from his advantage point. Dougal Patterson, as Louise had said, was *worthy* of notice! They stood feet below his towering figure. Viking prowess had been handed down through the blood-line of this man...legally or otherwise.

Kitty held out her right hand and put her other one on the ship rail.

'Oh NO!' Dougal Patterson moved with the speed of a blood-hound and rough, calloused fingers unlocked hers from the rail. She staggered back, amazed to see him wipe his hand down the length of his trouser leg as though it had touched something offensive.

Henry's laughter rang out across the bay. 'Come on man, you surely don't heed such old wives' tales?'

Kitty's foot was already back on the boat, no man would put her off so easily. What had *he* got to hide, that he did not want her aboard? The next minute she was face down in the soft mud of the Ooze.

'No woman will step on any boat that I sail!' The man's anger spat across the bow, 'they bring nothing but ill-luck.' As he spoke, he crossed himself in a gesture reminiscent of Louise when Kitty had spoken of the *sleep that knew no waking.*

She struggled to her feet, black mud clinging to her skirt and hair, anger darkening her face beneath the dirt. Henry was a mixture of horror and amusement.

'I'm sorry, Kitty.' He handed her a pristine handkerchief and then helped to guide it across her cheeks, flicking away the Ouse slime with eager hands. 'So we're a superstitious lot on the island. No woman is allowed on a boat. I should have warned you.'

'Not even when invited by the owner?' Kitty managed a weak smile at her assailant but there was no answering acknowledgement. Dougal Patterson stood glowering down at her.

'So what happened to the boats of the Viking invaders? Did they all sink with their female booty on board?' Kitty echoed her pique. 'Take your pick girls, a watery grave or a pirate bed!' Determined to have the last word, she turned her back on the uncouth fisherman. Dougal Patterson was nothing but an *ignorant*, superstitious man!

His very name had been the one given to her by John Armstrong. Dougal Patterson, Captain of *The Sea Plunder* sailed the ketch owned jointly by Armstrong and Smythe. Her first meeting with him had been inauspicious. But the morning fray still brought a smile to her lips; for she had to admit that hill-country folk were as superstitious as seafarers, hadn't she herself bitten her bairn's nails in her first year of life, rather than cut them?

She looked for Patterson at the evening cards. But the handsome seaman was nowhere to be seen in the smart Smythe social gathering. Everyone in the world knew how to play Whist, but calloused hands could not be allowed to hold Mrs Smythe's packs! Instead, smooth fingers that had never pulled a ship's rope in gale or calm slid over the suits. Poor Marion and Louise if this was the extent of the Mother's chosen companions for her family. Henry was lucky he was free to go further afield to find his friends!

Pale and intense was Kitty's view of both the women and men assembled in Pilgrim House; there was not a whisper of the thrilling game of chance played by the sea. Not even a farmer stood stolid and red-cheeked in their midst. And judging from the stilted conversation little of note had occurred since their last card meeting! The advent of a new player caused hardly a ripple and Kitty was accepted into the circle as though she had only missed the last game. These people neither looked for, nor expected, excitement. It could be a long evening.

Her dealt hand was good, Hearts- Queen, King and Ace, Spades- Knave, Queen and King. She only had to concentrate and she could not fail to make a good showing. *Luck* was what card-playing was all about! She even hoped the second game would send her a more challenging hand; but then, she would soon become unpopular if she won too often.

And her popularity could wane no more so than with Louise. The girl had a gleam in her eye and her cheeks were flushed. Kitty was glad they did not play at the same table. From the girl's expression she was out to win from the first bell. Kitty sat opposite Henry, joint owner of the Sea Plunder, as he relaxed in the comfort of the parlour. Surely it was his sailing activities that paid for the gentility of the family! The mantelpiece held fine porcelain alongside the delicate bronze supplied by the son of the family. Did they come hidden amongst the legitimate cargo of his boat?

So someone was not playing fair with John Armstrong. Was it Patterson, captain of *Sea Plunder*, and the real reason why he had not wanted her on board?

She won the round easily and Henry gathered up the two shillings and placed it beside her as she saw Louise pick up the same amount on the next table. Kitty lost the next game, Louise harvested her winnings. Play was serious and conversation was brief before Mrs Smythe rose from her chair by the fire and rang the bell for an interval. The groups of four broke up, refreshment now uppermost on their minds.

Henry took her by the arm, 'I hope your treatment by Patterson this morning has not affected your concentration.'

'Oh never that! I hope to prove to Mr Patterson how wrong he is to listen to old wives tales. I'll step aboard his ship if it's the last thing I do!'

'Oh no, dear Kitty, it's my ship and I forbid you. Island lore is island lore and not to be broken.' Henry was still smiling - though not with his eyes- and his words were said slowly and distinctly so that there was no mistaking his meaning!

Kitty raised her eyebrows. 'But you are educated, Henry. How can you believe such nonsense?' So ship's captain and ship's owner were both ranged against her, and both were armed with a watertight excuse. Age old custom would keep her from the decks of the *Sea Plunder*. Astute Armstrong should have foreseen that obstacle!

'Island lore... Henry, are you instructing Miss Macnab in our taboos? I assure you they should be heeded, young lady.' Mrs Smythe nodded emphatically.

'Oh, don't listen to either of them, Kitty. Taboos are there to be broken.' Louise butted in to the conversation in a flurry of dissent as she looked rebelliously at her mother. There was an uncomfortable silence before the older woman, lips pursed, reacted to her daughter.

'One day Louise, you will go too far. Let us hope you learn your lesson sooner rather than later and that I am there to witness it.' The older woman's voice was haughty with anger and there was another uncomfortable silence. Not for the first time kitty saw the antipathy between the two!

An older man seated beside his hostess, and no part of the card-playing, intervened. 'Thou shalt not steal, thou shalt not covert thy neighbour's cattle, thou shalt not step on board ship if you are a woman.' The speaker's words brought instant relieved laughter.

'And Louise, always remember to honour your father and mother so that your days may be long.' The words of the island's vicar gently teased, his good humour written across his benevolent face. He turned to Kitty,

'It is also good to remember, Miss Macnab, not to speak of a pig or a rabbit on board ship or to mention the number thirteen. For someone in my calling, the latter is easy to understand; the thirteen seated at the Last supper was prelude to the Cruxifiction, the others I cannot explain. But then not everything can be reasoned.'

'Of course not,' Kitty smiled at the man. His face spoke of experience, his words spoke of tolerance. Not everything on the island reflected bigotry. Here indeed was someone who disproved her unthinking assessment of the gathering as pale look-a-likes. This man had his feet firmly on the ground. She almost expected to see him wink, but instead the island minister bowed and turned to go.

'Rector, Let us give our winnings for your endless good works.' Mrs Smythe gushed her benevolence, her eyes challenging the winning players. Kitty, surprised, took out the two shillings safely stowed away in her pocket and acknowledged the murmur of thanks.

'Louise!' Her mother's strident voice reminded the other winner and the girl rose to her feet, an obstinate retort quick on her lips, her hands tightly grasping the money.

'Sorry, Mr Brown…charity begins at home.'

Nine

The storm buffeted the island, tossing it like a stricken ship. The nor'easter began in the night hours venting it's fury on the vulnerable speck of land that lay open to the full force of the gale. It began quietly, whispering in the eaves then rattling the windows ever more loudly in its frantic demand for attention. Kitty, immediately awake, spied from her porthole anything and everything unfastened clattering along the street in an advancing wave of destruction. Perhaps it was the Reverend Brown's God out for retribution against sinner Louise on this so- called Holy island. Mrs Smythe surely would be the first to agree!

In the morning Mrs Smythe kept to her bed and demanded both daughters attend to her needs. There was no sign of Henry, but the Sea Plunder would be his one concern. However much protection the Heugh offered with its two-hundred foot elevated shelter, the ship's anchor would be in a tug of war with the wind. At least the boat was not out at sea. Kitty looked down at the empty street; fishermen and their womenfolk were locked behind closed doors. The tyrant wind had emptied the decks.

Jaded by a sleepless night, Kitty paced restlessly before finally seeking the kitchen in the hope of conversation, but the cook was no Pleasance. Short-tempered and brusque she dismissed the intrusion with a snapped, 'It'll last three days this one. The nor'easter never knows when to stop once it's got started.'

In an outhouse, rough trousers, boots and enveloping sacks for such weather lay amongst the clutter. Kitty eyed them with a sigh of relief. Three days confined in Pilgrim House held little attraction. Wind had never imprisoned her in the high borderland, nor would it now. There was no one about. In one deft movement, her dress was replaced by the all-weather outfit on the hook. Man-sized, it hung off her, but with some pushing and pulling and stuffing into the wide boots, she was ready. She wasn't convinced she wouldn't balloon into the sky when she was out in the full force of the storm! Adrenalin began to pump- she'd had enough of sedate parlour. Instead the smell and confusion of the storeroom lifted her spirits to a growing excitement!

The noise behind her made her jump, so sure had she been that she was alone. She spun round and there looking startled and embarrassed was the figure of Olaf Magson. Colour flamed her cheeks, incredulity and anger in equal measure making her stutter her shock.

'H-how long have you been here?'

'Just this minute.'

Kitty stared at him in disbelief, the moody Orcadian as unpredictable as the wind and an *unwanted* intrusion. Now he looked as displeased to see her as she was to find him here in the outer buildings of Pilgrim House.

'What are you doing here?'

'I might ask you the same.' He glowered at her and then his face relaxed.

'Kit—Kitty! You must be a weather sprite, first in fog now in storm.' His startling blue eyes were full of merriment. 'Look at you, what do you look like?'

'What do you *expect*?' Kitty pulled the sou'wester more tightly about her head, pushing her curls out of sight.

He eyed her ill-fitting, man's clothes, 'The name Kitty doesn't suit you when you're dressed like that. Come on, Kit, what are we waiting for? You look ready to face the storm!'

It was exhilarating. The first shock took her breath away and she staggered backwards, the boots big and unwieldy. But she steadied herself against the wall of the house and Olaf, making no attempt to help, strode ahead out into the full force of the wind. Kitty followed and separately they were blown as rubbish along the village street!

She followed him to the lea of the island, the wind losing its punch as the stone-walled lane beside the old church dropped down to the beach that faced the mainland. It was as though they had closed the door on an intruder. Safe on the other side the nor'easter could no longer take their breath and on it their words.

There were other figures gathered by the village pump.

'The women know to come down here to Jenny's well. In a nor'easter it's sheltered and they don't lose half their water.'

They watched as two women noisily clanked the pump handle up and down gushing water into the waiting metal buckets; filled, they grated against the cobbles, joining in a loud descant to the wind. Then, job done the women hoisted the buckets on to the wooden frame about their shoulders and turned in the direction of their homes. Kitty wondered if the Smythe girls even knew about the existence of the well or the bucket frames.

Olaf had disappeared down onto the shore. 'You must know the island well.' Kitty joined him.

'And St Cuthbert knew a thing or two as well.' He indicated a small island little more than a rocky outcrop that lay a short distance from the land. 'Even though it's sheltered, how would you fancy living out there, suffering for mankind and praying for the forgiveness of their sins?'

'St Cuthbert?' A childhood memory told her the local saint had wandered her hills. 'He lived there?' She pointed at the rock in disbelief.

'Yes... hard to imagine but so the story goes...'

'I've always thought of him in sunlit hills tending the sheep, never out in wind and rain.' Kitty laughed at her childish imagination. Here was reality; the rocky outcrop a flimsy boat on an insecure mooring. Beyond, the mainland towered dark and inhospitable, Cheviot and Hedgehope breasting the skyline in scurrying clouds that brought streaking rain onto the unprotected hills. What of her baby left behind in the hills? Fervently, she hoped that innocent dreams still filled her slumbers, that her reality was a warm kitchen and Pleasance.

'It must have been a constant contest between saint and elements... just to survive was an achievement!' Even Olaf looked impressed.

Kitty did not answer but lifted her face and felt only the faint brush of the wind before it bounced off and out into the unsheltered bay. She raised her arms as a gesture of defiance and there was only a gentle buffeting.

'You knew where to come to get out of the wind.' She turned to her companion, 'It makes these scarecrow clothes unnecessary!'

Olaf shook his head. 'Scarecrows have a place...'

She nodded. '...in planted fields... not windswept beaches. But at least I can stride out in these trousers.'

'Yes, we should walk.' He looked toward the sand yellowing now that the tide had retreated and the wind had become the towel. But he made no effort to move.

'Wait here, there's something I want to show you.'

Along the tidemark, pebbles and stones littered the shore and Kitty watched as her companion moved further down the beach, crouched on his haunches and began to sift the debris. There was a yell of satisfaction and then he was back beside her.

'Cuddy's Beads.'

Kitty eyed the tiny ridged objects. 'Are they shell or stone?'

'Neither. They're fossils laid down in the sea millions of years ago. It's said St Cuthbert used to gather them, hence their name.'

Kitty held out her hand and Olaf dropped the delicate limestone onto her palm. 'Not enough for a necklace, but then you are in men's clothes.' He winked at her. 'Never mind, you could make yourself one for when you are dressed in your more normal garb. It would ward off evil.'

'Is this an evil place then?'

He laughed. 'No more than most places.'

'You don't sound too convincing.'

He shrugged dismissively, 'It is best not to dig too deep below the surface.'

'Or it will fill up with water.' Kitty retorted and he nodded,

'Did you know seals carry the souls of dead sailors?' The teasing had gone and Olaf's searching blue eyes held her gaze.

'There are an awful lot of them swimming about out there then. The sea must be very greedy taking men as we take fish.'

'Of course… it's tit for tat. You'll soon see what it can do when it's roused.'

'You've changed your tune.' Instinctively she climbed back on to the land to the sheltering sandstone wall and he moved with her.

'Why is it you love the sea, Olaf?'

'Are you sure you want to know? It'll take at least an hour.' Again that mixture of serious and amused, she was beginning to learn his moods.

'Oh, not long then!'

'Wouldn't you rather be snug indoors in Pilgrim House?'

'No!' She shook her head. 'I'm happy if you are.'

He turned to look at her, an odd look on his face. His eyes reflected the sea, a liquid, changing expression of hidden and unfathomable depths. No, an hour was not long enough!

He said, his eyes fixed on her face, 'Yes I love it.'

'I know,' she laughed, 'you told me the first time we met and from the first moment when I stood on the shore watching the water ebb and flow all I could see was you- a man of changeable moods like the sea.'

He made no reply. Kitty hoped she'd not said too much and that, now, her silence would bring his words tumbling out as they had in the parlour at Barraburn and when they'd looked for the seals at Emmanuel Head.

'I grew up on an island- smaller than Holy Island. Sanday lies at the eastern extremity of the Orkneys. It's an afterthought of land.'

He stared down at the palm of his hand, fingering the tiny fossils that he'd found before suddenly tossing them like fives; they landed on his upturned fist then scattered back down onto the sand. 'The seals were my playmates, the driftwood on the beach my toys... even more so after....'

'I used to float sticks down the stream beside our cottage.' Kitty shared her make-use-of-what-was-lying-around childhood. It had made them both resourceful.

Olaf stared into the distance. 'I was only four years old when we went to live at Start Point; but old enough to appreciate what I'd been missing and what I'd been given. The sea, always there, always ready for an adventure and never quarrelling as we did at home. Arguing is a pastime in a lighthouse keeper's cottage you know.'

Kitty nodded thinking of the Smythe sisters equally confined in their island home.

'So you lived *on* the sea, a lighthouse must have been almost as good as being on a ship.'

Olaf pursed his lips, 'You could say that, one good thing- you don't get seasick... but it can be lonely.'

'Didn't you have a brother or sister?' Kitty had always regretted the lack of siblings.

'Aye.'

His voice was curt and Kitty looked at him in surprise, 'So you weren't the lonely child forced to befriend dumb animals on the beach.' She laughed 'I could have saved my sympathy.'

'Aye, but only after Ian...'

'After Ian?'

'After he died.'

Kitty flushed at her lack of intuition. 'Oh, I'm sorry.'

'My other brother came on the scene too late to be a playmate. I was fourteen when he was born. All I did was resent him for being too young to join in my escapades. He just got in the way, though I have him to thank for Sir Walter.'

'Who?' Kitty showed her surprise, 'Do you mean Sir Walter Scott...did he actually get to Orkney, even as far as Sanday? It's hard to believe when you make it sound as though it lies at the end of the world!'

'That's what appealed to him. He quests a story and he's not always been so lame.'

'So when did he visit?' Kitty strove to picture the writer as a younger more active man; but then he was still intrepid. Even in the last month his wanderings had brought him to the out-of the-way Armstrong farmhouse. He was certainly game!

'It was 1814, and he came on board the Northern Lighthouse Commissioners' vessel with Robert Stevenson, the great lighthouse builder. Two famous Scots..!' Olaf paused and she knew the scene was forever printed on his memory. '...you can imagine how excited I was. For once I felt proud of my home, proud they should want to come to see our lighthouse. You know, we had the first revolving apparatus in the whole of Scotland and Stevenson had brought Sir Walter to see it! *Every half a second* it beamed its warning!' His eyes flashed and Kitty could see rays of light piercing the Orkney water.

'So Sir Walter was impressed?'

'Of course,' Olaf was dismissive, 'but you'll never guess what struck storyteller Scott above anything else that day?' He grinned at the memory. 'It wasn't the new, impressive light, but the sight of my mother holding a six day old infant in her arms, one that she had delivered herself without any help.'

It was Kitty's turn to look impressed, 'No wonder!'

'Yes, resourceful if nothing else my mother, as strong as any lighthouse, no childhood tears moved her. Then I never saw one tear on her face even when our Ian drowned!' He stopped and the set of his jaw told her she should not question.

Kitty said quietly, 'A hard life quenches any self-pity.'

'Aye...' He laughed dismissively. '...anyway it wasn't just my new baby brother whom Sir Walter noticed that day. When he got back to the mainland he wrote to ask if... if I would like to come to Edinburgh-to finish my education!'

'Oh how wonderful!' She imagined the impact of that letter on the remote Orkney home.

'Yes, I study in Edinburgh, first at school and now at the University.'

Kitty took in the full significance of his reply. 'But Edinburgh is not by the sea. Do you miss it?'

'Aye, but then I would have gone anywhere to get away. Besides it's a means to an end.' His soft voice echoed resolve and Kitty caught hold of Olaf's hand. She was seeing him in a very different light. His past held deep unhappiness, *just* like hers.

She said 'Your story is a Scott novel. Don't tell me you're a character in one of his books, if so- hero or villain?' As soon as the question was out she regretted it.

'Villain of course, how did you guess?' Olaf almost spat out the words, 'But Sir Walter is a kind man and he wouldn't knowingly gain from real-life tragedy.' A thin smile shadowed his face, 'He has written a novel, called The Pirate, based on his travels in Orkney and Shetland. I think it's near to publication.'

'That I must read...so you are no hero...' she strove to make her voice light, 'then I seem to remember you didn't see me in a heroine's role either. How discerning you are.'

Olaf looked at her 'At Barraburn you were Kitty, on Holy Island you are Kit. I don't go in for coy female leads. Why have you come to the island, Kit?'

'I might ask you the same question!' And as Olaf made no reply she said, 'I came to see the sea. You'd made me curious to see it for myself.'

Blue eyes stared at brown and Kitty knew that the water between them was calm, sheltered from the storm. Yet somehow she knew that like her, Olaf's reason for being there would not be quite as he told.

'You're a mystery man, why were you in Pilgrim House?'

'Easy answer, I'm a keen wildfowler and so is Henry, unfortunately the storm has interrupted our pastime.' She was silenced by his reply; here there were as many birds as people, even more at the summer migration, their distinctive cries the noise that dominated the island. Wigeon, duck, geese, curlew shrieked their presence; and no doubt young Olaf had wielded a gun since his early youth. What could be more natural than him seeking such a spot? Very different fortune had led them both to this sea-buffeted island off Northumberland.

She watched him as he jumped back down on to the beach again and from his tense stance she knew he thought he'd said too much. The past hung heavily on his shoulders as it did on hers.

'Kit,' she ran his name for her through silent lips. It sounded right and his attitude to her had changed since the christening. She liked it, 'Kitty' described the luxuriant-haired girl that men openly admired and wanted- 'Kit' sounded like an equal companion for an intrepid wildfowler.

And like her, Olaf was a conflicting mixture. Could such a man believe in fate? She wondered if his brother's death lay in its fickle hand. Olaf had said there was a logical answer to everything when she'd feared the eerie noise in the fog; but only a few minutes ago she'd heard him say that seals carried the souls of dead sailors.

He was standing now lost in thought, eyeing the far mud flats. Once the storm had passed he would be off with Henry on their chosen sport. The tide was out, but she had no desire to follow the guide posts that linked back to the mainland; she was free to go yet already the island held her in its thrall.

In the distance, birds circled and called.

'Do you need flat calm?' Kitty joined him on the beach and away from the shelter of the wall again she felt the wind.

'For what?' Olaf jumped.

'Wildfowling of course.'

'Oh, no, it is best when the force of the wind drops slightly, then the birds come low across the island to get out of the buffeting and into our range. The cry goes up- '*The geese are in.*' She could almost hear the flutter of wings, the cries, and then the sharp thud and silence. She shivered, suddenly aware that she was cold. The wind was eddying about them. She shivered again and Olaf said,

'Come on, Kit we've been sheltering too long from the storm. Let's test its teeth. You'll find it exhilarating.'

Down by Jenny's well they'd been lulled into a false calm but out beyond the Ooze there could be no more words. The wind screamed its vengeance in a tirade of venom. It tore at her clothing, so that the added din was of flapping, agitated cloth. Suddenly her sou'wester was no more and her hair whipped about her head as though it resented its own mass and length. She watched the flying headgear and Olaf in full flight after it before it became lodged in a prostrate thorn bush. He retrieved it with an inaudible yell of triumph and then he was back tying the ribbon under her chin, biting his lip as his numbed hands fought to keep control.

Then, her hand firmly in his, they faced the elements. The sea thundered upon the rocks, giant-high waves in a lather of hate, spitting their fury at the unprotected shore. Sand blew in her eyes and mouth, her cheeks ached from the biting onslaught and she clung to Olaf knowing that without his strength she would be but flotsom. He squeezed her hand and she could feel his serenity. How often had he stood watching the fury of this playmate, delighting in its dominance, but knowing it would subside as quickly as it had risen?

He let go of her hand and simultaneously they lifted their arms outstretched into the wind. She watched his feet shift as he slid forward lying prone upon the wind and it bore his weight. She followed his example and felt the unseen support buoy her up to become a hovering bird. She turned to face him, a smile of wonder etched on her cheeks and, laughing, he bent and kissed her, brushing her lips. His lips tasted of the sea, salt coarse and biting.

They ran all the way back to Pilgrim House, hand clasped in hand at first, Kitty unsure whether she ever drew breath. She was aloft with the wind and like the birds her feet no longer touched the ground. And then they were in the village and there were cottage eyes, he let go of her hand and she was adrift, a hostage to the storm. Olaf had been her anchor, without him she was a rudderless boat. They reached the blue door and he strode off down the street.

In the outhouse she retrieved her dress but, reluctant to take off her borrowed disguise, retreated to her room. She stared at herself in the mirror. A shapeless, seal-like creature gazed back at her with enquiring eyes. Her unruly hair, released by the sou'wester's disappearance, stumbled about her shoulders and impatiently she scrapped it back into a tight bunch. Uncluttered by curls, her face was different. Her chin showed resolve, and her high forehead complimented her eyes, unblinking and determined. This was the image that Olaf had liked, Kit, not Kitty. A wayward curl fell back across her brow and hurriedly she swept it back. She thought, 'for *him* I would cut it all off!'

Ten

Afternoon tea! No tempest could interrupt the daily formality. Noises from the parlour told her the family were gathered for the ritual. Female laughter met her as she descended the stairs but it was Olaf she saw as soon as she entered the room. He was seated by the fire as though it was something he did every day at four o'clock within the walls of Pilgrim House. It was a homely scene, tea in Indian tea- cups and saucers, seed cake on delicate plates, honey biscuits that melted in the mouth, all offered by two sisters dressed in pink-hued gingham dresses.

'Kitty,' Marion greeted her with a petulant smile. The older girl, slimmer and more petite than her sister, looked the very essence of simple elegance as she welcomed the late arrival.

'Where have you been? Do come by the fire, though I'm sure you cannot have been outside in that.' She waved her hand in the direction of the storm that had had no impact on her day. Every hair of her fair locks was prettily in place. Kitty regretted too late that her hair combing had been careless.

Even Olaf looked the gentleman in high collar and tight waistcoat, his years spent in the capital city clearly evident. He had risen at her entrance and she thought, *he's a chameleon, able to fit into any situation!*

Marion simpered up at him, 'Olaf Magson, Kitty Macnab.' Smiles, handshakes, their morning kiss had been in the wrong order of formalities!

Without a word Olaf offered her his vacated chair. She already knew his lips, but his blue eyes offered no recognition.

She smiled her thanks, cursing the curls that lay unbidden about her cheeks. For him she wanted only to be Kit!

Marion was eying her closely for Kitty's cheeks had flushed. 'To be sure I do believe our island suits you. You look better already. Does she not, Henry?'

'Indeed, I was just about to say the same.' Marion's brother proffered her a teacup and hovered behind Kitty's chair.

'My sisters stay by the fire on such a day, but you choose to go out at the height of the wind?' Henry Smythe raised his eyebrows. 'I saw you return to the outhouse. One can hardly imagine what could draw you out on such a day?' His dark features held calculation that made his facial scar even more prominent.

'Why not?' Kitty laughed, 'You should remember, the Cheviot Hills are hardly an afternoon tea party. I traipsed them in all weathers.'

'But you know them well, the island is different.'

Kitty nodded her agreement, 'So the more reason to go out and explore.

'So it was good that you met up with Olaf and he could see you home to the door.' Henry's voice had changed.

'Oh Kitty, I cannot think why you like to do such things,' Marion pouted her surprise, 'Still, it was good you found Olaf!' The older girl smiled up at the silent Orcadian and Kitty looked away. Amidst the crumbs she could still taste his salt on her lips.

'I wanted to see the storm in its fury, it was exhilarating. B-but Olaf knew where to find shelter.'

The Orcadian said nothing as Marion moved nearer to their visitor, the plate of biscuits her excuse, 'Hardly surprising, he knows the island like the back of his hand, don't you Olaf?'

'…do I?' languidly Olaf lifted his arm and studied his fingers in a frown of concentration. Then, slowly and deliberately he stretched out his left hand and with exaggerated movement traced around the outline of each finger with his other hand like a small child at play.

'All the ins and outs of this coast…it's quite a network!' Forcibly he separated each digit, 'In that cove the brandy is put ashore; in that one, the tea, between the index and little finger is the whisky, and then of course the tobacco goes there.'

There was a stunned silence and Louise giggled. Mrs Smythe who had been dozing by the fire, her face reddened by the heat, frowned at the young man beside her.

'What nonsense you do talk, my lad.' Playfully she reached out and gently slapped him across the knuckles. She said emphatically, 'Why don't you put those fingers of yours to better use. Come, Olaf, play something for us on the piano, you know we always enjoy that.'

'That's a good idea!' Louise, unusually siding with her mother seized Olaf's hand, led him across the room to the instrument and lifted the lid. Without protest their guest sat down at the piano stool and began to move his fingers across the keys.

He played well. *The Bluebells of Scotland* filled the room and then without any bidding there followed a Scottish reel. When he stopped there was spontaneous applause and Marion exclaimed,

'Let's dance after supper. That would be fun. The reel is my favourite dance.'

'Not tonight, dear Marion,' Louise was quick to contradict her sister, 'Olaf owes me some money from the last time we played cards. This is my chance to get it back.'

'Oh, girls, do stop it.' Brother Henry thumped his fist down on to the piano in his growing impatience.

'Kitty, you can see why we don't keep bees. They're reputed not to stay in a household that is at war with itself,' Henry was rattled both by his sisters and by Olaf with his childish finger display!

'Olaf, give us another tune. Our piano's a bit tinny, but it will help to drown out the storm.'

Louise glared at her brother, 'So you think *our* piano inferior to the ones found in the fine houses you frequent on the mainland? We'll...'

Olaf interrupted the rest of her outburst with a loud crash of keys and there followed another spirited reel. Again there was applause.

Kitty, do you sing?' Henry turned to their other guest.

She shook her head, it seemed like only yesterday her duet with Olaf had summoned the seals. She would remember it forever.

Olaf began to play, this time a gentle refrain. It was the calm after the storm and it washed over her like a retreating wave. Olaf had music for all emotions.

It was Louise who interrupted the appreciative silence.

'Thank you, Olaf for that.' She gave an impatient nod, 'But as Henry so rightly says our old instrument copes better with more rousing tunes.' She had a mischievous smile on her lips. 'Of course it could never be as good as the piano back in your lighthouse, could it Olaf?' She turned to Kitty.

'Would you believe it, Kitty, at chez Sanday they actually have a *grand* piano?' she emphasised the 'grand'. 'Yes, a real beauty by all accounts.'

'A-a grand piano?' Kitty had no idea what the girl was talking about, but it sounded most unlikely to fit into a lighthouse cottage.

'Yes, isn't that surprising?' Louise looked about the group, 'It's amazing what can be *found* on the beach,' Louise burst out laughing, 'be it on the coves of Holy island or in those of Orkney!'

Kitty thought, 'even Olaf isn't safe from this girl's sarcasm'. She's paying him back for his jibes about the hiding places on Holy Island! But with that thought, John Armstrong flashed into her mind and the reason why she was there. The Smythes, Olaf, were they *all* involved in the island illicit trading?

Henry snapped, 'Oh, Louise, how you like to make trouble.'

Louise giggled. 'It's true, oh brother mine, what else is there to do here?'

She turned her innocent blue eyes on Kitty, 'What about our other visitor? Did you find anything of interest on your travels today? Something that his Majesty's customs officers might be interested in? If so you'd better hide it away.' She turned back to Olaf, 'Of course it's more difficult with something like a Baby Grand.'

Olaf had stopped playing, the atmosphere in the room ruined by the girl's flippant nonsense.

Kitty spoke into the silence, turning to Henry, who still hovered at her side.

'I hear the best time for shooting is when the wind drops.'

'Shooting, shooting what? Louise pounced, 'Could it be excise men, perhaps, Kitty?' The innocent change of subject had played right into Louise's hands.

'I meant the geese and ducks that crowd the mud flats.' Kitty clenched her hands tightly together; that perverse girl had wittingly brought the storm into the Pilgrim House parlour.

Louise still looked dubious, 'So, Kitty, if you really do want to shoot ducks, its Henry you will have to smile at, certainly not our friend Olaf here. You won't find him in a punt with a gun in his hand. He can't kill a fly. *That isn't why Olaf is here.*'

Eleven

The Brent Duck was inches from her gun. She looked straight down the barrel into the innocent eyes that awaited the inevitable. Slowly, she lifted the rifle and aimed. As she did so the face before her changed into excise-man Byres. He was taunting her, goading her to pull the trigger. The crack of the shot resounded around her head, it was deafening. She clapped her hands to her ears, but there was no rifle to let fall; she was standing in the dock before Magistrate Armstrong, and she was handing him her child. Like *Pass the parcel,* passing him a tiny baby who clawed the air, reaching desperately back to her uncaring mother!

Kitty awoke with a stifled scream on her lips, and bathed in sweat. It was but a dream… her child had been safe in her womb when she had stood in the dock! She trembled at the memory of the expression on the Magistrate's face. Armstrong was the man with power, prosperous farmer, local upholder of the law, smuggler? Why *had* he been merciful? Why had he saved her from transportation? Would she have kept her child or would it have gone to the poor house orphanage? John Armstrong had held their fate in his hands, and now, in the latest twist, he had sent her to Holy Island and there she had found Olaf!

She lay tossing and turning, troubled by her dream; she'd handed over little Katherine to Armstrong just a few days ago, almost without a second thought. And for what but a final adventure before the growing child substantially limited her life? How *weak* she had become, how easily she'd succumbed to the allure that was Olaf Magson.

Of course, it could never ever be!

Past and present eddied in a whirlpool with a layer of scum muddying the surface. So the Smythes knew of her past? Had they told Olaf? She cast her mind back to the parlour scene in which he had not spoken a single word directly to her? No, his mood had been strange. His gaunt face stretched about his high cheek bones, his eyes watchful and alert. She moistened her lips but the salt had gone, washed away by Louise's snide reference to Kitty's past life. Could she *ever* explain herself to him and find acceptance? She knew she would never have the nerve.

But Olaf had hinted his past was not all good and Louise had been eager to water the seeds of doubt with him. Kitty sighed, had she misread the Orcadian companion to Sir Walter Scott, the university student freely admitting his obsession with the sea? And the fact he was a keen wildfowler- that lie had come from *his* lips.

So why was Olaf on Holy Island? Did he really study in Edinburgh and did he play a piano in his Orkney lighthouse home that he'd found on the beach? Kitty involuntarily giggled. It was something even Sir Walter could not have dreamed up for one of his novels!

Night thoughts were like the tide, advancing, retreating, ebbing away her peace of mind as her belief in Olaf came and went in a choppy sea. The storm! Did it still rage? Her noisy thoughts had shut it from her brain. She lay perfectly still.

Yes, the windows still rattled, a Scottish reel dancing out its strident rhythm, resonant and now, very out of tune. Bang, bang, bang, it tuned her disquiet. Life had taught her not to trust, why had she thought it could be any different? The island and its surrounding sea had lulled her into a false sense of happiness. Yet it had not taken her long to learn that the sea did not play a lullaby. How foolish she'd been, to close her ears to the warning tap-tap-tapping of the threatening tempest.

She climbed from the bed. The rattling of wooden window frame was a dispute she could no longer bear. She needed something to place between the sparring partners, something small that would block the irritation. She thought of the Cuddy beads given to her by Olaf. How quickly they would be worn into dispersing dust by the friction. They would never make the necklace promised to her by Olaf.

The new noise came suddenly, a great tirade of sound that drowned the insistent annoyance of the frame. From the window she watched the sleeping street spring to life at the command of the Church bell. Stridently it pealed out over the village - opening cottage doors as with a communal key.

Clang, clang, clang! A procession of lights answered the summons, streaming toward the sea like a burning fuse and into the middle of the column emerged a figure she knew, dragging a ganzie over his head as he joined the line of men. It was taller than Henry, even though he was bent against the wind. It was Olaf.

At that moment there was a loud thump nearer home, a meaningful battering on her door and she heard her name. 'Come on Kitty, here's something to stop our boredom!' Louise shouted her excitement as her footsteps retreated and Kitty saw the small, slight girl, draped in a long cape, run to join the line of villagers; Louise Smythe was in on the men's work. Kitty felt the adrenalin rise, the bells and scurrying figures drew her compulsively out into the night commotion.

Minutes later she was beside Louise, grateful the borrowed storm garments had been heaped on her bedroom floor. The wind beat in her face and tore at her clothes as they all marched out towards the sea. She felt an excitement bubbling up in her ribs; intrigue… the unknown… danger? Not a night for the faint-hearted to be out in the roaring nor'easter. Not a night to be at sea. The bells could warn of one thing and one thing only - a ship in distress.

'T'is the Plough,' The name reached back along the column, borne aloft on the crashing waves storming the shore, a strident herald of the first morning light, an angry yellow, lining the black waves. Her eyes followed the pointing fingers. Half a mile off shore and barely visible above the torrent, a ship floundered.

Kitty fixed her gaze on the tiny shape dwarfed by the crashing sea; it looked a toy, baby-rattle shaped, being thrown from hand to hand in a playful game of chance. In view, then lost below the water then tossed back into sight. It mesmerised and Kitty's heart began to race; on board was a horror only to be imagined, men and women, perhaps even children, playthings at the mercy of the storm. Desperately she shouted at the man beside her,

'What can be done to save them?' He towered above her and then she realised she was looking up into the wizened features of old Janet.

The streaming eyes of the island woman registered the question but there was no word in reply. Kitty shouted into the wind as it threw back the inevitable answer. The situation was beyond help. Kitty turned away, suddenly she could no longer bear to look; men could seek for animals buried deep in snow drifts for up to a fortnight! There was no such reprieve in a merciless sea.

The stinging wind made Kitty's eyes weep, tears trickled down her face. Janet beside her was not crying, just wiping away the seepage of old age; the old woman faced the storm, a figurehead standing arms akimbo, her spindly hair flattened to her head by the near horizontal wind. She was muttering something, concentration etched on her weather-beaten face. Were her old lips reciting a prayer? Prayers, it would seem, were the only choice left.

The line of fishermen stood immobile, paralleling the shore as though built into an instant human sea wall, a barrier without chink, each one a masoned stone to form the whole. All rugged men appeared hewn by the elements so that their faces no longer showed even a fleeting glimpse of fear. But then neither did she see compassion. The reality of life had made them hard.

Where was Olaf? She struggled to find his known face. Surely he would not just stand and watch? She caught sight of Henry Smythe shoulder to shoulder with two fishermen whom she could not name. His dark looks and dress not out of place amidst the cottagers, then only Mrs Smythe and Marion put on airs of gentility.

'Henry, can't you do something?' She was tugging at his jumper, the wool hard and unforgiving as the look on his face as he turned in surprise at her voice, then impatiently he turned his back on her.

She scanned the crowd for Olaf's familiar figure. She could not see him. 'Olaf....Olaf!' her impotency sounding the only name that she could trust, *he* would know what to do, he was used to gales that hit his northern isles for six months of every year!

'Olaf!' and there he stood a few feet from the wall of men,

'Do something, Olaf, do something!' She faced him, her distraught face pleading in words he could not hear. He looked down at her, his eyes flickering at the sight of her concern and then he too turned away. 'What can be done?' He shouted his denial, 'We are all impotent against the sea.'

Here was true hell; a treacherous place with fatalistic people in the face of uncompromising nature. Kitty's shoulders sagged. She alone was affected by the stricken ship. How she hated these uncouth people!

The vessel was already lower in the water. There was a murmur from the crowd and Kitty saw- with a flash of revulsion- that the stricken ship was nothing but a spectacle for an invited audience; the bells had not rung to gather help but to announce the show, and she had followed sheep-like to her place on the front row!

'Kitty...' Louise was at her side, cheeks lashed red, hair streaming in tight ringlets, her face alive with excitement. '...how about this for a storm?' Her new friend's face peered into hers and shouted, 'this doesn't happen every day of the week you know. This one has been specially put on for you, you've been lucky!' Louise was another front-seat member of the audience.

Was the wind easing, the storm at last abating? The Smythe cook had said it would last three days only but Kitty had lost all track of time. Perhaps, by some miracle the ship would see out the gale. But the faces of the onlookers held no sign of hope just blank acceptance, and then a low growl swept through the crowd like the chorus in a Greek tragedy and Kitty knew the muffled sound foretold imminent doom. Old Janet's voice rose above it in a shriek,

'Lord, send her to us.' Her incantation rasped into the cold dawn,

'Lord, send her to us.' And her audience- to a man- echoed the words as one by one they fell to the ground on their knees. Louise took up the chant, mouthing the prayer in a piercing shriek above the wind.

'Lord, send her to us!' All eyes scoured the sea and the stricken vessel.

'The devil *strike* her, she must not get away!' Louise's young, excited, pleading rose above that of the crone.

Kitty froze, her senses numbed, she could not believe what she was witnessing. Then came an exultant cry- a roar of satisfaction, like onlookers at a cock-fight! Kitty knew without looking that the ship had gone.

The onlookers' prayer for blood had been answered.

She stood above the bowed heads of the supplicants, a church-like silence reflecting their rapt devotion. Only one in the congregation stood at her level, and she ran towards him. Olaf alone offered sanity...surely... but as she neared the upright figure, he too sank low to the ground.

Old Janet raised her voice in triumph. 'It is the will of God,' she declared 'such a storm comes *only* from the Almighty!' She laughed exultantly.

Twelve

Kitty stood, a lone figure, watching the sea ebbing, flowing, coming and going, but advancing to the tenuous strip of land that was Holy Island. How could *anyone* defy it? Were the islanders truly God-fearing but alienated from reality by the shifting nature of their land? Or did the sea slowly and surely eat away their very humanity?

On the lonely north coast the dunes rose above her, in a ripple of transitory land that was friable and disintegrating. Her feet began an avalanche of sand as startled brown shapes disappeared into a network of holes. Dozens of rabbits were making the most of their insubstantial world; agitated, white tails disappeared underground and out of trouble! Kitty watched them vanish to safety.

The stricken ship had had no such chance of escape. If only they had heard the seal music warning of danger! Instead their bodies floated with the selkies, rotting and bloated, coming ashore with the new tide; the water running red.

She turned her back on the sea to face inland and there was a figure moving across the sand dunes, a hand raised in greeting. She'd been seen! More than ever, she envied the underground rabbits. The *last* thing she wanted was to face anyone from the village. She waved back reluctantly.

'Kitty!' Henry did not hide his delight and she smiled. He was easier to like than his sisters. He was easy to read, a spoiled young man but with a scar to show that he didn't always get his own way. Then, he was the lucky male in the family able to choose where he went!

She'd even flirted with him before the shipwreck on the previous evening, as Louise with Olaf had become ever more the smug winners at cards. She had wanted to make Olaf jealous. It was as simple as that.

Henry seemed surprised as he came to stand beside her. 'What brings *you* to the Snook?' He waved his arms in the direction that she was headed, the only part of the island she had not yet explored. It had looked the isolated wilderness she needed.

'You'll find only rabbits here. The Snook is nothing but a vast warren.'

'So I can see, the only obvious thing is their droppings.' She kicked the hard, dark pellets with her boot. 'So that's what they think of the place!'

He laughed. 'Yes but it shows me they're here in their droves and a sitting target.'

'*Target* - so no-one's safe after all!' Kitty looked up at him. 'Do you know, I was just thinking how lucky they were to be able to escape down into their burrows away from any predator?'

'Unfortunately for them, there is no real escape. That's life.' Henry Smythe grinned cheerfully revealing his island fatalism. 'Come, Kitty, surely you catch rabbits in the hills?'

'Yes, but...' How could she explain that there it was a fairer contest, here the sea stopped *any* escape!

But she thought of the farmers at harvest time driving the hunted animals into the centre of the field. She had wielded a stick with the rest of them! She sighed, Henry was right, it was the way of the world - but *now* she minded! Had the wreck been the way of the real world? Olaf, Louise, Henry, old Janet all with their feet on the ground awaiting the inevitable outcome?

'Anyway the Bishop is too fat.' Henry grimaced.

'Bishop?'

'Aye, his grace the Bishop of Durham, owns all the rabbits, just as he thinks he owns our souls.' Henry smirked at her.

'Rabbits are easier to control.'

'...and easier to catch...' Henry indicated the bag he clutched and with one deft movement he lofted a squirming creature whose eyes bulged under his restraining fingers. Kitty looked at the ferret with disgust. Its mean, thin face showing its evil intent. The morning wreck-watchers had had such faces!

'Why should the Bishop fill his fat gut?' Henry knelt on the ground, 'The rest of us like nothing better than a good coney pie.' With a meaningful shove he pushed the hunter deep into the sand.

Mean mouth, teeth, blood, body; mean mouth, teeth, blood and body. It was as easy as the harvest of drowned souls delivered at the invocation of the villagers. It was sickening. She watched as the bloodied rabbits began to fill the empty sack.

And Kitty thought, my role here on the island is to be the ferret.

Henry stood smirking, his sack full. 'Why should the Bishop own the lot?' His eyes narrowed as he scowled down at Kitty. 'In fact - just like Armstrong! Why should Our Respected Kinsman think all the cargo on the Sea Plunder is rightfully his when it is Patterson and I who risk life and limb?'

'Just think of it Kitty, Bishop or Magistrate, they're only placed above the rest of us so that we can double-cross them... wouldn't you agree?'

She watched the anger on Henry's face, his unguarded words fuelling a growing excitement in the hard-done-by man.

'He's just a bit too smug, our John, too impressed with his own duplicity.' Henry was warming to his subject and out to impress his audience.

'D-duplicity?' Kitty stuttered her surprise.

'Of, course, dear Kitty, you know all about him, no need to pretend otherwise.' Henry's eyes narrowed in a glint of malice. 'Doesn't it ever gall you that he can be both figure of the law and flaunt it as well?'

He seized her hand. 'Come on, now I've got my bag of Bishop's rabbits, let me show you my takings from the Magistrate's ill-gotten gains!'

Along the shore the lines of sand suddenly gave way to high cliffs with gaping holes in the rock, looking for all the world like enlarged burrows created by the sea.

'It's amazing what the land can provide.' Henry was enjoying himself, 'And it would be foolish not to take advantage, wouldn't you agree?'

Kitty's eyes glinted, nodding assent. She was about to find the answer to her quest without *any* effort on her part. Henry was going to reveal what Armstrong had guessed, that he was the double-crosser!

Tomorrow she could retreat back across the mud-slakes to her solid hills where her child waited for her return. Time to recount her discovery and then she and baby would be gone. But already she knew the silver ship would not go with them. The early morning tragedy had changed her, what was not hers was not to be taken.

The cave was dark and chill. It smelt of rotting seaweed and she almost choked. Henry held her hand in a tight grasp, his fingers hot and perspiring, but she did not pull away. The blackness like a tight blind-fold about her eyes, she could see nothing but the shadowy figure of Henry alongside her. She stumbled with him across the uneven floor, her feet striking boulders and pebbles so that their progress was accompanied by sudden, startling noise as they displaced the sea-strewn floor. Water splashed about her legs, relict from the previous tide. At high water the sea would be back.

Henry was inches ahead, his good humour echoing around the cavern in his obvious self-congratulation, 'It's a warren isn't it? Even the rabbits are outdone here.' He broke off as a solid wall blocked their way. He let go of her hand, and she could hear him fumbling with something and then suddenly there was light; a candle flickered on a ledge of rock above them.

'How's this then- for Aladdin's cave, Kitty?'

The flickering candle danced on to the limestone walls, casting shadows that were solid and bottle-shaped, piled in crates high on the ridge of rock above the water-line.

'Here's brandy, enough for you and me both?' Her companion's face was only inches from her, his breath stale from the night before. He grabbed a bottle and lifted it to his lips and she could smell the spirit as the already-open bottle reached his mouth. It was his welcome-to-the-cave tipple! She looked about her at the stack of liquor piled high to the roof in this north coast cave. And she thought of Olaf's pantomime outstretched fingers in the Smythe parlour. Unbelievably he had voiced his own knowledge of it. Had he too drunk from the bottle? She closed her mind to the hateful thought.

Darkness, illegal spirits, this was Slymefoot all over again! Only the crowded camaraderie was missing, the black humour absent in the chill cave. She shivered and Henry was at once concern, the bottle at her lips, the smell rasping her nostrils.

'Come on Kitty, let's drink a toast to you and me - us against the Magistrate!'

She heard the bottle crash on to the hard rock floor as his arms were about her and the taste of brandy was from his lips. He had her pinned against the cave as his hands sought her breasts.

She could hardly breathe as he forced her against the hard unyielding rock. She closed her eyes shutting down every sense to what was happening. How often had she done that - painfully learning that once a man was roused he would *not* see her lack of response?

But in that, arrogant Henry Smythe was different. He drew away from her, his eyes just inches from hers, showing his surprise in the shadowed light.

'This cannot be your first time!' The young, handsome squire was now intrigued that here was a girl that did not fall gasping into his arms. He pressed himself hard against her and she wanted to cry out in her revulsion. Her, *no, oh no*, was an unvoiced prayer.

'What's the matter? Last night you gave out a very different message.'

'I'm sorry, it was wrong,' she tried to squirm from under his imprisoning arm, but his manhood dug into her, his arousal now fed by her reluctance. His head was sunk on to her breasts and his teeth were about her bodice. Her dress tore like the opening of a tight sack and triumphant hands and hungry mouth sought her nipples; octopus hands had her skirt above her waist. His thrust was hard against her as she bit his arm.

'You little *d-devil*,' his voice was slurred, but furious at her resistance. 'You know now that this cave hides things not meant for other eyes. REMEMBER THAT!' His lips again sought her mouth and this time she did not shrink away. She'd heard the threat.

Henry had shown the cave and its illicit horde to the girl who teased any male in sight. Kitty, the flirt, an easily donned role, played to perfection in the Smythe's parlour the previous evening. If Henry had been so fooled, what had Olaf made of her performance?

Henry groped her buttocks and his hardness was an iron rod, his scar scoured her cheek as he whispered, 'So now you know the cave and its cargo,' his hands were now at her throat, 'my secret is safe with you I am sure dear Kitty- cross your heart and hope... to...die!'

His threatening laugh echoed around the walls, suddenly, above it, she heard a different sound, the swish, swish of advancing water; insistent and loud behind Henry's back at the mouth of the cave. The tide was returning, coming to her rescue!

'Oh, *blast* the bloody sea!' Henry was already in retreat. The same noises of feet in water, the same chill of spray, but accompanied this time by the fury of her guide as sudden daylight showed the advancing high water.

'Time to lift your skirts again, Kitty' Henry shouted his ribald comment above the noise of the waves and then they were out onto the ledge of rock that stepped the entrance to the cave. His hand was tight on hers as they slipped and slithered on the narrow shelf. Visions of the Plough Rock swam before her eyes. But this time the sea had been her saviour.

Thirteen

Now Kitty knew what she had come to discover. But Henry knew her knowledge! He had trodden in her footsteps all the way back to the village. And for the rest of the day- if he was not close beside her- Louise was there at her elbow.... or so it seemed!

At the night session of cards Henry watched her every move, by the end, another loss of 1s 6d was writ large on her slate. So the tide came and went and there was nothing she could do about it. In the night hours she did not dare to attempt the crossing of the mud slakes. But she guessed that Henry would not trouble her in the Smythe family home!

By morning the tide was back again and he had gone.

And now her card debt was a debt of honour. Before she could leave she needed *one* last winning session.

In the dawn the Monastery lay deserted and sacred still. It was the only place on the island where Kitty knew she might find solace. She picked her way amongst the ridges and bumps that carpeted the past. The glassless arch soared heavenward, the ornate carving- pink in the rising sun.

The returning sunlight warmed her face, but there was little comfort for her bruised body or for the wreckage of bodies lying strewn upon the water. The procession of looters weighed down by booty would not have stopped throughout the night hours.

And it had been old Janet and Louise who had led the voices calling for the destruction of the ship! Kitty shuddered. It was a scene that would stay with her for life; she saw again the lone figure of Olaf, and he too had followed the herd, sinking to the ground, leaving her the only unbeliever in the worship of Satan.

She felt empty and leaned against the monastery's stone pillar for support; throughout father's years of misusing her, she had clung to her belief in a God who was good. She'd never knelt in prayer- though she'd fallen to her knees beside the cot of her baby at Barraburn. She felt a sharp stab of reproof, silver rattle and silver ship swam before her eyes. Were they really what this was all about?

There was a face watching her, a cheerful, wistful expression that was hard to read. The carved gargoyle was young, with a grin that promised mischief. A self portrait of the mason starting out on his career... or one of the monks, *still* filled with youthful optimism? Whoever it was, some of his zeal had been removed by centuries of wind and rain but there was enough to see that he still eyed the world with trust. Kitty smiled back at the cheerful pink stone cheeks and she was still smiling as she turned to face whoever it was who stood behind her.

Immediately, her expression set hard as stone as she stared in to the blue eyes of Olaf; his look questioning hers.

He pointed to the gargoyle, 'This place has put a smile on his face it's only worn a bit thin over time.'

Her expression was cold but her cheeks flushed. She tossed her head. 'Well I find little to smile about. This island has taught me your sea is cruel, Olaf Magson, and that you are callous too.'

'*Callous*! Is that what you really think of me?' He put out his hands towards her but lowered them again as she stood rigid. I'm sorry that the wreck on Bishop Rock ruined our storm.'

'*Our* storm?' she snapped back at him, how could he think she was so easily won. 'This whole village is callous and cruel. Why did no one try to save the ship?'

'But you saw the waves. Nothing could be done.'

'Nothing....' The repetition showed her hopelessness.

'The island has a surf boat, given by the Lord Crewe Trustees, but in such a sea it could not be launched.'

'I- I can understand that,' she saw again the mountainous waves, 'It's the prayers I cannot accept.'

'Prayers...?'

'Yes, the islanders praying for the ship to go down. How can that be? I am no believer, but *my* prayer would have been very d-different...,' Kitty's voice faltered. Olaf stood silently, his hands down by his sides clenched.

'It was sickening!'

'Yes, but life has made the villagers hard. These people struggle for survival, they've had to be tough; the men have immense strength, the women are brawny and resilient but all are child-like in their fatalism.'

She watched him, his face was creased in a deep frown, and she knew his words were a hard-won judgement learned elsewhere. He spoke of the Holy Islanders, but she knew he thought of a northern isle. Had he witnessed his mother and father prostrate on the shore of Sanday?

Of course not, his father was a lighthouse keeper. It was his job to keep ships safe at sea!

'Why did you join their prayers, Olaf?' She whispered her accusation and watched the heavy flush as it spread like the incoming tide up his forehead to his hairline.

She continued, 'I *watched* you. You were the only person standing upright and then you too joined the bent knees. How could you do it?'

The rooks were cawing on the high wall of the ruined church, raucous and insistent just like her accusations!.

'Kit, you wouldn't understand.'

'Try me.' Her laugh held no mirth.

'I stood out in the crowd and I hate that.' He sounded bitter. 'One day, Kit you will understand.'

'I find that hard to believe.'

'So be it.' His eyes were veiled.

'You and your sea are best avoided.' She turned away from him. He grabbed her arm.

'The sea is just like people, it has moods.'

She laughed scornfully, 'And *my* mood is bad.'

'No, you're not like that...' he shook his head, 'see, Kit- today the sea has a smile on its face. Please give me the chance to show you its other side.'

Fourteen

The boat carved its path across the water like a skilled chisel in the hands of a master mason. The water parted before them, unresisting, submitting to the curves of the boat controlled by its intent oarsman. Kitty sat opposite Olaf, stiff and silenced by the proximity of the water, by the spray splashing her bare flesh, by the dark unseen depths below. She kept her eyes averted from the retreating land. Yet in spite of a nagging fear she knew she had complete faith in Olaf's seamanship.

Olaf held her gaze. Every sinew in his body strained to the rhythm of the boat and she watched his brawny arms flex and tighten. Determination and concentration narrowed his eyes and firmed his mouth; but there was a hovering smile that told he was where he loved to be. The noise and confusion of the harbour had given way to the soft swishing of water and the thud, thud of the oars. Birds accompanied, swooping and calling, the gulls, their soft, white feathers gliding through the air, only their beaks and beady eyes revealing nature's other side. How well they reflected the sea in its veering temper!

She was surrounded by sea but it was Olaf's sea. Kitty leaned back against the hull. She should be terrified out in this flimsy craft, just a slither of wood and two oars and a sail between her and the impenetrable depths! The southern sun blinded her eyes and she closed them. She drifted.

When she opened them again the specks on the horizon had become land spread out in a haphazard sprawl of rocks and islands.

'Welcome to the Farne Islands.' He handed her ashore and she felt his heat and the pain of his effort; it had been a long

row. He collapsed onto the sand and began to sift the grains in his fingers, lifting it high before it avalanched back...
'I once buried our Ian right up to his neck. And he couldn't get out! Needless to say I got into trouble.'
He got to his feet and she watched as he man-handled the boat higher up the beach. The versatile Northumbrian coble with its high bow and flat bottom could land anywhere. Olaf's face was set hard as though the effort needed all his concentration but she could see his mood had changed.
Wordless, he dropped back down beside her on the sand; his hands were worked red. She had to stop herself from seizing them in hers to soothe away their hurt.
She said, 'I'm glad I came.' Rocks surrounded in a clasp of protection the sandy cove retreating into bright green grass and a necklace of small pink flowers straddling the tide line.
'Sea Thrift- its tough Kit, a bit like you... able to withstand unpromising surroundings.' She made no reply their eyes were level and she retorted,
'It looks as common as a weed.'
'Yes, that's why I like it. It covers Orkney as well. When I come here I almost feel I've come home.' He fingered the small tufted flower.
'*Almost..?*' She wanted him to talk, to talk of his homeland to her.
'Yes, islands are islands, Sanday, Farnes or Lindisfarne- the big difference, there is always a wind in Orkney and it's usually gale-force.'
'No wind here today.' She licked her finger and held it up as she had done so many times in her sorties in the border hills. 'It's set fair.'
'Aye.'
She asked, 'Did it blow a gale the day your brother died?'
'No, it was flat calm, one of the rare days in November...the kind of childhood day that promises to last forever... but you don't have to grow up to find that it doesn't.'

'No...' *how long before baby Katharine discovered just that?* She reflected bitterly

'The baby seal was days old, its cream coat vivid against the far rocks. Ian and I found the dead mother, half skinned, its flesh ripped. I should have waited for the tide to return, perhaps the young seal would have made its way without our help, but its cries were pitiful. So I took the boat, it wasn't far but I knew four- year- old Ian wouldn't be much help. But I was twelve and impressed with my strength. We got to the young seal and I clambered out on to the rocks. I'd never been so close to a youngster before- mothers are belligerent in their protection.'

'Yes, I suppose they are.'

'It looked like a small puppy, large trusting eyes, cute face, but I could see it had a wound. The only thing to do was to take it home. I almost had it into the boat when it turned on me sinking its razor teeth into my hand, tearing the skin. Ian rushed to help, his thin stick arms useless on a squirming slippery animal. The frenzied selkie turned on him. It caught him in the neck and I heard the skin rip and saw the surge of blood.'

Kitty took his hand. The scar of that day stood white and jagged, evidence of his lasting pain. 'Oh Olaf!' She didn't say stop punishing your self, though she could feel his guilt. No wonder he'd escaped to Edinburgh!

Kitty could feel the sun and hear the soft swish of the water in the cove; the birds' cries were soporific. She could not see, but sensed seal eyes watching them. Everything looked sparkling clean, scrubbed by salt spray and wind. That included Olaf. She had a vision of the sea dousing the Orcadian; his clear skin and high cheek bones made him look the innocent, only now she knew he wasn't!

His telling of brother- Ian's death had been terse; how easy now to defend Olaf's mood swings. His childhood had been lonely because of the death of a beloved brother; and it had been his fault. She sensed the resulting rejection by his parents, and an early self-sufficient manhood. She saw him for what he had become, aloof and remote.

It was as though he could read her thoughts, 'Do you know, Kit, in spite of everything I still accept the Orkney belief that seals unite land and sea?' He frowned, 'The story goes that selkies swim ashore at night, throw off their pelts and dance on the sand just like human beings.'

'Oh, I like that!' How he could charm!

She said flippantly, 'Perhaps they do it on Holy Island as well?'

'Perhaps…,' he turned eagerly toward her, but her tone took the smile from his face. 'Of course it's only a legend.' He sounded cross.

She shivered, 'It's hard to imagine it ever being dancing-on-the-beach weather for either seals or humans, besides wouldn't they trip over the washed-up wrecks?'

He was frowning now, 'Aye, Sanday is hardly visible on a dark night, there have been many wrecks.'

'Hence the grand piano in your living room?' Kitty had longed to question the claim made by Louise.

'If you were caught wrecking, it was seven years transportation to the American Colonies.'

'Oh.' Kitty shuddered.

'We didn't worry that much, the authorities were far off in Kirkwall; the prayer was not *'send her to us'* like the Holy Islanders, but it was similar,' he paused and then said quietly, '…*inflict the doom of total loss.*'

'Oh.' Kitty's strangled cry rang across the cove.

'You know, Kitty, a child finds it hard to separate legends from truth. Do the selkies really dance like humans on the sand? Just because I'd never seen it, didn't mean it never happened.'

'No.' Kitty thought of her fourteen year old self, newly living with a father not knowing what was right what was not. She shuddered again. 'But, *'inflict the doom of total loss,'* that is barbaric.' Olaf was losing her again.

He muttered, 'They told me if you saved a man you had deprived the sea of its prey, and in revenge it would take you or one of your family.'

'Oh.'

'It was a terror I lived with even when the sea was in a good mood, so that I wasn't surprised when it claimed our Ian.'

Kitty thought, Olaf is the tide-tossed pebble in gale-whipped seas. She could find no reply.

His arm swept the rocky outcrop. 'You can see there are no trees on these islands, just like Orkney, we used the driftwood from wrecks for building boats and houses and fences.'

'And grand pianos?'

'I know someone with a fence made from mahogany!'

'*Finders- keepers.*' Kitty's voice was sharp. She'd taken pretty things, just frippery, not something for everyday necessity, but did that include a piano?

'Living in a lighthouse set us apart, my father was a threat to their livelihood.' Olaf's face showed his hurt.

She took his hand as though he was still a child. 'Olaf, *I* need to be accepted too. We see the Smythes and we envy them their secure place in the family, however much they argue.' His blue eyes met her brown ones and she smiled; was she beginning to understand him?

He squeezed her fingers, 'Come on, my stomach's rumbling and Mrs Darling is an excellent cook. Her stew is big enough for all the family and for two others besides.'

On the other side of the island, the lighthouse towered above them. It looked solid and unmoveable, built with as much skill and dedication as any medieval monastery; the circular stone-tower all of forty feet.

'Grandfather Darling came to Brownsman at the end of last century, it's been modernised since and now his son William is Keeper, the light revolves and shows the full face of the reflector every half-minute. Come on let's go and meet the

Darling family.' Olaf pointed to the small cottage attached to the lighthouse and his face was all smiles.

He knocked but briefly, and not waiting for an answer lifted the latch. Lowering his head, he strode into a room crowded with furniture and family. There would have been no space for a grand piano!

'Olaf!' He was greeted with cries of surprise and pleasure; then hand-shaking between the men and hugs from the woman who was obviously the man's wife. Olaf indicated Kitty. 'This is Kit,' and there followed again the unstinted welcome.

They had interrupted the family meal, a fish stew sat on the plates, its aroma high in the rafters.

'Hitch up our Grace, there's room for two more beside you!' A small girl of about seven years smiled shyly and did as she was bidden.

'Hello, Grace,' Olaf nodded at the girl, 'how's your garden?'

'We eat our first cabbage today!' Grace proudly indicated the plate and the cooked greens on it.

'All we needed was some soil and the shelter of a stone wall.' Her mother beamed. 'Our vegetables and the mutton, all home grown on the island!'

There was silence until the last morsel was cleared.

'Good thing we can produce some of our food, it's been a stormy early spring.' Mrs Darling grimaced as she turned to Olaf,

'We've never known anything quite like it. In February a brig went down on the east end of Brownsman and five other ships were lost on the same day.'

William Darling frowned. 'Mr Magson and I have business, our Gracie, why don't you take the young lady and show her the island?' Benches scrapped across the bare tiled floor, 'Though, I admit there's not a lot of land to be inspected above the twelve foot mark!'

'Don't forget, Kit would love to see inside a lighthouse,' Olaf smiled at the girl, 'She'll be able to see that I've been speaking the truth!'

Kitty pulled her shawl tightly about her, the warmth in the cottage quickly lost once they were out in the bracing air of the island. How did she manage on the long sea-crossing-? The girl, Grace, did not bother with such things, her ganzie proof against all weathers. Kitty imagined it had been knitted in the long winter evenings after animals and garden and cleaning had filled the light hours. The mother's eyes looked tired, then little wonder, close work under the gas lamp would be a nightly strain.

The girl was a funny little thing, Kitty studied her companion. She was slight, thin hair tied in a short pigtail-uncomfortable in its lying.

Kitty said. 'Do you like living here?'

'Like?' the girl raised her eyebrows, 'where else would I live?'

The inevitability of the reply made Kitty smile, it was like the tides coming in twice daily, and nothing could stop that. Kitty envied the child her conviction. She thought of Olaf; he had lived on a remote sea coast, now he called a city home. Had Edinburgh changed him, so that now he no longer knew what he was?

'Come see the Tommy Noddys,' the little girl slipped her hand in Kitty's.

'*Tommy who?*'

'Noddy, that's what we call the puffins. You'll see why in a minute.' The child was earnest, even the childish name did not bring a smile to her lips. Kitty could feel the strength of the thin arm as her young guide led her to the cliff face. 'Look,' Grace pointed, 'there they are.'

Kitty burst out laughing, 'What a funny bird. Your made-up name is just right.' Chunky black and white birds straddled the island edge, their large, distinctive heads shaking from side to side revealing their brightly coloured bills, a vivid orange like their feet.

'You certainly couldn't miss them,' Kitty smiled, 'so these are your noisy playmates!'

'We do not have time to play,' Grace frowned, her tone was condemning, 'we share Brownsman with the puffins; the soil is deep enough for them to build their burrows, and deep enough for us to have a garden.'

'Burrows? That's strange for birds.'

Grace didn't answer, then as one strutted towards them, 'Can you see its feet? They use their bills to loosen the soil, and then their webbed feet shovel it away. The burrows can be several feet deep.'

Kitty moved forward eager to see the birds' nests but Grace's thin fingers pulled her back. 'It's the breeding season now, and there is a large white egg in each burrow. We have to be careful where we put our feet.' The girl's tone was matter of fact and Kitty felt like the child being told by the teacher.

'It must get even noisier when all the babies are born.'

Grace smiled for the first time, 'It's a good thing the nights are short. By next month it's only dark for three hours so none of us sleep very long. The noise can be deafening. Oh, look, there are my father and Olaf now.'

They met up outside the lighthouse, a tall very obvious intrusion into the landscape unlike the puffin burrows successfully hidden below the island soil. The two men watched Grace and Kitty's approach and Olaf greeted them with a smile, a half questioning look on his weather-beaten face. Their day had again darkened his skin leaving little trace of city pallor.

'Has the girl shown you the island?' William Darling's voice was brusque, but he fondled his daughter's hair as they drew alongside and his eyes were friendly.

'Oh, yes,' Kitty smiled, 'I was introduced to the Tommy Noddys, though I guess some of the birds must be called Thomasinas!'

Olaf saw her good mood and laughed, he looked relaxed and happy, 'Everyone loves the puffins? They're so much more colourful than the whitemaas.'

'Whitemaa?' Grace raised her eyebrows.

'Yes, that's our name for the seagulls back home in the Orkneys. We all have our pet names- you know Grace.'

The girl nodded thoughtfully, 'I'm going to call them whitemaas from now on. Oh, look they've already learnt their new name.' A couple of large white gulls swooped over their heads and then drifted lazily away out to sea.

'Time for us to go as well,' said Olaf. The lighthouse keeper's daughter held out her hand and they both solemnly shook it. Kitty thought you *know where you are with Grace Darling!*

Kitty and Olaf walked back to the boat, and only when they had reached it did she turn to wave to the little girl, but she knew as she did so that the child would already have disappeared. Olaf was whistling as he pushed the boat back into the water, it was not hard to see the island boy. She studied him as she trailed her hand through the water. She could see the shape of Holy Island on the horizon.

But the island tour hadn't ended. Another island and the boat hauled up onto a narrow beach.

'This is Longstone, you can see why it's so called, no soil here for Grace or the Puffins. This is just bare rock, a few feet above the sea and constantly swept by storms.' Olaf frowned. 'I wonder how she would adapt to living here.'

'Do you mean Grace? Kitty looked about her, it was desolate,

'I'm sure the little girl would accept it- doubting is not part of her.'

'No.' Olaf sounded his own doubt. 'Let us hope so.'

Kitty laughed. 'You're not really serious, Olaf, I can't imagine anyone living here.'

'Can't you?' He stared down at her, 'So it would not be for you?'

Kitty didn't answer, her companion's easy manner had gone with the landing on this stone outcrop.

'Yes, I think even Grace might find it difficult,' he stared down at Kitty, his conflict obvious. 'But this is where the lighthouse should be. Right here on the very edge of the archipelago in full view of the shipping.'

'Wouldn't it be a struggle even to build it?' Kitty grimaced, lethal rocks littered the sea.

'Oh yes.' Olaf's eyes gleamed and she thought how he would welcome the challenge! But he said,

'Kit could you believe that these rocks were placed here by God to wreck and tear ships apart?' His tone was strange.

'Oh no.' Kitty shook her head at the absurdity of the idea.

'That's what the locals think about the Farne Islands. If God had meant there to be a lighthouse here, he would have built it himself.'

Kitty laughed, 'That's primitive.'

'But we sailors and islanders see things rather differently from you, Kit.'

She made no reply and Olaf sighed. 'You saw the storm and how the islanders reacted- they truly believed it had divine beginnings.'

'That just cannot be.' Kitty shook her head, 'Whatever the cause it was not the work of God. Sadly the ship was in the wrong place at the wrong time. All I know is, it was the most sickening sight I've ever seen, that boat adrift, knowing that fellow human beings were going down to a watery grave and no-one raising a single hand to help them,' her voice reflected her continuing horror.

Olaf fixed his eyes on the horizon. 'We islanders believe flotsam and jetsam are ours for the taking and if we can move it in our direction so be it...' His bleak words were as harsh as the rocks about them, and she knew he was testing her,

'...so Kit, is there no forgiveness for a wrecker?'

'No, how can there ever be?'

Fifteen

No forgiveness for a wrecker *or* for letting emotion rule the head.

The time had come to leave behind her the temptation that was Holy Island. Here the sea and Olaf Magson had been wearing away her resolve. The trip to the Farne Islands had been a glimpse of happiness that could never be. All she needed was a winning hand of cards and then she could go.

The stakes were high. In the hills they played for joints of beef and wooden walking sticks, in Pilgrim House they played for money. Kitty knew as she descended the stairs that night that she could not let continue the one- way drainage of shillings to the grasping hands of the youngest Smythe girl. Another evening of loss would mean an empty purse and the debt would be way beyond her paying. She needed trump cards in her hands!

Henry was on his feet as soon as she entered the room and his arm guided her to the seat opposite him at the green baize table. She smiled up at her partner, and her eyes flashed her intent. Attack was the best form of defence,

'I feel lucky tonight.' The show of optimism masked her hidden repulsion. She wouldn't miss Henry Smythe, could she say the same about Olaf?

'My dear Kitty, you look every inch the winner.' He squeezed her arm and the pressure almost made her cry out. She relived his hands on her body in the cave and she bit her lip to stop the involuntary shudder that would reveal her true feelings.

'Louise,' she said provocatively, 'Henry and I will be the winning team tonight, at cards I mean' and she flashed a disarming smile at the younger girl.

'We'll see come ten o'clock. You might be the one who's disappointed, dear Kitty.' Louise's smile did not reach her eyes and the set of her mouth showed her resolve.

Henry still hovered at Kitty's side though Marion and Louise had taken their places, unlikely partners! That could aid her chances! So where was Olaf? Kitty had looked for him as soon as she had entered the room, expecting to see the taciturn Orcadian seated at the Smythe fireside with no hint of the young man that day who had confessed his demon - his part in the death of his brother Ian.

Louise said, 'Olaf's gone, wanted to catch the tide. Presumably he didn't want to lose any money, must have thought his good luck couldn't last. But he always was one to get cold feet. I tell you Kitty, female backbones are....'

Mrs Smythe interrupted, 'It's female tongues rather than backbones you should be concerned about, Louise, *yours* drives all away with your nonsense about equality!' The woman glowered at her younger daughter. 'I should have used the cane more often to knock some sense into you!'

Olaf gone! It could not be true, not after their day together. Inner Farne, Brownsman, Longstone the differing outcrops had felt their feet, heard their happiness and she'd seen his need, glimpsed the haunted child, loving- then hating his lighthouse home -that set him apart from the rest of the community.

Why had he told Louise and not *her* that he was going? Not a hint of goodbye. His departure filled her mind. No Olaf and an amorous Henry still very much here. She would have to watch partner and cards like a hawk.

Henry was restless, his mind other than on cards, though they managed to win the first game. Kitty's mind fought to concentrate on the proceedings. She tensed when he got to his feet and came to stand behind her, his hot breath on her bare neck, and then he was caressing her hair, his intrusive fingers winding a tight, tight ringlet.

He bent down so that only she could hear, 'your hair is as dark as a rabbit burrow, dear Kitty, but don't worry, I tease rather than ferret.' He laughed at his unpleasant comparison; ever tighter- ever tighter he wound her hair so that the roots felt they were being tugged from her scalp. She sat rigid.

He said more loudly, 'Don't ever cut your hair, dear Kitty, though like the pelt of a coney it could fetch good money- it might even cover your card debt!'

She said in a flash of her old spirit, 'Rabbit skins are ten a penny on this island, my hair would buy a warren.'

Louise clapped her approval, 'Well said, Kitty, that's you told, Henry. Come on, do sit down and leave Kitty alone.'

Kitty didn't know which was worse, the close presence of Henry behind her, or him sitting opposite -his eyes devouring her. She stared back at him, her gaze steady. She wasn't born yesterday, she'd survived on native nous into her twentieth year, and she had no reason to think she could not outsmart him now. Her knowledge of his illegal plunder of Armstrong's cargoes would bring his downfall sooner or later!

She shrugged off the vestige of fear that had kept her awake the previous night; however much Louise irritated, however much sedate Marion bored her, she was safe in the bosom of the Smythe family. The mother dozed by the fire, a joint of pork with all the trimmings already making her eyelashes droop. Yes, Henry could be easily repelled by a cloak of women.

Up until now Henry had been clever and she careless! She'd followed him into the cave, gloating at how easy it was going to be to solve Armstrong's problem, but he'd outmanoeuvred her, his secret making her his accomplice. She gazed at the cards in her hand.

Red cards when the trumps were black, black cards when the trumps were red. Kitty could hardly believe the dealing. Lady luck was neither on her side nor that of Henry for that matter. Louise and Marion could not loose. Kitty's purse was light on her lap.

Louise was laughing, 'Good Lord send them to us. You're on the rocks you two, another night when the wreckers will take the spoils.'

'Never', Henry was looking flushed. He drew out his pocket watch and glared at it. 'Time for one more game and it is make or break.'

'It's like taking sweeties from children, dear brother.' Louise laughed as she turned to their guest, 'you'll have to play for both of you, Henry's mind is on other things- even you Kitty, cannot distract him from his regular Friday night pleasure.

Louise was right, the game was quickly over. Anger simmered behind Kitty's smile in defeat. She had been playing not two but three people in the room. Henry's mind was not on the game- obvious from his repeated removal of his pocket watch and the drumming of his fingers on the table. He'd been partner only in name.

At the end of the debacle Louise spread her arms about her gains. 'Here it is Kitty, all for you to win back from me tomorrow. My gain in more ways than one, it means you can't leave the island until all the money is back in your purse. So with a bit of luck you'll be here the whole summer. And who knows by then, Henry's Friday night antics will be other than at the Fisherman's Arms!'

Kitty sat before her mirror brushing her hair in long steady flowing movements. The image that stared back was less than pleasing. The thick mass of curls and ringlets were an annoyance, an intrusion, that distracted one man, repelled another. She clutched the brush ever tighter, scouring her head so that she could feel the sharp barbs of the pig bristle between the thick strands of hair. She flinched, though it was a better feel than Henry's fingers violating her curls.

The door opened behind her and Kitty started, then her shoulders drooped in relief, reflected in the mirror was Louise, so Henry had already retired to The Fisherman's Arms. Kitty did not turn round, there had been no knock, no plea for admittance from the girl, and Kitty had had more than enough for one day of the Smythe family company.

The girl moved to stand behind her and playfully caught hold of Kitty's hair winding her fingers round and round in a tight spiral of soft black wool just as her brother had done.

'So you want to buy a rabbit warren?' Louise pursed her lips.

'Hardly...' Kitty was unsmiling, 'I was just pointing out the real price of my hair. I thought Henry under-valued it when he compared it to a coney pelt.'

'I would agree with you.' Louise still held Kitty's hair, idly playing with the long tresses. 'It's beautiful. It would fetch a high price at an Artificial Hair Emporium. Do you know I always dreamed of having thick black ringlets? Instead I got thin brown rats tails. We're never satisfied with life, are we?'

Kitty didn't answer.

'No, I'm not happy with my lot and neither are you Kitty, though you pretend otherwise.' As she spoke, Louise suddenly tugged at the long lock in her hand. 'Dear Kitty I find you hard to read, are you a Marion or a Louise?'

They stared at each other through the mirror and Louise bent forward and whispered, 'Go on admit you're more like me!'

Kitty raised her eyebrows, they were as dark as her hair and Louise, letting go of the curl, gently smoothed her finger across the arch of Kitty's brow. Kitty did not react. There was silence. Why had the girl come? It was already late. Was it just to annoy, as she so often did her elder sister, her brother, her mother? Kitty swivelled round to face her uninvited visitor.

Face to face and she was staring into a large pair of gleaming scissors. Shocked, she recoiled as Louise took a step towards her brandishing what she had kept hidden so carefully behind her back. Kitty felt the metal on the side of her neck.

'Perhaps it isn't a rabbit warren you are after, Kitty. But your hair could get you what you want.' Louise giggled as she wound a strand of hair between the blades. 'What do you think, your card debt cancelled in return for your hair?'

'For heaven's sake Louise... do stop playing games!'

'It's not a game, I'm serious.'

Kitty raised her eyebrows at the unexpected tempting offer, her loss at cards hung heavy.

'Do you really mean it, Louise?' She turned back to the mirror eyeing her crowning glory, her curls gave her beauty that she no longer wanted. Without it Kit would suit her so much more than Kitty. A faint flush crept up her cheeks, though Olaf might appreciate the change, is that what she would want?

'Come on, Kitty, snip, snip, snip and we'll make it quits.' Louise was giggling.

Kitty sighed, 'I'm tired, Louise.'

'But you can't be, the night is young. I've said before you and I both like excitement. We're never meant to stay at home by the fireside - not like Marion!' The girl seized Kitty's hands, 'Come on let's have some fun. The first time I saw you I thought, *she'll be game for anything.*' Now she was pulling at the reluctant Kitty.

'Your idea of adventure and mine are not the same.' Kitty snapped, remembering only too vividly the young islanders' game of chance in the cruel storm. She looked at Louise, there was a wild excitement about her, her usual cynical smile had gone.

'Please, Kitty, don't be a Marion.'

Kitty laughed. 'I could never be that.'

'There I told you, I know you've been hiding your light under a bushel, come on- what the men can do, so can we! You'd make a good man.'

Kitty could feel the blades of the scissors on her neck. There would be no money left on the card-debt slate, her daughter awaited a mother. Her hair would be no loss for no man would look twice at her after that. Louise raised the scissors... the long dark tresses would fall to the floor in a silent shower of black sleet. An unknown face would look back at her no longer made pretty by false curls.

Louise giggled as she seized one of Kitty's ringlets but instead of cutting it off she held it under Kitty's nose.

'A moustache would be a splendid disguise. No one would recognise you. It makes you look quite sinister, no more the voluptuous Kitty.'

Kitty laughed. 'Come on, Louise,' as the girl lowered the scissors, 'You can't get cold feet now. My hair for the debt you said?'

Louise frowned.

'*Do* get on with it,' and Kitty made an effort to grab the scissors.

Louise threw them on to the floor and there was a look of cunning on her face. 'No, your hair is too small a price in return for the money you owe me. What else can you add to the bargain?' She towered over Kitty her hands on the seated girl's shoulders and her eyes flashed.

'Let's go out, it's Friday night- why should it just be the men allowed out after dark? Let's have some fun with your fisherman disguise then I'll give you your money back, and you can go.'

'Go?'

Louise snapped, 'Yes, you've already tired of us.'

Kitty shook her head, 'O-of course n-not.'

'I don't blame you; imagine pretending I was going to cut off your hair just for a cheap bit of excitement and what a damp squib that turned out to be. You actually agreed to do it to cover your debt; that's how much you want to leave us.'

Kitty made no reply to the bored girl driven to play games that even sank as low as shipwreck.

'Let's go to The Fishermans Arms in disguise. Ritchie Gardiner, the landlord always enjoys a joke and two disguised visitors would appeal to his sense of humour.' She fingered her purse hanging at her waist, 'not much to ask is it, in return for your money?'

The public house at the top of Marygate echoed revelry around the silent cottages. Women left at home had darkened the fires and gone to bed; Friday night meant just one rendezvous for their men-folk. Hadn't they worked hard all week for the reward of a night's drinking?

The girls in fishermen's trousers, ganzies and woollen hats pulled low over their ears, hovered on the cobbles below the open window at the back of the alehouse. Kitty felt the adrenalin pumping in her veins, night shadows and men's clothes had been her border-sortie life, though surely it was alien to the well brought-up Smythe girl.

She'd surmised Louise, all talk, would lose her courage. But when a small man, consumed by a large apron, came into the back yard and left the door open, Kitty followed a triumphant Louise. They went cautiously into a small alcove adjoining the fire-lit kitchen... so this wasn't the *first* time Louise had been here! What attracted the girl to the island drinking den? Was it her thwarted sense of adventure, doing what she shouldn't, or did she have some other motive?

The kitchen was crowded and men stood or lounged about the walls, their hands wrapped round a pint. Kitty peered into the room, the smell reminded her of Slymefoot minus the fish and she felt a strange wave of homesickness. There they'd accepted her into a man's world; shepherds were straight forward, obvious not the devious, changeable men of the sea. She peered into the room and recognised Dougal Patterson, his solid frame filling the small kitchen, but as he bent to his tankard she saw Louise's brother, Henry already the worst for drink and beside him a figure that made her gasp. Olaf Magson was there as large as life, he had not left the island as Louise had said.

Kitty could feel herself trembling, why had he disappeared after the trip to the Farne Islands only to turn up in the Fisherman's Arms? It didn't make sense. Here he was amidst the men she had just deemed devious and changeable and now it included Olaf!

Had Louise known that Olaf would be at The Fisherman's Arms when she'd suggested the ploy? She'd known he wouldn't be at the evening cards.

Unquiet questions tumbled about her head as they clung unnoticed to the shadows; noise, laughter, and camaraderie echoed around the fire-lit hostelry; the girl's entrance had coincided with what was obviously the highlight of the evening.

Louise whispered, 'They're sharing out the week's takings from each coble, the most successful first. As usual, Dodie's boat will have more money than the rest of them to spend on drink.'

Kitty watched the four fishermen, all looking smug with hands raised to seize their wages as Gardiner, seated at a small table, counted out the money. There was a mixture of approval and an undertone that could only be resentment.

Dodie George, a fresh-faced young man grinned, 'wahey lads, as usual we've landed more in two days than the rest have in a week.' It brought a sarcastic cheer. 'So tomorrow we lie in our beds whilst the others go out agen.' He raised his glass to his three crewmen and there was silence as all took the invitation to down their ale.

Another of the successful crew smirked, 'The herrin' is good to us, but you lads, yer'd be better off with mussels, even though it's women's work!'

An old fisherman in the corner wagged his finger at the lad.

'Take care yer don't take all the herrin', so that next year there's nowt for any of yer and yer're all be forced to seek other employment.'

Dougal Patterson nodded at the man. 'Aye, Tommy we forget that at our peril. When ah was a bairn and the stocks low ah was forced to pick whelks for the baiting. Ah'd not want to do that again in a hurry.'

The village sage nodded, wizened by weather and years, now harboured in the ingle-nook seat, he sought to make the most of Patterson's attention, 'Ah mind that time, Dougal when first yer were made a fatherless bairn, yer were a credit to yer widowed mother.'

'Aye, Ah've no forgotten. Ah was forced to become a man overnight.' So saying, Patterson finished his pint and called for another; his voice gruff at the memory.

In the following silence the distribution of earnings continued until all coble crews had been paid, but the set faces of the other men showed the weather had badly interrupted their trade. Kitty felt no sympathy. Only yesterday these same men had achieved illicit gain from the sea. Still she could not get the wreck out of her mind. The firelight flickered on weather-beaten faces, hard men locked in a hard life.

The boat crews crowded together in threes and fours as though, by rule, they not only worked but played together. Tankards were filled and downed. Gardiner the landlord was almost run off his feet. The aroma of sweat and ale and tobacco mixed with the roasting dried salt-cod joined the rising wave of noise.

Still no suspicious eyes sought the shadows where the two girls, woollen hats pulled low, eavesdropped. Kitty thought gleefully, if women were not allowed on the fishing boats then Patterson and the rest would be horrified at the girls' presence here at their drinking session. She had to curb the urge to reveal their bad luck presence.

Henry Smythe was in the thick of the fishermen and already his speech was slurred.

'Come on Gardiner, more beer over here.' The girls saw him down a tankard without hesitation quickly followed by another.

'You're in good form the night!' Dougal Patterson now on his feet stood beside Smythe's table with almost a full drink in his hand, his speech distinct; he was cold sober.

He looked down on his ships owner, 'Yer'll be claiming the prize tonight.'

'P-prize? Henry turned bloodshot eyes on to his companion, 'wa'as the matter with you Patterson, 's-usually you downing the glasses as though there's no tomorrow.'

'Oh, ah'll see the morrow alright but it'll be late before yer do, sir,' the Sea Plunder captain laughed as the landlord put down another pint in front of Louise's brother. Publican Gardiner, steady on his feet, hummed as he kept his customers happy. He was clean shaven and looked younger than most of the fishermen, his only pressure the flow of beer rather than that of a fickle tide.

Patterson winked at the landlord and money exchanged hands as another drink found the young Smythe's shaking fist, without him rising from his seat.

Kitty whispered, 'Patterson is trying to make your brother drunk.' And she saw Olaf put out a restraining arm, but Henry bad temperedly pushed it away.

Gardiner with yet another drink banged it down on the table that was now swilling with beer and they all watched as Henry emptied the contents.

'Why aren't you drinking Patterson?' Henry's unfocused eyes surveyed the room, and he shook his head as though to clear it, 'Look at you, your glass is still full!' His voice was now shrill with suspicion.

'Ah can't compete with yer the night, Henry, no one can.' The unusually sober seaman winked at the landlord, thoroughly enjoying himself at the other man's expense.

'Smythe, you've had more than enough.' Olaf spoke out of the shadows.

'No need to interfere, sir.' The dismissive landlord already had another beer in his hand, 'So Mr Smythe you've won tonight's prize and that means payment excused for the next two Fridays.' Gardiner grinned as he wiped the young man's table so that not a drop fell on to the winner's immaculate breeches.

There was a murmur from the other men scruffier and less able to pay for their enjoyment, one or two openly muttered aloud their resentment. But it was followed almost instantly by a roar of satisfaction as, bang, a loud crash and Henry was prone on the floor, his head hitting the hard stone. He lay still.

'That'll teach the bugger.' Patterson laughed without sympathy, 'with a bit of luck Ritchie, yer should have quenched his thirst for some time to come.'

Olaf said, 'It would be best if you saw Maister Smythe home, Patterson.'

'Aye you're right,' Gardiner's voice was edged with concern as he peered down at his legless customer spread flat on the ground.

'Let him see himself home.' The Plunder's captain drank his drink in one gulp and banged the bar with his other hand. 'Ah'll have one for the road, Ritchie. It's not Mr Smythe who is goin' to be my companion tonight, but the fair Miss Smythe.'

There was a roar of surprise at Patterson's preposterous claim, ribald laughter, and Olaf's voice was drowned in the tide of hilarity. The Orcadian pushed his way out into the centre of the room to stand in front of the boat captain and this time his words filled the room, 'Hold on Patterson, before you go I want a word with you.'

'Another time,' the strutting man, lapping up the limelight, turned his back on the Orcadian, 'ah've got better things to do. Its female company ah'm after the night. What better than the virginal Miss Smythe- and with nee brother to protect her?'

'Hey yer've really got it in for yer boss.' Dodie George frowned as Patterson kicked at the immobile Henry still out cold. 'Ye're a dark horse, Patterson no mistake.'

Kitty was aghast, hardly able to believe her ears but there was no reaction from Louise to the seaman's outlandish bragging.

'So which Miss Smythe would it be, Dougie? ah fancy they both carry a candle for you,' coble skipper George smirked.

'Aye, they'd be fools not to.' Patterson thrust out his chest in a gesture of self-satisfaction and again there were guffaws.

'Ah fancy the prim one, Marion, it would be a rare game teaching her the birds and the bees. What do you reckon, lads?' Another fisherman drew cheers from the assembled room.

'Na, it's the young one I fancy, she walks round with an invitation card held out in her hand; often thought ah'd try my luck there.' A fisherman close to the bar grinned appreciatively and still Louise close to Kitty remained impassive.

The landlord tutted his displeasure, '...and you a married man, Fleming, you should watch what you say. And you too, Patterson, or you might be looking for another boat.'

Patterson laughed. 'It's ma ship as much as *his*.' He threw a disparaging gesture at the owner cold on the stone floor, 'Or it *will* be.'

'So which sister?' A chorus of voices echoed their intrigue.

'Why, Marion of course.' Patterson thumped the bar with his glass, 'She's the beauty!'

That made Louise gasp.

'Though beauty's not everything...the younger one has guts for them both.'

'Oh yes, Dougal Patterson you speak the truth, I've got guts,' Louise stormed into the bar tearing off her hat as she did so her fair hair falling into the shocked silence. Eyes blazing she tossed her purse to land at the astonished skipper's feet.

'Gutsy Louise can also play cards. I promised my winnings and here they are.' Her voice was brittle. 'Do stop teasing Dougal, just for *once!*'

'What's *she* doing here?' There was uproar. Angry shouts echoed the men's horror and many crossed themselves.

'We'll no be able to go out the day now- the woman's mired our path.'

'*Get her out!*' The mood was hostile. The landlord stood immobile, and Kitty in her hiding place could only watch in disbelief as the fisherman close to Louise grabbed her arm.

'Get your hands off her.' Olaf, the silent spectator moved to stand beside the girl, glowering at the aggressive fisherman who swore loudly and spat into the fire saying,

'…a woman interfering, and now a bloody foreigner..!'

His words cleared the room, leaving Patterson, Louise and Olaf; Gardiner, a mixture of annoyance and bafflement retreated, passing within inches of Kitty still crouched in the shadows.

Patterson peered at the Orcadian, 'What's yer problem? Does it concern the girl?'

Olaf said, 'No-it's you… I want a word with y-you, on another, very different matter.'

The Sea Plunder captain raised his bushy eyebrows in surprise; Olaf could have been speaking a foreign tongue- his Scottish accent thick in the fug of beer, fish and his hardly concealed unease.

Kitty noted his discomfort, what did Olaf have to say that was of importance to Patterson? She watched as he stood eye to eye with the fisherman, looking slight against the seaman's brawn.

'I have a confession to make to you, Dougal Patterson.' Olaf's voice cracked and he struggled to clear his throat, 'I have something that I want to get off my chest. I've wanted to do it for a long time.'

'So we have a confession,' the fisherman sneered his delight, 'Can yer smell incense, Louise, does Gardiner's kitchen remind you of a church? Is that why you've no drunk your ale the night?'

'Like you, I had good reason, neither of us would want to end up like him,' Olaf pointed at the now snoring Henry.

Patterson shrugged his shoulders, boredom written all over his handsome face and seizing Louise's arm he said sarcastically, 'Come on, hinney we've got better things to dee than-.'

'Hear me out, Patterson, my guilt has waited a dozen years.'

Patterson snapped impatiently, 'Ah divint trust Scotsmen boasting of their sins, ah've telt yer, you want the building doon the lonnen.'

'No, it's here and now I must speak the truth. It concerns the past, *our* past man.'

Patterson let out a grunt as he sought to remember a connection one with the other, 'How come? Where?'

'In Orkney.'

'Orkney? Never been that far north,' Patterson's frown reflected his bafflement, his disinterest and then a flicker of comprehension swept across his face,

'Nay niver me, b-but ma faither d-did.' He broke off and then a dark cloud of anger suffused his skin. 'Is it about ma faither?'

'Aye.' Olaf was trembling, and he clasped his hands together in an effort to control himself.

'Are yer talking wrecks?'

'Aye to my shame!'

'My God...' now Patterson was trembling. '...after all this time!' He lifted his fist to within inches of Olaf's face.

'Hear me out before you hit me.'

'So the truth at last,' the Holy islander's voice was heavy with emotion.

'Aye, and it's no pretty.' Olaf mopped his sweating brow striving to keep a measured tone.

'Ah'm all ears!' Patterson sank on to a stool and buried his head in his hands. 'It was November 1815 and me faither was first mate on the Albion out of Blythe on its regular run to Orkney.'

Olaf nodded, 'Aye! It was a freezing, dark night and the boat had just left Stromness when it went aground near the Old Man of Hoy.'

Patterson lifted his head and his eyes pierced those of the Scotsman. Olaf, pale cheeked, beat his scared hand on the bar table in a gesture of despair.

'I-I was there that night, helping out my fisherman uncle and his mates.'

Patterson's heavy breathing filled the silent room.

'There were two survivors.'

'S-survivors? Patterson stuttered his confusion. 'Survivors..?' His voice was a storm blast. 'Why didn'a they make it home then?'

Olaf struggled to find the right words. 'We... uncle and the other men - unloaded the cargo from the ship and when they had finished they tied one of the survivors to the rigging...' Silence, '...the other we carried ashore, he was injured, but he breathed his name, Dougal Patterson from Holy Island.'

His son groaned, an animal cry caught in a snare.

'The men had drunk most of the rum they'd found on board.' Olaf breathed in heavily, 'They left your father on a shelf on the cliff.'

Patterson screamed his agony. 'But you were sober.'

Olaf held out his arms in a childish gesture imploring understanding, 'I dared not go back to help him.' His voice was a sob, 'I was but a boy and I well knew that if you saved a man from drowning you deprived the sea of its *prey. Next time it would take me or one of my family.*'

Sixteen

Patterson hit Olaf a death-wish blow. The Orcadian fell to the ground. Kitty crouched paralysed, her limbs dead. The full horror of the recounted crime swamped her mind and her reasoning; Olaf was a wrecker just like the Islanders of Lindisfarne. He was no better than the rest!

A laughing, untroubled group of men intent on resuming their evening entertainment, returned as Louise crept from the room. They stopped abruptly when they saw not only Henry out for the count but Olaf as well and their fellow islander towering over him. One did not need to be sober to see that Patterson was speechless with rage.

'What's up with yer, man?' Dodie caught him by the shoulder, 'Have we missed some sport?'

'Aye, if yer call it sport, him leaving ma faither to *die* - alone on a foreign shore!' Patterson pointed down at Olaf, 'Then yes.'

Their revenge clamour was instant. Young Fleming, already the worse for drink kicked at the prone figure. 'We'll kill him.'

'Aye.' Dougal Patterson nodded his agreement. 'He deserves such an end. We've no high cliffs, but plenty of isolated wave-washed beaches. He'll have time to repent.'

Kitty inhaled her fear, now her limbs began trembling so uncontrollably, that she feared her gibbet-bones would give her away. But at that moment Olaf groaned and opened his eyes to see Patterson just inches away. He lay unresisting.

Patterson repeated the confession slowly and painfully to the men fuddled by drink but still able to take in the impact of the truth told at last. It made stark hearing; Dougal Patterson had grown up fatherless together with six brothers and sisters because of the Orkney Islanders' treachery. Little wonder his mother had sought the comfort of an early grave.

Fleming growled again. 'He deserves to die.'

'Aye,' Patterson kicked a booted foot at the prone figure, 'no one niver larnt me to read, it was tossing ship's deck not classroom where I grew up.' His bitterness was tangible. 'Death's too good for him.'

'Aye.' They spoke with one voice.

Fleming spat into the fire. 'Ye ken I'm from Eyemouth, I'm ashamed to call him a fellow Scot.' He kicked out at Olaf's buttocks and then again as there was no reaction. 'He's inhuman, he should be wetting his breeks by now, the scumbag.'

'Aye, that's all he's good for!' Patterson snarled his contempt.

'And lads, we know a way of making him do just that.' Patterson's laugh was demonic as he and Fleming bent to Olaf and dragged him to his feet.

'Come on, we'll take him to the herrin' sheds.'

The village street was deserted, houses shadowed the cobbles in a conspiracy of silence; there was no moon. Kitty, some distance behind the men thought, *thus has it always been, night raids, fleeting figures.* And, like the innocent monks, she was helpless as a pebble tumbled by the incoming alien waves. But this time she knew the retribution was just. An eye for an eye... had the besieged monks felt the same...or had they turned the other cheek?

She followed, past the eerie monastery ruins, its night-invaded terror long since forgotten. Then onwards they all went, down to the harbour and its ships that had always offered island men the lottery of a living or a watery death.

That distant November the local Albion had sailed unknowingly to its doom on a far Orkney shore. Thus had it always been. Sea-loving Olaf knew that as well as the next. He walked, upright, a lonely figure crowded by his tormentors. He had shaken off his escort's hands and they had not argued; they knew, as did Olaf, that the surrounding sea made escape impossible. And Kitty, following at a safe distance, guessed it had never entered his head. He had confessed and was ready to take his punishment.

His question to her as they had stood together on Longstone Rock hammered in her brain.

'Kit, can there ever be forgiveness for a wrecker?' And she had replied, 'No never.' It had been *her* words that had triggered his confession to Patterson, driven him to owning up to his part in the long-forgotten tragedy!

The party came to a halt beside tall, dark buildings that cast ominous shapes. A beam of moonlight broke the clouds in a warning flash revealing the hard, silent huddle of men. Kitty could hear the waves pounding on the jetty in a song of retribution- hungry and cruel. This small island had become the universe and, here, man was playing out his fate. Kitty cowered back into the shadows.

The herring sheds backed the harbour and Fleming undid the door of the tallest building with a key taken from its hiding place. The lock groaned and the men disappeared into a fug of fish and tobacco. She was alone. She would neither hear nor see what the baying hounds had in store for their quarry but she'd watched frenzied teeth tear apart a male fox and these men had come for the kill. Whatever their intent she could do nothing about it.

She put her head in her hands and wept, salt, bitter tears of fear, of anger, of knowing that punishment followed sin as surely as the tide ebbed and flowed on this unholy isle. Helpless, she leant against the herring-house wall hearing only the whisper of the wind. She clapped her hands to her ears to shut out its menace but as she did so, she heard another noise.

Men's voices! She started fearing a new danger, but the voices came from within the herring-house.

She stood beside a gap in the wall, ear-high; it was a large slit, herring- sized, where the fish that were kept in the sheds in water containers, were fed from outside. Inside the building, hastily lit candles showed long wooden troughs to catch the fish and beside them baskets and barrels waiting for the final gutted catch.

She could not see Olaf and a tinge of fear ran through her. Surely he had not been despatched already to the bottom of a barrel where a thousand herring could weigh him down? Oaths and ribald laughter echoed from the same men who'd watched the wreck on Plough Rock. It had taken unknown lives, now they punished a similar crime, but *they* could put a name to the victim. Dougal Patterson was the man who died, and it was a name still carried by their fellow islander. Unforgiveable! The Orcadian had walked into the lion's den to admit his guilt. He was an honourable man!

Kitty forced herself to look again and recoiled with horror. A coil of thick rope had been tied across the rafters into a makeshift noose and below it stood the recognisable figure of the Orcadian though his face had been covered by a lint bag. He stood stock still. Rancid tobacco escaped through the herring-hole and she covered her nose, nauseous at the stench. Mutterings and laughter, a feeling of carnival filled her ears as she saw the bag removed from the victim's head. Olaf stood pale and uncomplaining. She heard Patterson roar, ''tis time lads...' and Kitty struggled to keep watching, '...'tis time for the ritual.'

Olaf did not flinch as Patterson emptied a jug of beer into his face- a signal for the rest of the men to empty their tankards over their victim.

Ringleader Fleming strutted forward with what looked like a loaf of bread, and seizing Olaf's chin he shouted. 'Swalley the breid,' as he tilted the man's head back, forcing the crust deep into his mouth.

'Heap on the salt,' the men roared in unison, and Olaf spluttered, trying to spit out the foul mixture as more and more of the vile concoction was rammed down his throat.

Patterson stood apart, hands on hips, his mouth twisted into a cruel satisfaction. Then slowly he lifted his hand for the men to cease their fun. He began to pull the noose about the Orcadian's neck tighter and tighter, 'Divint weep or fill your breeks,' he shouted over and over again and the men took up the chant. 'Tighter, tighter, divn weep or fill your breeks,' the foolish words screamed now in a mad drunken frenzy- feet stamping in time with their loathing.

And then their vengeance was over, Olaf slumped forward into unconsciousness and a pool of water was at his feet. The men cheered the smell of urine. Then, quickly satisfied as children, they turned to the door, their thoughts already on The Fisherman's Arms.

Kitty drew back into the shadows, praying the men would not lock the herring house behind them.

Once they had gone she would go to Olaf.

Seventeen

In the night silence the boots of the fisher-men marched in unison, loud and insistent, an army stepping out, exultant at the defeat of a despised enemy...back to the Fishermans' Arms and their half-drunk ale. Their vengeance reeked.

Kitty stood waiting for the sound to fade; she could hear the gentle lap of the waves and the distant calling of the birds. She stood breathing in their normality...but the air tasted of days-old herring, and seaweed rotting on the harbour wall.

Silence! Emerging from the shadows she ran to the door of the herring shed. It was locked. With frenzied fingers she felt for the key on its ledge. Had the vengeful men taken it with them? Panic! But the metal fell with a loud clatter to the cobbles. Down on her knees she groped to retrieve her quarry. 'Oh, thank goodness.'

Her cry of satisfaction was drowned by a new noise. Horses hooves and carriage wheels! An intermittent sound- soft on grass, then strident on the causeway behind her. Kitty froze at the shuffling of hooves...then approaching *footsteps*!

'So what have we here?' the man's voice was triumphant. Kitty cowered as hands seized her. 'So! ... We have a lady of the night!'

A face thrust into hers.

'Leave me! How dare you!'

An exclamation of amazement, a belch, then slurred words,

'Kitty... what yer deein'?' His grasp tightened on her shoulders. 'Yuv larnt *nowt* ...this is nee place for a lady!' The

Northumbrian burr was pronounced as Armstrong grappled with his surprise. Taking note of her men's clothes, he shook his head in disbelief... she could hear his anger.

'You're nee lady! So *madam*, your time here appears misspent!' He seized her waist, 'Still the same old Kitty!' His voice rebuked and then changed to a gratified hiss, 'you seek night shadows...that can mean but one thing...' his nails dug into her flesh and his face was close to hers. His breath was like the fetid seaweed of the harbour.

She stayed stiff and mute but the ribald surprise in his voice turned to anger. 'You can only be here for one thing- to liaise with a man!' Silence... as the implication of his words took hold of him,

'Well, am telling yer - *am* head of the queue,' Armstrong gloated, swearing an obscene oath as he pushed her to the ground, struggling to pull down her trousers.

He had the strength of a drunken man. The smell of whisky entered deep into her cowering body like a dose of medicine gulped against her will. A turning away of her head, a flailing of arms, he was heavy upon her...loud protesting, useless sobs- a child resisting the unwanted attention of yet another man.

She lay, remembering the dark nights, her father's insistence and afterwards the cold dawn.

She walked out into the waves, waist high and the cold made her gasp; she choked and vomited as though in that way she could rid herself of his vile intrusion. She scooped the salt water high between her legs, time and time again, bitter tears and stinging brine joining to wash away her shame.

Cuddies beads lay in a pool by her groping hands. In the early dawn light she felt their tiny insignificance; and knew that somehow through thick and thin they had survived. A curlew, its long crown feathers open to the wind, stood uncertain at the water's edge, one leg planted straight, the other bent ready for flight…to go or to stay? There was only one place for her to go; back to her child… the bairn's innocence and her burden.

And as the chill crept into her being there came the knowledge that Olaf had deserved and had wanted his punishment; surely, her humiliation and punishment had never been wanted *or* deserved.

Across the bay, grey-blue sky, taffeta-shot by the first orange of sunrise, reflected back over the water. Somewhere out there, the camouflaged blue-grey figures of the seals swam free and uncaring. Her plight was nothing to them.

Eighteen

'Don't worry the young man was found and despatched. He's left the island... he'll not be coming back.'

Kitty stared into the face of Magistrate Armstrong on the other side of the breakfast table, an inscrutable expression on his rugged features. And all she could think was that, in last night's confusion, he had not recognised Olaf as Kitty's night-time tryst.

Armstrong's mouth was set in a firm line, only relaxing to shovel in another forkful of herring. The smell of the fish sickened her. Kitty shut her eyes but could see only the herring slit feeding the long thin troughs and barrels packed to the gunnels; even the tobacco lingered stale and pungent on Armstrong's waistcoat. He was dishevelled.

She was numb. The night had been short, and Armstrong had made little effort with his morning toilet. Kitty in contrast had put on her best dress, powdered her wind-blown cheeks and brushed her hair into a neat, tight coil above her troubled eyes. She stared at the uncouth man in front of her- so unbothered by appearances (except hers). He'd seen fit to send her to his relations for her to learn to be a lady...only to do to her what he did to those who were *not* ladies!

He was studying her, his thoughts half on his fried herring, the rest on her. She hunched under his penetrating gaze. Abstractedly she wondered if she was holding her knife correctly as in the houses of the gentry.....anything to numb her brain! For unconventional Armstrong, fingers to his food were acceptable, but for a young lady to rise in the world there was a right way and a wrong way. Surely the reason for her stay with the Smythe family could not have been just to make her good enough for him? She shuddered. His eyes held no memory of the night, just as her father had been his normal self over his breakfast crowdie.

Kitty stuttered, 'I-I have discovered who is double crossing you.'

'...as long as it isn't you Kitty...' Armstrong scrapped the final piece of herring from the plate and then, ignoring the napkin, wiped his hand across his face and rose to his feet.

Louise entered the room, there was no sign of Henry, then no one would expect to see him on a Saturday morning before midday at the earliest! No one spoke. The girl took the seat opposite Kitty; her toilet was immaculate; thin fair curls coiled about her face making her look soft and feminine. She had piled on the powder as though the island wind should have no say in her colour!

Kitty did not try to catch the girl's eye. Last night she too had been humiliated. She'd thrown herself at Patterson and he had laughed in her face. Was sister-Marion really a rival in love; after years of quarrels did the two sisters have this real issue between them? Had Louise really planned to give her card-winning money to the handsome boat skipper in the hope of them quitting the island together? Kitty crowded her mind with trivia- anything to keep her thoughts from her own *horror*.

She would not be here to witness the sister's cat-fight. Armstrong's parting night words had barked his intent.

'Have your valise packed for the early crossing.'

The words repeated like a tempest in her brain, over and over and over, trying to drown out Armstrong and his mocking, opportunistic rape of her in the early hours of the morning. Fumbling lust, in the dark shadows of the island where ill fortune had placed her within his grasp; his drink- fuelled reasoning-*why not take what he had paid for*? Cruelly, her abusing father's friend had reminded her that even now her body was not her own.

She thought of Olaf's dancing seals. She had dreamed of casting her whore pelt. But now- it was way too late.

The sea! -one minute friend, the next foe! Which guise would see her cross the sand-flats never to return? Would the seals sing or would silence be their mute farewell? She remembered their cries piecing the fog, the whitemaas calling as they swooped over the rocky coast... and bodies from the wreck coming in with the tide.

'Ten minutes and we must be on the road, so do not linger over your farewells.' Armstrong's voice broke into her thoughts and she sprang to her feet, upsetting a plate in her confusion.

'Yes, I have good-byes,' she forced herself to look him in the eye, 'I look forward to seeing Pleasance a...and little Katherine.'

'Unfortunately not!' Armstrong frowned.

Kitty stuttered her surprise. 'The...the child has not come to any harm?'

'No, when I left she flourished, it is to be hoped she always will. But I have other plans for *you*.' His voice was cold.

Kitty squeezed her napkin into a tight ball, the Magistrate's words carried threat. Was the child an innocent pawn in yet another of his games...*you do what I want then you will see your child again*?

The carriage waited at the door, inside sat Armstrong. Alongside him sat a bleary-eyed Henry and sister Louise, who feigned sleep. The coachman handed Kitty into her seat and, promptly, they were trundling along the chare to the sea then out beyond to the waiting mainland. Kitty sat huddled, her eyes closed; she heard the swish of the wheels in water and felt the gentle give of the wet sand. The horses' hooves gained speed when they reached dry land. The state of the tide had perfectly colluded with whatever Armstrong planned for the day ahead. Where could they be going?

Land, the coastal plain; fields filled with burgeoning crops, animals grazing, and beyond- hills as unpredictable as the sea. When they reached the Great North Road they turned northward in the opposite direction from her waiting child. What possible destination had Armstrong for the unlikely travelling companions? Kitty struggled to keep her composure. Louise sat impassive. Henry's head lolled forward on his chest, oblivious.

'We are all off to Lamberton, just the other side of the border...' Armstrong broke the silence, a Magistrate making utterance, 'far enough, I think for our first stop to rest the horses.'

He laughed mirthlessly, 'and what better place than the village of Lamberton for an eloping couple to seal a runaway marriage? The Old Toll House there is almost as popular as Gretna Green for such occasions.'

He had their attention. 'What say you, Kitty...' he waved his hand in the direction of the bemused girl, '...is not my young nephew Henry a good catch for you?'

He bent forward and whispered in her ear, 'Reason enough, last night, for the *owner* of the bride to first sample the prize?'

Kitty drew away from him in a shudder of revulsion. The coach had halted besides a small building on the left of the road. Her heart beat fast, this could not be happening and yet...

Louise giggled nervously and the sound was offensive, the earlier subdued girl, agog now at Armstrong's words. She sat bolt upright, eyes gleaming,

'And am I to be the bridesmaid?' She shrieked with laughter as she dug her brother, seated beside her, in the ribs. 'What a reward brother, just what you would have asked for!'

'Aye it's his reward alright and justly deserved I think. This is where you Cousin Henry, get out of the coach.'

Armstrong opened the door and with a hard shove in the small of his back, Henry Smythe was down on the grass verge just feet from the Toll House door, staggering in his hang-over surprise. He leered into the coach; Kitty recoiled as a bemused but now grinning Henry leant in and held out his hand to her.

So *this* charade was the reason why she would not be seeing her daughter that day.

'Look at her face, I don't think Kitty likes the idea too much,' Armstrong's voice bellowed into the country quiet. 'What say you, my dear... surely Henry fits your needs?'

A bemused Kitty shook her head. Armstrong laughed. 'It looks as though there must be a change of plan. Sorry cousin, no honeymoon tonight after all, you'll be spending it on your own. And it's a long, lonely walk back to the island, so you'd better get started.'

He turned to Louise and Kitty, 'Wave good bye, girls.'

He glowered at Henry, 'You should all reflect on the fact that no one double-crosses John Armstrong without paying for it.'

Armstrong shouted a command to the driver and, with a lurch, the coach shot forward, Smythe's baffled face in full view of the occupants.

Kitty leaned back into the cushions that padded the walls and began to laugh hysterically. John Armstrong was known for his practical jokes, funny unless you were on the receiving end. She was trembling- the man's humour had also been at *her* expense. He was showing his power over her and over them all. His face was implacable as if he sat in court, *I'll tell you when to laugh, when to cry.*

But she'd waste no sympathy on Henry, the double-crosser deserved all that he had got. Yet she hadn't told Armstrong of the northern shore- cave stacked with plunder. With a start she realised it meant only one thing- *Armstrong had known all along who was stealing his profit.* Kitty's mission to Holy Island had been but a ruse. Why? She could not believe the reason was purely to exert his control over her. How the man liked to play practical jokes... on his victims!

She stole a glance at Louise- the joke against her brother had appealed to the girl's strange sense of humour. But as the carriage continued ever further away from the butt of the jest, Louise sat pale and unsure, twiddling with her skirt, a nervous habit that betrayed her concern. Kitty raised her eyebrows at the girl. Slowly Louise shook her head. So she also did not know what Armstrong had in mind for them. Was it to be another silly prank or something more sinister?

Kitty felt anger bubbling inside her, furious that they sat trapped in the coach with Armstrong. She would act when next the horses stopped. And then, as if in tune with her thoughts, the coach wheels suddenly juddered to a halt. Kitty's hand was already on the door, ready for any new mischief.

There were voices and immediately she felt relief, here were other people; the unmistakeable sounds of a man issuing orders, the neighing of horses, the stamping feet of reigned-in mounts. The coach was surrounded by a posse of horsemen in uniform. A face appeared at the window, the unsmiling aspect of a blue- uniformed officer with flowing horsehair on his helmet. Official business!

'What now…' Armstrong wound down the window and the soldier manoeuvred his mount closer to the carriage, '…what is the matter, Captain, is there trouble?'

'Nothing to worry you and the ladies, sir I do assure you. We are deployed here a-bouts to enforce the King's law and order on the highways and byways. In the past few months there has been some unrest in the shires, radicals you know, barn-burning and the likes; we are here to reassure and to keep an eye out for any suspicious characters.'

A smile spread across Armstrong's face and his voice boomed. 'Then we have *just* the man for you, sir. We passed a fellow a few miles back along the road, about Lamberton way. He looked highly unsavoury. So let us not keep you from your duty. It is reassuring, is it not ladies, that patrols protect the road for we innocent travellers? Where rumours abound, the King's Highways need your presence!'

Armstrong winked at the girls. Kitty's face was impassive but inwardly she was a mixture of emotions; with the soldier's words came the realisation that her idea of escape would appear to be foolhardy; the highways were unsafe for everyone- and not just for lone female travellers. Kitty watched the troops move off in the direction of Lumberton as Armstrong murmured to himself, 'So many rumours, but only one to interest us.' His narrow eyes glinted across at her. Kitty feigned sleep for she'd no intention of letting the man know her disquiet. The horses returned to their steady rhythm. What lay in store for her, for Louise, when next they came to a halt? It was musical chairs but played out on the trot; the music provided by the drumming in her brain was loud and discordant. And when it stopped they might know their destination.

Part Two

Nineteen

Smoke from coal fires blanketed the city rooftops in a choking black haze, as ominous as any storm cloud crowning the top of Cheviot. The wind, as in the hills, scurried in a flurry of unexpected gusts lifting skirts and hats and dust. The streets were as dirty as any upland path. But here was noise, new vistas and new happenings!

Edinburgh lay unravelled before them, and Kitty could only marvel at the sight, just as she had marvelled at her first view of the sea. Buildings towered to a dizzying height. Worked stone piled layer upon layer and windows heaped one upon another, defying nature. They dwarfed one-storey hill cottages, the three- floored Barraburn Farm and even Pilgrim House! Roads, wider than a river, throbbed with life; more people than she had ever seen in all her years congregated along the Princes' Street thoroughfare. Its pavements were fronted by stately mansions, whilst carriages bowled along the wide road, each one of them fine enough to carry the King himself! Kitty felt a stirring of excitement.

'I've dreamed of Edinburgh and now here we are!' Louise wore a permanent smile on her face. They had been in the city one whole day, and the Smythe daughter had found nothing to fault. Kitty had not heard her utter a single cross word!

'Yes, it's been a dream of mine as well.' Early morning and Kitty was by the window of their lodgings gazing at the busy street below. She could not imagine ever tiring of the scene; even sleeping had seemed a waste of time and she had crept to the window to watch the city- busy even in the night hours. Carts had trundled along the darkened street, and shadows moved; intrigued, she'd marvelled that folk could be abroad at three o'clock in the morning. The capital city of Scotland did not sleep whatever the hour.

'We must be the luckiest girls alive!' A refreshed Louise came to stand beside her, and Kitty nodded agreement. She had decided not to think beyond the other girl's unquestioning acceptance of their destination. Kitty hid her unease; time would tell what Armstrong expected of them in return. She clutched at the fact that he had not attempted to molest her again. Louise was a natural restraint on her uncle and for that Kitty was thankful. Perhaps this was the Holy Island girl's ordained role?

Armstrong treated both girls with a cool indifference, though she noticed he watched their reaction to their destination with childlike interest. 'Didn't I promise Sir Walter Scott I would bring you to Edinburgh?' He'd looked smug. Kitty had not replied, leaving the gushing to Louise. She knew there must be other hidden reasons, but one day or three days here, in this new world offered a very different way of life for both girls; Kitty in spite of herself could not quench her intrigue.

'What are you going to wear Kitty?' The fair girl frowned down at the state of her dress. 'How was I to know we were coming to Edinburgh and that we are to meet with Sir Walter Scott this very afternoon? Sir Walter of all people! Wait till I tell Marion, she will be green with envy!'

Kitty said nothing but she smiled, already she anticipated the planned meeting with the eminent writer. At Barraburn he had been friendly, naturally interested in Armstrong's young ward. Not like his young companion. Olaf had been aloof to the point of hostility; had hardly deigned to acknowledge her existence! Yet on Holy Island she had seen both his see-saw friendliness and his cool indifference. She acknowledged that he was a fellow troubled-being.

Down in the street, a group of young men were laughing, playing the fool, a clutter of heads of all colours, black and brown- no light sandy hair to spoil the uniformity. Where now was Olaf? Was he back in this sprawling place- a small pavement-sized speck lost in the throng? From the moment she had entered Edinburgh, her thoughts had been on the Orcadian, would their paths cross? The city was large, but he and Sir Walter had been travelling companions; the writer, even now, paid for Olaf Magson's education. What if he were also there at number thirty-nine Castle Street?

She breathed in quickly and, like Louise, gazed down at her travel-crumpled dress.

'It doesn't matter what we look like. It's just an informal visit to Sir Walter.'

'But we have no calling-cards.' Louise wailed her concern. 'When I think of the pile I have at home. It is too bad.'

Kitty giggled, 'I've never left a card in my life, afternoon tea parties were not common in the hills!'

'We are talking of Edinburgh, Kitty and it's no laughing matter.'

Louise seized her companion's hands in her concern, 'We do not want to appear the country bumpkins.'

'But, Louise, Sir Walter is himself a country bumpkin, never happier than at home in Abbotsford and out walking the hills. He will think us a breath of border country air!' Kitty spoke to convince herself that the storyteller would accept her for what she appeared to be. He must *never* know her clouded past.

Louise's face showed she was unconvinced. 'How can you think that? Well, you do as you please, you *are* a country girl - I decidedly am not!' She flounced away from the window, 'I am going to stand by the fire and hope that the creases will fall from my dress.' Resolutely she turned her backside to the fire in the grate, her blue crepe in danger of disappearing up the chimney.

Kitty grinned, 'don't go too near the flames, I wouldn't like to see you become part of the pall of smoke that hangs over the city. It isn't called Auld Reekie for nothing.'

Number thirty nine, Castle Street facing west, reflected the afternoon sun, its bow windows with square panes like gleaming spectacles on a venerable face, its cheeks polished above high cheek bones. Three steps and curving hand rails led to the solid front door. Armstrong and the two girls heard the bell ring in the inner depths and Kitty tapped her foot impatiently. The city of Edinburgh held no greater man than the occupant of the fine town house that awaited their calling-cards; for Armstrong had vacated their lodgings early morning and now both girls clutched delicate parchment oblongs that told of their worth. Kitty who'd never dreamed of holding such a possession could hardly take her eyes from the delicate gold-leaf lettering.

Of course, Sir Walter did not answer the door himself and a uniformed servant led them across the stone flags of the large entrance hall to a room at the back of the house. He read the cards and then announced the visitors in a strong border accent. They were not the only country folk in town. Sir Walter attired in blue coat and white linen, rose beaming from a table by the fireplace.

'What treat is this?' His voice boomed his welcome and there were handshakes all round. He bowed low over Kitty's hand before greeting the newcomer, Louise. Formalities over, he turned back to Kitty. She noted that his limp had become considerably worse in the few months since his visit to Northumberland.

'I thought it appropriate to welcome you in the Library young lady,' he extended his hand to indicate the book-lined walls. 'I remember books are your particular pleasure, and whilst you are in the city I would hope you will avail yourself of my collection.'

Kitty raised her eyebrows, astonished that their host remembered their conversation at Barraburn. In his busy life he had retained what for him must be less than a significant fact, 'It is indeed kind of you Sir Walter. Though I do not know the duration of our visit to your beautiful city,' she looked at John Armstrong her voice questioning.

'Young lady, you've only just arrived and you talk of departure. That cannot be.' Sir Walter landed a good-natured hand on farmer Armstrong's back, 'The city Summer Season can only be enhanced by the arrival of two beautiful young ladies, autumn is many months away. There will be plenty of time for you girls to raid my shelves.' He pointed to three chairs pulled up to the fire and sank down thankfully into his vacated seat stroking as he did so the head of an enormous dog, limpet-close to her master, their mutual devotion obvious.

'Don't worry Maida is a gentle giant and ageing like her master. No need to fear her even though her head is as high as the back of my chair.' He fondled the deerhound's head. 'She is missing the country, as do I; there are seedlings of cedar and oak to plant not to mention the need to install gas lighting throughout Abbotsford; we have sickened of the smoke of wax candles and whale-oil.' He sighed at the thought of the accumulating tasks that awaited him.

'But it is to be hoped you do not return there in the near future, Sir Walter?' Armstrong unsettled to be in such an unfamiliar room absent-mindedly stroked a cat who had taken a fancy to his lap. A further tabby complained loudly as Kitty put her hand on the chair it occupied and, disgruntled, moved away to the window. But if it was sunlight it sought, there was none to be had, for the room was dark and hidden from the afternoon light at the front of the house. In this room it made sense that there was a fire in the grate on a July afternoon.

'No, unfortunately, the seeds and lamps will have to wait. I am needed in Edinburgh. It is a momentous time for the capital and for m...' He stopped in full sentence and smiled guardedly. 'You know John…. of the likely happening, though to be sure, the possibility changes *every* day.' He shook his head and Kitty thought he is an old man with much on his mind.

She said, 'So you did not exaggerate, Scotland really does have a fine city for capital, I am sure there is none more beautiful.'

Sir Walter beamed. 'You haven't seen anything yet my dear, when all the new buildings are complete, Athens in all its glory will have a rival.' Kitty heard the pride in his voice and felt again her liking for this Scotsman who showed his feelings without any false restraint. His manner towards made her feel good. But she felt a stab of concern at his appearance; he looked older, there was dark shading under his eyes and his cheeks were puffy.

'Unfortunately we do not have the Greek climate to go with it; the erratic wind on the Mound being built to join the Old and the New town is very unpleasant, in truth I have hardly left Castle Street on foot what with that and the uneven flagstones.'

He was a caged animal; Kitty thought of the hard streets, the high buildings, the throng of people, there must be some big reason why the eminent borderer was spending his summer cooped up in the city away from his beloved Tweedside.

'We are used to wind, sir, as you know Northumberland gets it from all directions and Miss Smythe lives on Holy Island which is in the path of every gale God sends.' She indicated her friend who as yet had had no part in the conversation.

'Ah, the isle of saints and kings, Miss Smythe, a proud tradition for such a wee piece of land, rather like here in Scotland. Have you heard of our great find? It was one of the most sacred moments in my -. Oh dear, forgive an old man his enthusiasms.'

'Please tell us, Sir Walter,' Louise was beginning to thaw to the friendly unassuming man, a household name with few pretentions.

He smiled at the invitation, 'Imagine young ladies, if I told you I found buried treasure...' He stopped to achieve full impact and then when both girls looked suitably impressed, '...not just jewels but the Crown Jewels; Scotland's Regalia lying dusty and forgotten in the Castle and unseen for centuries!' He frowned, '*Now*, I am glad to say they have been returned to their proper place.'

'Did you find the crown?' Kitty could imagine the patriotic Scot, his hands on the lost treasures of his country, what a discovery it must have been for him!

'Yes, and orb and sceptre- all there in the lost Honours so integral to our history. I fervently believe our past can redress the problems of the present and that the treasure can make us a nation again. But forgive me, I am an incurable romantic and think of the past when I should be concentrating on the present.'

He rang the bell beside him and, as though she'd been waiting outside the door, a young girl appeared. She carried a tray of refreshment; lemonade and the type of tart made both sides of the border, the pastry filled with dried fruit and covered with icing that melted in the mouth.

Armstrong ate loudly, his fingers garnering the last crumb and only then did he turn his attention to their host, 'Your suggestion that we take rooms at the top of Leith Walk for the duration of our stay appears to be a happy choice.'

Sir Walter beamed. 'I do not believe there is a nobler avenue than Leith Walk in the whole of Europe; fine buildings parted by a wide thoroughfare and in the very heart of the city. You are minutes from the Theatre Royal and that is something the young ladies will wish to attend I am sure.'

Louise could hardly contain her excitement, 'Oh, yes, a real live play- that I would dearly love to see. What is playing in the Theatre?' She sounded as though she was acquainted with the very latest performances.

Their host smiled, 'Would you be surprised to hear that William Murray is putting on a stage performance of my *Heart of Midlothian* and his sister, Mrs Harriet Siddons is playing Jeanie Dean?'

'Oh h-how wonderful,' Louise was almost speechless.

Kitty smiled her agreement. But it was all too good to be true. Even now as they sat in one of the most fashionable houses in Edinburgh worry clouded her view. Why had Armstrong brought the two girls to the city? And why had he placed them and him in the very heart of cultured life when that was so alien to them all?

As if Sir Walter could read her thoughts he said, 'Miss Macnab I am sure you have already noted that close to your dwelling is Calton Hill; for those used to green spaces it is a pleasant retreat. Yes, you will be happy with your lodging and who knows within a week or so it might prove to be the most advantageous position in the whole of the city.' He smiled at the two eager faces.

'You mention Mrs Siddons, Sir Walter, I believe you said besides acting she is teaching Court manners and deportment to the young ladies of Edinburgh.' Armstrong, his face now red from proximity to the unseasonal fire, looked increasingly out of his depth; theatre, actresses and young ladies' deportment not his usual topics of conversation. Kitty thought, surely the heat of the room has addled Armstrong's brain that he should make such enquiry!

'Yes, she lives in Picardy Place just minutes from your door. I am sure the young ladies will find a few sessions with Mrs Siddons to their benefit.'

'We are to learn court manners?' Kitty could not hide her chagrin. 'Are we such country girls that we cannot be accepted into Edinburgh society?' Her face was now as flushed as Armstrong's.

Sir Walter threw back his head and laughed, 'Miss Macnab I am more than happy with your manners, not to mention your deportment, but even the finest Edinburgh ladies are receiving tuition on the likelihood that one day they will be received by his Majesty King George the Fourth. For, if I have my way, His Majesty will one day agree to grace Edinburgh with his presence.'

Twenty

At last the city lay at their feet. The front door closed behind them. To the right, Castle Street fell away down to farmland and the Firth of Forth. To the left, the Castle towered into the dour northern sky, its ramparts lost in a mist that had fallen over the city. Both girls were of the same mind, green fields and open spaces held no draw for them.

An earlier shower of rain had helped lay the dust, but there was an overpowering odour of horse manure mixed with the descending smoke from Sir Walter's library chimney and from those of his neighbour's. Kitty sneezed and then sneezed again. Horses' hooves vied with the sound of metal wheels as they clipped the cobbles- relentless sounds as the busy city moved about its business. Above them, seagulls wheeling in from the sea circled low around the castle, but Kitty's darting eyes were on the city buildings.

It hadn't taken long for their host to fathom that the girls wanted to be anywhere but seated in a stuffy library. In no time, Sir Walter had instructed Armstrong to tarry behind for a discussion of mutual interest, whilst producing a young under-footman to accompany the girls on their first foray out into the streets. Young Alec would be their chaperone.

'Come on Kitty...we might get lost.' Louise almost collided with their escort so eager was she to keep up. But she had no need to hurry her companion, Kitty was right behind her- on the bustling pavements it would be easy to get lost.

She followed Louise's smile; it had appeared as they had approached the capital on the previous day and Kitty swore it must have been evident throughout the night hours. She'd not heard her friend complain once!

They reached Princes' Street, green grass and trees on the castle slopes, but grime-covered, and Kitty found it hard to equate the green here with the vegetation she knew back home. Lack-lustre horses waited patiently at the coach stand, their coats likewise grimy from city life.

Kitty breathed in heavily, she said, 'Louise why are we here? Do you know?'

'*Why?*' Louise stared at her as though she had taken leave of her senses, '…why not?'

'But that's no answer.'

A puzzled Louise pointed at their young-faced guide. 'You're my chaperone, I'm yours. Even so, Alec was thought necessary to be with us on our trip into the city.'

'But…' Kitty trailed off, how could she explain that she was no virgin to save from molestation? Cynically, she thought, apt employment lurked for her in the city back streets. But Louise had no inkling of Kitty's past and the child that she had left behind. She must *never* divulge her dark secrets to her new friend. Louise would make a meal of it- that she knew! And now to add to it, was her new bitter shame in the dark shadows of the herring sheds. It bore down on her like the smoke from the reeking chimneys when she longed to see Edinburgh in transparent blue sky.

Kitty fixed her eyes on their guide. They reached Princes' Street and the young man turned eastward into an even noisier, jostling crowd that spilled off the pavement into traffic on the road.

'O, look Kitty, there's the Theatre Royal that Sir Walter mentioned. Oh surely, Cousin John will allow us to attend?'

'Probably- as the play is taken from one of Sir Walter's novels.' Kitty stopped in front of the theatre billboard and young Alec immediately halted. He said in an apologetic voice,

'The Theatre is rather shabby from the outside but opulent inside.' Kitty stared at the low-storeyed building- she'd expected a much grander edifice. It hardly merited a second glance except for a carved pediment that graced the entrance, 'Who are the three figures?'

'Who else but William Shakespeare in the middle, and flanked either side by the muses of Tragedy and Comedy.' The young footman was ready with the answer almost before the question had formed on her lips! Slight and pale-faced, he, like the building, appeared unremarkable, but his eyes flashed with interest.

'Why we must be with the most knowledgeable person in the whole of Princes' Street!' Kitty grinned appreciatively, 'Then it's hardly surprising when you're in the employ of the most famous man in Edinburgh.'

That made the serious lad smile, 'Sir Walter likes to educate us. But sometimes I can tell him something that he didn't know,' Alec looked positively pleased with himself.

'We'll hope to do the same, shall we not Louise?' Kitty was beginning to succumb to the obvious promise of the city.

'I'll leave any learned stuff to you, Kitty. I'd be quite happy just to go to the Theatre dressed in a beautiful gown on the arm of a handsome young man.' Louise sighed and Kitty laughed.

'Sorry to disappoint you, I think your middle-aged cousin will be our only escort but, no matter, to visit the theatre would be a highlight for us both.'

Kitty refrained from repeating the girl's heartfelt sigh but she too felt a rising surge of expectation. To hear professional actors and actresses perform on the stage was something she'd only imagined and now it was almost within her reach! She didn't care that the theatre had seen better days, for it offered a glimpse into a world of romance created by the man she admired above all others!

On the arm of a handsome young man, Louise's words rang in her ears. A handsome young man- the image of Olaf Magson came easily to mind and her heart missed a beat.

Could he be her desired escort?

Perhaps he would be her desired escort; listening intently to every word of the play and then expounding to her on the plot; giving explanation and answer. And then, satisfied, surely he'd return to the topic closest to his heart, the uncomfortable truth that a lighthouse was needed not on Brownsman Island but on Longstone and his regret for all that would mean for the Darling family.

So as to rid herself of the image, she said to Louise, 'So do you have a likely man in mind?'

Louise frowned, 'I thought I did,' and Kitty knew she was thinking of Dougal Patterson, 'Anyway Olaf Magson could do very well, though his introverted island upbringing isn't really what I'm looking for…'

'He's serious-but only over things that matter.'

Louise laughed, 'He can be very annoying. Have you noticed, he always takes the opposite stance…like quarrelling with his lighthouse keeper father?' She laughed at Kitty's expression of surprise. 'You don't have to remind me that I do that with my mother. But he's become rather priggish and I can tell you he's not the innocent he appears.'

'Well *who* is?' Kitty snapped and then quickly, 'Olaf is no different from any of the rest of us,' she said, 'We all know that Tragedy and Comedy hold equal sway whether on a theatre facade or in real life.'

'Tell me more.' Louise looked intrigued and Kitty said quickly,

'Forgive us, Alec we delay your errand,' the lad was looking restless, 'but everything is new for us.' They moved off. So Louise did not know of Olaf's childhood tragedy. Whereas he had freely admitted it to *her!*

Louise peered at the stream of passers-by, all unknown faces, 'So we're all in Edinburgh. I wonder where Olaf lives…'

Kitty sounded disinterested, 'He could live anywhere…' she pointed to the high tenement buildings that crowded the skyline.

'Did you not say he was an acquaintance of Sir Walter? Perhaps we can make contact through him.'

'Perhaps…' again Kitty was non-committal.

Edinburgh was hilly! They climbed steadily, crossing a tall bridge that spanned the drained N'or Loch and immediately the atmosphere changed. Gone the wide thoroughfares lined with the elegant buildings of the New Town; suddenly the city had another face. Narrow streets, crowded housing… no room here for mews stables! Smoke spiralled from chimneys that mushroomed from jutting slate roofs. The grime mingled with the sounds and smells and all was made more intense in the confined streets. Kitty looked at the mass of people that thronged about them. She saw the same confusion- tall hats atop smart trousers and jackets fashioned the affluent, whilst the poor walked in their steps, wearing trousers without knees or ragged skirts that trailed the city dirt. Elbow-less shirts showed match-stick arms.

She'd never seen such a gulf between those that had and those that had not. It was like comparing Sir Walter's library to Slymefoot tavern. And yet the huge difference seemed to go unnoticed- rich and poor, bad and good, mingled side by side in the melting pot. Olaf could pass by on the other side of the road unnoticed. And what about her…how easy to become lost in this amorphous city… and then what would become of her daughter?

The little girl figured ever larger in her thoughts. A woman passed close to her, a toddler of similar age held tight in her arms. Kitty had to turn away. Her little one's distinctive smell invaded the senses, as though that tiny hand did indeed clutch hers. She choked back her regret.

'Oh, what a smell…' a disdainful Louise held her nose. A couple of ragged boys tracked their steps, 'Kitty, do you think there are pickpockets? I have heard such fellows exist.' Louise edged closer to her friend as she spoke, and for the first time her smile was unsure.

'I hardly think they would want our visiting-cards and that's all I carry upon me.' Kitty was flippant, 'But yes we should have our wits about us. Edinburgh is not Holy Island.'

'No, thank goodness.' Louise's eyes gleamed, 'We must take full advantage of our time here.'

'Sir Walter has offered us the use of his library!'

'That's not exactly what I was meaning.' Louise grinned, 'Still as long as it has novels I'll be content. I'll leave the learned tomes for you.'

'Your cousin can't have brought us here,' Kitty raised her eyebrows, 'just for us to read books?'

'Oh, Kitty you do fuss about needless things. But if it will make you any happier we'll ask Cousin John his reason for coming.' So saying, the girl dismissed the subject with a touch of her old impatience and Kitty sighed. She did not share Louise's confidence that they would get a satisfactory answer. There must be more to it than just the invitation issued to them by Sir Walter on his Northumberland visit.

Again Alec was waiting anxiously for them to catch up and now with a fierce expression on his young face, he waved away the two lads still close behind them, 'young ladies be vigilant at all times.' He sounded older than his years and Kitty smiled to herself; then he was city aware, they were not.

'Here we are at the University where I have papers to deliver for Sir Walter.' They stood before the arched entrance to a large and imposing building. Eagerly they followed their guide into the busy quadrangle centred by grass with wide walkways all round. 'If you would like to wait here, I shall be brief.'

They had entered an oasis of peace just steps from the outside world! Kitty glanced about her, small groups, of young men carrying books, moved with purpose. Within these walls favoured sons and brothers studied subjects at their will. Kitty, who'd received no education other than at her grandmother's knee, could only wonder at their good fortune. She couldn't remember learning to read, it had seemed to come naturally, but she'd put it to little use.

'How I envy them,' she said aloud, 'I hope we stay in Edinburgh long enough to make use of the Castle Street library if nothing else.'

Louise shook her head. 'What a waste that would be. City life offers something more than that. Oh, come on Kitty… do stop being such a kill joy!'

Suddenly the peace of the afternoon was shattered as a door opened and a noisy throng of students erupted into the quadrangle. Louise disappeared in a melee of rowdy, caged boys who, at sight of the surprised girls, let out yelps of delight. One minute they were scholars, and next, they were healthy young blades surrounding a delighted Louise. Kitty pushed back against the wall and surveyed her friend's entanglement with amusement. This was what Louise's dreams were made of!

She was beside the open door and without thinking she went inside; she'd no wish to be caught up in the noisy fray. Rows of benches tiered up into the roof of a vast cavern like an amphitheatre, empty, except for a solitary figure seated on the front row engrossed in a pile of papers. Silent concentration, tufted hair, he was bent forward from squared shoulders in a stance that told her she had seen the long thin neck -just days ago- noosed in the herring house of Holy Island. He lifted his head and she looked straight into the eyes of Olaf Magson. She gasped.

Olaf's pale face lit up in a brief flush of surprise. 'K-Kit-Kitty?' He looked abashed, and she flushed a deep crimson. Olaf looked every inch the young city gentleman, in high collar and dark green trews- whilst, instantly, she felt like the country cousin. Was there pleasure before she saw his expression change, his mobile face closing to a look of disinterest? They stared at each other.

To break the uncomfortable silence she said, 'What's so interesting?' pointing at the sheaf of papers.

'Och, this is the account of the building of the Bell Rock Lighthouse...' and now his face was animated... 'a most remarkable feat of engineering- and it happened here in Scotland!'

'...where?' Kitty peered down at what was focusing his interest.

'...eleven miles out in the North Sea, on a treacherous sandstone reef.' He moved his satchel to make space for her on the bench beside him and she needed no second bidding. He hadn't said it wouldn't interest her or that a mere girl would find it boring! The seat was hard, the back dug into her shoulder blades and she thought, *this is the best place in Edinburgh!*

The top paper was a mass of words, of tight-spaced lines and scribbled corrections.

'It must have been a difficult task.'

'Building work could only take place during the calm summer months and then only for two hours each low tide...' Olaf's eyes reflected his passion,

'...my goodness!' Kitty was impressed.

'Yes, but it was more than necessary. Before the Bell Lighthouse was built the rocks claimed hundreds of lives; in 1804 HMS York went down with the loss of 491 lives.' Kitty shuddered.

'It is Mister Robert Stevenson's greatest achievement. He's been asked to publish an account of the work and he wants me to comment on his manuscript.' Olaf could not keep the pride from his voice as he fingered the great man's work. 'Already it's taken him eleven years to write it up. Then I have to admit he is a perfectionist.'

'All that time, that's dedication!' Kitty looked impressed. 'And you likewise! You've stayed behind whilst all the other students made a hasty exit.'

'Yes,' Olaf looked defiant, 'Mr Stevenson is my mentor. He has always been greedy for knowledge, unflagging in his task of self-improvement. He too came from poor beginnings. I would emulate such a man.' Kitty stole a glance at her companion. A frown furrowed his brow and she could almost imagine him eleven years hence, still glued to the scroll of papers.

He said, 'Do you know that the famous artist Mister JMW Turner has promised to provide an illustration for the cover of Mister Stevenson's book?'

'Oh my... even *I* have heard of him!' Kitty looked suitably impressed. How different were the circles that Olaf moved in from hers! She stared at him. Here was the focused man she had first seen on their trip to the Farne Islands. She said,

'How proud you must be that such a famous engineer has asked you for your opinion.'

'Oh, yes.' Olaf looked smug, knowing himself to be a young man whose opinion mattered -and to the leading engineer of Scotland. Just a few days had passed since the Orcadian's ignominious return from Holy Island and now he sat comfortably in his persona of valued student!

She thought, *he has put his demons behind him, whereas mine still sit below my skirt.*'

She said stiffly, 'I must not keep you from your studies,' and rose from the bench. The yawning gap between their lives was painfully obvious.

He looked up at the clock on the wall, 'Gracious, I shall be late for my next lecture!' Flustered, he rose to his feet and, gathering the pile of papers together, disappeared like a startled rabbit out into the courtyard.

She stood and watched him go, her heart heavy. She still did not know where he lived. Nor had he questioned her presence in the city.

Twenty One

Kitty sat huddled on the bench, head in hands. Olaf had gone without a second glance. Disinterest in her! His intelligent eyes were a luminous blue reflecting his many changing moods. She'd noted his disdain for her at their first meeting and it had rankled. In the time on Holy Island she had dared to hope she'd gone up in his estimation, he'd even deigned to share his beloved sea with her and now it was if he was rowing away in the opposite direction. Seated on the hard, ungiving University bench, she saw clearly his new horizon- and it did not include the likes of her. How could she *ever* have considered otherwise?

The lecture hall was dark and eerily quiet. She shivered and pulled her shawl about her. Through the open door she could see the quadrangle bathed now in sunlight. But still she lingered in the smell of learning, the feeling of worth crowding about her head.

How she wished her life had been different; if Olaf's brother had lived and she had been a boy... then they too might have shared this bench. Their heads could have been bent close and they would be seated near the sandy- haired young man who filled the front row with his ambition. But wishful thinking would not bring dead Ian and *whore* Kitty to the City College.

Louise popped her head round the door. 'Kitty, there you are! Why on earth are you hiding in here? I've been looking for you everywhere.'

'Louise,' Kitty shrugged her shoulders, 'sorry, I've never been in a lecture theatre before and I was just imagining what it must be like to sit here and listen to someone like Sir Walter filling my empty brain with fascinating facts.'

Louise laughed. 'Don't worry about your brain- it's your face that's your fortune. Men don't want clever remarks, they want black curls round a pretty face. Look at you Kitty, you are beautiful, you should be thinking of fine salons not fusty student rooms. Ugh, it smells rank in here, too many unwashed bodies after too many late nights in the taverns.'

'If only I'd been born plain... in fact... I wish I'd been born a boy.'

Louise laughed. 'Sorry, I'm no fairy godmother to grant that absurd wish. Just be thankful for Cousin Armstrong. Come on, we are going to be late for our appointment if we dally a minute longer.'

'Appointment...what, has your cousin arranged something else for us?' Kitty frowned. The girl obviously knew more than she did and it annoyed her. 'Louise, do you really know why we have come to Edinburgh?'

'Oh for goodness sake, Kitty, are you not happy to be here?'

'No I think perhaps I am not.'

'But why...' Louise looked mystified, '...here we are in Edinburgh when we could be kicking our heels in Pilgrim House or in B-Barraburn? That sounds like the back of beyond and a bit further!' The girl's eyebrows were reaching her hairline in disbelief!

'Barraburn is where my...my little sister awaits me. She grows bigger every day and I am not there to see. She will not recognise me when I return.'

'You seem to have a greater fondness for sisters than I do! I flourish in our separation. What is so special about yours?'

Kitty shook her head and laughed. The thought of her neglected child brought again an intense wave of longing, but also of shame that she could not acknowledge her baby. Instead she was playing Armstrong's game by calling little Katharine her sibling. That wasn't the bairn she had brought into this world after hours of painful labour! If Louise but knew, how she would pounce on the fact- her eyes a sly incredulity. If it was the last thing she did, Kitty vowed she'd keep her secret from this girl who shook and played with every snippet of gossip just as a cat played with a mouse. She must hope that she was never the tossed victim caught in Louise's claws.

'Where is our guide, have we lost him?' They emerged out into the afternoon sunshine. She didn't know why but she would not tell Louise of her meeting with Olaf. The Quad was deserted except for a hurrying figure at the far end. 'O, there's Alec. He looks rather anxious... perhaps he thought we had given him the slip.'

'Something to do next time perhaps, but he knows where the dressmaker lives, and we must rely on him to get us to the fitting by four thirty. It's important to be prompt- she is a busy lady by all accounts.'

'We have a dress fitting?' Kitty automatically looked down at her shabby dress that passed for best.

'Yes, sometimes I think you're resentful of Cousin John but...well, he's arranged through Sir Walter to provide us with dresses fit for city wear.'

'Oh.' Kitty could think of no appropriate reply and knew that any protest would be useless.

'We must hurry ladies if we are to reach Princes' Street in ten minutes.' Alec looked at their feet and saw the country shoes of the girls; Kitty grinned to herself guessing he would have stopped at a fashionable shoemaker on the way if there had been time. So, all outward appearances were to be satisfied- but for what? New dresses, deportment classes, and book- learning- it could mean only one thing. Her mind reeled. Prostitution did not flourish just in tenement hovels. It was also to be found in the smart town houses of the New Town. She shuddered in the afternoon sun.

Mrs Hamilton's establishment looked down on a Princes' Street thronged with late afternoon traffic. The street resounded to the noise of carriages and their horses and the cries of their drivers but in the hallowed precincts of the salon there was a revered hush. Even Louise had ceased her chat and, like Kitty she seemed overcome by the superior silence of the place. They waited expectantly, Kitty morose, nursing her unease. Her indebtedness to John Armstrong was piling up like her card debt to Louise. The girl had wanted her hair, what would Magistrate Armstrong bill into his account? Little Katharine played innocently about Barraburn farm. To the child it was now home. Was she the mother that the child really needed? By now, surely Patience had supplanted her in that role.

With a start she brought herself back to her present situation, a huge leap from Cheviot farm to city sophistication. She gazed about her. Thick green wall to wall carpet, rich red damask-covered chairs- but just the two so that there would be no unseemly queue. At the far end three shallow, curved steps led up to a double door tightly closed. There was no sound and even Louise was lost for words. The perfume of red musk roses hung heavy in the waiting room like an expensive drape. The flowers were perfect in shape and size as though they too had been chosen by tape measure. It was obvious that Mrs Hamilton had exacting standards.

'You go first, Louise.' Kitty's whisper sounded like an aside in church, any moment the vicar would frown down at her from his pulpit.

'Oh, no, Kitty I would rather it were you.' Louise calmed her unruly curls as she spoke and her quick reply was in a whisper. She too felt threatened by the place.

'But I feel uncomfortable here,' Country Kitty spoke her unease, 'and besides, I shall never be able to repay your cousin. For you it is different- but *I* do not like it!'

Louise frowned both at the words and the level of deliverance. In her mounting concern, Kitty had raised her voice.

The younger girl whispered her reply, 'Would you feel happier if I told you I have passed your card money on to John? You are paying for your new dress yourself.'

Kitty raised her eyebrows at the plausible solution but any finished article from this establishment would far out-weigh the debt she owed to Louise.

She said, 'Dear Louise, you are very kind.' with a finality sounding in her voice that she did not feel. The argument would have to be continued elsewhere, when she could raise her voice and her objections.

'Miss Macnab, welcome to my establishment.' Mrs Hamilton, seated in the centre of what Kitty had already christened the holy of holies, smiled her greeting, though it was distant and her lips hardly moved with the words. Kitty gave a short bow in return, determined she would not be over-awed. A silent assistant had led her up the sweeping steps into the church silence of the fitting room. It was the colour in the room that was loud, from the cherry red gown of the owner, to the bales of cloth stacked on shelves, a veritable library of material.

The seamstress held court; straight back and head on long graceful neck gave an instant feeling of aristocratic superiority... genuine or rubbed off from her clientele over time? Kitty straightened her back as she met the woman's unblinking gaze. Kitty's eyes flickered, and she saw the overall impression of supremacy was but skin deep- thick powder was needed to camouflage the woman's heavily pock-marked face!

But her hands were unblemished... long delicate fingers ended with manicured nails unused to toil, and the smooth skin was un-pitted by needles and pins. That was left to the ghostlike assistant who wielded the tape measure and carefully noted the measurements in a book attached to her. As the tape circled her slim waist, Kitty breathed normally, smugly thinking Louise would have to hold her breath for an acceptable reading! Her own waistline would flatter any dress, however humble the material. Still, it would seem that need was now a thing of the past...

Mrs Hamilton studied the results without comment then she looked the girl up and down from head to foot and extended fingers to indicate three rolls of cloth.

At last she spoke, 'I believe Miss Macnab you come from Northumberland.' Again her mouth scarcely moved as though she permanently held a line of pins between her lips. 'City fashion is somewhat different.' Then silence, sign language between her and her assistant, the other woman the one with the real pins in her mouth. Discretion was not the only proviso keeping her mute.

'I shall endeavour to have your choice round at your lodging the day after tomorrow.' Mrs Hamilton did not add, *I think it best if you stay indoors until you can be suitably attired,* but Kitty guessed her thoughts. Measurements taken, style and material chosen -all with minimum effort- only then with a perfunctory nod did Mrs Hamilton again address her client. She spat out the words,

'You are to dine with Sir Walter two evenings hence. He keeps a sophisticated table.' She had no need to add that the fashionable dressmaker's part in the proceedings would save Kitty from disgracing her host.

Kitty returned to the waiting room with a mixture of emotions. The dress already on its way to the stitching room was everything she had ever dreamed! The material chosen by Mrs Hamilton, a subtle pink, showed her dark skin and hair to perfection, and the new fitted style accentuated her waist...no more Empire Line.

A dress fit for Sir Walter's table but where besides? One word swam before her eyes 'PROSTITUTION,' though not cheaply dressed in tenement backstreets, but in the fine-gowned elegance of Georgian Edinburgh. The country whore-transplanted to a sophisticated world, and all thanks to Magistrate Armstrong.

She shook her head to rid herself of the dread that had constantly filled her mind ever since his island abuse of her. The dress was beautiful, it's acquisition a story for her daughter; somehow wherever they went she would take it with them, so that one day it would cut down to fit a slim, beautiful girl about to enter society.

For now, it was Louise's turn to go through the torture of pins and open condemnation... or perhaps Miss Smythe was more acceptable. Later, they would laugh about Mrs Hamilton, though not in earshot of Armstrong- he'd be impressed by the woman. And what did Sir Walter make of the larger than life character? Had she already appeared in one of his novels?

'Gracious, there's someone else here, oh, dear how I shall be frowned upon sharing the room with another client!' The young woman- bursting into the room-saw Kitty and giggled, her hand flying to her mouth in dismay,

'Two sins, filling the waiting room and talking as well... whatever next?'

So Kitty had perfectly read the expected protocol. The girl held out her hand, 'Let us introduce ourselves, it's important to know who is breaking the rules with me!'

The girl's voice was loud and she made no effort to lower it. In spite of her protestations, the place held no menace for her as it did for Kitty.

'I'm Charlotte Naismith.'

'Kitty Macnab.'

'Why I know that name, I heard it but yesterday...' she frowned as she tried to recollect.

'You know my name? I think not, I am a stranger to Edinburgh.'

Charlotte Naismith pursed her lips, though her eyes sparkled, 'Oh now I recall. Papa told me you are to attend our class in the morning.'

'Class?' Kitty looked mystified, 'May I ask what we are to learn, you and I?'

'My father is Alexander Naismith.'

'Oh,' Kitty flushed. His daughter expected her to know the name. 'Forgive me, I am newly arrived in the city, in fact it is my first visit to Scotland.'

The girl laughed delightedly, 'So Miss Macnab, perhaps you can spread the word when you return south of the border, though I do believe he has a following even there.'

'Please put me out of my misery, so I'll not appear ignorant next time.' Charlotte Naismith's openness encouraged confession.

'My father is a well-known artist in Edinburgh and you are to attend his painting classes for young ladies.'

'...painting classes?' Kitty could not hide her astonishment. 'But I have never held a paintbrush in my life!'

'That will please my father- no pre-learned bad habits!'

'Miss Naismith, we are ready for you, though you are *early* for your appointment.' Mrs Hamilton had emerged from her cocoon, followed by a chastened Louise.

'We shall see you tomorrow then, Kitty Macnab. I look forward to it.' Miss Naismith waved a hand in Kitty's direction as she turned to Mrs Hamilton who was smiling unreservedly at her new customer,

'How is your esteemed father?' Her mouth had opened wide on the greeting, no metaphorical pins to hide her warmth now! Fascinated, Kitty stared at the woman's teeth, yellowed and jagged, two sparkling white pearls falsely intruded in the front gaps. Mrs Hamilton had reason to speak sparingly.

Charlotte Naismith winked at Kitty as she fell in behind the precise steps of Mrs Hamilton.

'Don't forget Kitty to wear your oldest clothes for the lesson. Its great fun and the paint goes everywhere!'

Twenty Two

The cords of the sash window were like the ropes tethering her to the apartment. Kitty paced the room backwards and forwards, always returning to the window- outside there was fresh air or what passed for it in the overcrowded city. The cords were white and unworn as though they still awaited their first movement up or down. Her fingers itched to release the window, but she knew, without trying, that it had been too long closed. Below, the street bustled, figures and carriages and carts moved, insect-sized below her crow's nest view. She sighed, an uneasy restlessness threatened to become a headache. She thought longingly of her home hills, of climbing trees to get a better view or even to hide from trouble if some gauger stalked the valley.

Louise's head was buried in a book, she looked up, 'Oh, Kitty, do stop pacing about, can't you find something to do? You'll give yourself indigestion after the mutton stew Mrs Laidlaw made for our dinner.' Kitty didn't answer, afraid she would say too much.

Louise had refused to see Mrs Hamilton as a figure of fun and there'd been no shared mirth after the dress-fitting session.

'I'm sorry, Louise, I forgot to bring my needlepoint with me.' Kitty was flippant and her companion frowned, but as Kitty retreated to the window yet again, Louise's head was already submerged, engrossed in her book. It was obvious Miss Smythe intended to read all of Sir Walter's prodigious output before the girls departed from Edinburgh... whenever that was going to be!

Before that, there was the dinner invitation to Castle Street. Kitty thought of their genial host-to-be, how he too chaffed at being confined in the city. Sir Walter, like her, was a borderer, who loved nothing better than to trek the hills, and yet this year serious business required him to spend the summer in his city residence; he'd shown his frustration at that. Intuitively he'd seen that Kitty too would become the caged animal.

'Remember my dear young lady you can always escape to Calton Hill, your lodgings are just minutes away.'

She glanced at Louise, sometimes she seemed like her gaoler, always there, always watchful...surely she was not imagining things... she knew instinctively she'd not be able to leave the apartment without the girl insisting she go with her. But all Kitty wanted was her own company. Armstrong had cast Louise as her nursemaid.

The inert figure of the girl sat by the window to catch the failing light which already dripped into dusk, she looked up at Kitty whose face was now pressed against the window glass. Louise, an exasperated scowl on her face, slammed her novel shut and flounced off into their bedroom. Kitty grinned triumphantly and, seizing her new shawl, made her escape!

The sea sparkled in the distance but, in the opposite direction above the rooftops, green slopes provided a backdrop. Her spirits lifted; all she needed was to feel grass beneath her feet, and hilltop air about her cheeks for she could still feel her urban pallor. Smart town houses fronted the street in a terrace of stone, but she guessed that somewhere a narrow passage would seek the hill that rose steeply behind.

She was right, there by the sign announcing the name of Baxter Terrace, a small cobbled road skirted the end house to its back gate- and beyond to Calton Hill. She stopped, drawn by the elegant house three storeys high with basement and attics. The middle layers were of fine worked stone, the bottom and top were coarse and pitted. Instinctively, her eyes went to the attics; on that top layer, city life for her would surely have been played- drudge, maid of all work. And from that dismal prospect John Armstrong offered something else.

Her gaze scoured the attic windows, did girls like her look out - longing for escape? Nothing, the panes were dark vacant eyes. But there was movement on the third floor, where folk like the superior Mrs Hamilton lived out their lives, tight-lipped, whilst assistants hovered in their shadow awaiting every command. She stared enviously at the fine moulded window that hinted of the luxury behind it and saw a figure retreat back into the room. She felt a stab of jealousy for the unknown watcher; why should it be basement or attic for her or her daughter? Armstrong offered a ladder up to the desired height, however steep the rungs would prove to be.

She tossed her head in a gesture of defiance and pulled her shawl more tightly about her shoulders; with the wearing of the Paisley she had climbed the first few rungs. The expensive new shawl wasn't something she could ever have afforded to buy, she hadn't even known of its existence. It was Mrs Hamilton who'd informed them that the beautiful Kashmiri silk was desired by all the fashionable ladies but few of them could afford it! Louise had answered for both of them that Armstrong's purse was full and open.

The soft green grass of the hill sank beneath her feet, the trees canopied her head and she could hear country rustle, the hum of the city receding as though she'd closed a door behind her. The shawl caught on a twig and she knew how foolish she had been to wear it on such a foray. She'd left her common sense behind, somewhere in a Cheviot clough!

But now she was out above the tree-line on a slope as steep as Barraburn yet in the very centre of the capital. Late sun tracked eastward over jutting rooftops in a blaze of red that patterned the verdant green hill, reflecting the colours of her Paisley shawl.

The Hill was deserted. She had it to herself! She threw her arms wide and began to dance, swirling this way and that to an imaginary tune that resounded loudly in her head. How good to be free of her watcher, Louise, and free of Armstrong. But if I play my cards right she thought, I shall no longer *be* the misfit. *I can rise like this hill into a world in which I have every right to be!*

Kitty stopped abruptly, righted her skirts, patted her hair, and giggled sheepishly- suddenly aware that anyone could be watching. She began the walk downhill, time to return to try to tread Armstrong's line. Though here was a place that offered escape whenever she needed it!

What was that...a noise... someone was there behind her? She was down amongst the trees again, rats, rabbits must live here, even a fox out for his early supper. She walked on, but there was the soft rustle in the undergrowth and when she stopped, it also stopped.

How foolish she'd been, to think that Calton Hill would be as safe as her country slopes. She thought of pickpockets or worse, all drawn to the city and its easy takings. She glanced back over her shoulder and there was distinct movement in the undergrowth; picking up her skirts she began to run. She was only minutes from the busy Leith Walk and safety. The unseen tree trunk sent her sprawling.

'Are you alright?' A figure bent over her. She struggled to sit up as the man repeated the question, but this time he added, 'Kit.' She peered into the dusk, the shock at hearing her name made her speechless, but she would recognise anywhere the Orcadian lilt that was Olaf's.

'Olaf?' she got to her feet unaided, 'Olaf -you were following me!'

He frowned down at her a mixture of guilt and defiance.

'Remind me sometime,' she said standing up and dusting herself down, 'to give you lessons in stalking- you'd be hopeless out on open moorland! Your prey would easily escape.'

'Prey...hardly that!'

'Then why didn't you make yourself known?' She frowned, 'You surely didn't think I needed protecting alone on a dark hillside? I've been in worse situations. I can look after myself, you know.'

He laughed, 'I seem to remember on our very first meeting I had to save you from falling into the sea.'

'But it was a thick mist...' she remembered it as if it were yesterday, '...though I admit you kept me from a wetting... and then, when the mist cleared we... we made the seals sing,' she added lightly. She smiled up at Olaf and saw that he too was remembering the scene. Striving to keep her voice steady, she said,

'You've been behind me ever since I came on to the Hill. Was it you in that house, watching me from the window?' She peered up at him suddenly intrigued, 'And it wasn't from the attics or basement, but from the fine worked-stone level. My word Olaf Magson, you live in a grand place!' She didn't add, *you've come a long way from your cramped lighthouse home!*

'It's the home of Mr Robert Stevenson and I have the honour to live there with him and his family.' He was sounding pompous again. 'It's a fine house as you say, with many large elegant rooms,' adding as an afterthought, 'and an infinity of cellars, garrets, apple lofts and a long garden that runs down to the foot of the hill.'

'You spoke of the famous engineer before, when we met at the University.' Kitty was amazed to hear that Olaf actually lived with his mentor.

'Yes I am lucky to reside with the finest engineer in the whole land, England included.'

'Then you have the right to feel yourself fortunate.' Kitty put out her hand in a gesture of pleasure resting it lightly on his arm, and she saw his face stiffen, so that she withdrew it quickly. 'Tell me what do you build between you?'

Olaf smiled sheepishly, 'Is it that difficult to guess Kit?'

She looked up at his face, enthusiasm lighting his eyes, yet Olaf stood feet firmly on the ground, like a lighthouse on a rocky shore.

She said, 'is it lighthouses...hence your fascination with the Bell Rock one?'

'Of course.'

'Of course...' She repeated his words, why had the obvious truth never dawned? This man with the sea in his blood was atoning for his childhood misdemeanour in the only way he knew how. She wanted to hug him. Instead she said, '...now I understand.'

'Understand what?'

'Why you were less than truthful about your mission to Holy Island...your chosen career puts you in opposition to the wreckers... and... also... why you go to the Farne Islands.' Again she wanted to hug him close.

'Yes, a new lighthouse is mooted, the Darlings will have to move from Brownsman to Longstone.' He shook his head, 'Grace would lose her garden a...and the puffins.'

'She will always have the whitemaas,' Kitty grinned and Olaf smiled reluctantly.

'You worry too much, Olaf, I've seen enough of that little girl, just seven years old but already able to accept and make the most of any situation.'

'Do you think so?'

'Yes, and I envy her. It's a good lesson to learn I think.' There was silence and Olaf turned away as if blinded by the setting sun, his face inscrutable in the shadow.

Kitty shivered, pulling her shawl closer, it was getting late. She must return to her new world the one that hovered; fine gowns, painting lessons, and then...

'I must go.'

'Yes, back to your new city life.' Olaf laughed dismissively and as he did so, an owl screeched.

'Kit you don't belong here.' He took a step towards her, 'You should return to your old world,' he was scowling now and she felt his displeasure.

'And I don't like your expensive shawl. It is as out of place as are you. Do you wear it to blot out your past?' He caught at the edge of her Paisley and his hands crumpled the fine wool.

Angrily Kitty jerked the offending article from his grasp, 'It is none of your business. I can wear what I like, when I like. You're a hypocrite, Olaf Magson. YOU sit long hours on a student bench so that you can get away from YOUR beginnings.' She was breathless in her anger and, as their feet reached the cobbled road, he turned away from her and continued in the opposite direction.

The owl called again, faintly now, retreating back into its known world within the trees, and she called after Olaf, 'Do you know, Olaf Magson, up on that hill I thought I heard the seals sing. But of course it was an IMPOSSIBLE illusion.'

Twenty Three

Louise was already dressed in her finery, paisley shawl clasped in her hand, ready to brave the inclement Edinburgh evening. Kitty stood reluctant, still in her undergarments, a disapproving scowl on her face. She slipped the new gown over her head and Louise did up the back. Kitty fiddled with the neckline that scooped low, exposing the soft white skin of her breasts.

'Your dress fits like a glove. You look lovely, Kitty.' Louise's good mood had returned.

Kitty smoothed the tight satin over her flat stomach and smirked, 'I should have breathed out on purpose when she measured me. I bet Mrs Hamilton is never wrong. And that makes me want to rebel.'

But, Kitty it's just perfect, your waist sets off the conical skirt. Don't you think the new fashion is so much more becoming than the tight skirt of a few years back?'

Unconvinced, Kitty scowled into the mirror seeing the figure that Olaf Magson would see; slender girl in blue, sea-blue. Only, all he would note was a country girl aping a society lady and he would not like what he saw... then neither did she.

Ahead, stretched dinner at the most sought after table in town, if not country. You did not have to be bookish to join the guests of Sir Walter Scott -they could include smugglers, even lighthouse builders! She struggled to keep her composure. She hadn't been told, but she knew instinctively Olaf would be there.

Louise draped her shawl about her shoulders and swirled in front of her friend. 'And our Paisleys are the very latest style, according to Mrs Hamilton. Not long and thin but squared to fit the fuller skirt.' She fondled the soft material. 'They look as expensive as they actually are! *I* shall never cease to be grateful to Cousin John.' Her tone showed disapproval of Kitty for her lack of appreciation.

Kitty could not hide her gasp of admiration as a footman in blue and yellow livery opened the door to them. She saw Louise smile with triumph; *this* society was what the Holy Island girl had always dreamed of! Hill-country- girl Kitty, straightened her back- she could and would rise to the occasion. Besides Mrs Hamilton's sea blue satin gown was perfect camouflage for a girl unused to such company.

Sir Walter greeted them unreservedly, their warm-hearted host's face was bright with pleasure.

'Miss Kitty, no whisky keg on your shoulder, when on such a dreich Edinburgh night the sea-haar would keep you hidden from the excise man?'

'Indeed, sir.' Kitty's smile was that of a conspirator, but she was glad that they were the first to arrive and there was no one else to hear his words except for his wife.

'Take no notice, my husband lives his whole life as though it is a page in a novel.' Lady Scott, dark-haired and slight, shook her head. 'He would make us all into something exotic if he had his way. Walter cannot bear to think we live but ordinary lives.' The kindly woman smiled at Kitty.

'But, my dear Caroline,' Sir Walter's voice rose, 'Life is *stranger* than fiction, I could not have dreamed up the Laplander who recently resided on Calton Hill together with his family and reindeer, a man no more than the size of a twelve year old child, do you not call *that* exotic?'

Lady Scott sighed, 'There you have me.' The self-effacing woman smiled and Kitty thought, *they are excellent foils one for the other, one up in the air, the other feet firmly on the ground.* The woman was wearing a long sleeved dress with high collar, her hair neatly curled. Sir Walter was in a midnight blue coat and dark trousers, his white linen shirt was high collared and inset with intricate lace. But above it, he looked tired and his eyes were puffy.

The momentary silence that followed was broken by the door opening and a new visitor ushered into the room. Both Sir Walter and his wife greeted the young man like a son. Olaf had come as she knew he would. He showed no surprise to see her, his city face registering polite welcome. Had he likewise guessed that she too would be invited? Kitty stood apart as Louise gushed and Armstrong bowed stiffly; she thought *there is no need for any other exotic guests we are as ill-met as any freak Laplanders!* Did Sir Walter have any idea of the mixture around his table?

He said beaming, 'Olaf, you will remember our visit to Barraburn and of course you have but recently been to Holy Island.' He indicated Louise. 'We are all fortunate indeed to be able to know such a place.' He turned to his wife in triumph, 'I can assure you my dear, my pen was not needed to create such a fascinating island.'

He began to recite-his voice clearly moved by the scenes the words had conjured,

'*For, with the flow and ebb, its style*
Varies from continent to isle;
Dry- shod, o'er sands, twice every day,
The pilgrims to the shrine find way;
Twice every day, the waves efface
Of staves and sandalled feet the trace.'

Olaf said, 'Marmion,' his voice matter of fact as though he heard such poetry every day of the week. Sir Walter inclined his head. Kitty could not speak, the novelist's words had evoked an instant longing for the island. How happy she had been there where Olaf's sea ebbed and flowed with the tide. She felt his penetrating eyes on her. Could he read her thoughts?

Sir Walter addressed his protégé, 'I hope you found your visit there profitable, Olaf? Do you know ladies- this young man is a very good engineer, one of Mr Robert

Stevenson's finest apprentices?' Sir Walter's words reflected a father's pride.

He turned to Louise, 'Young lady your island coast is dangerous, tell us Olaf, and are there plans to build a lighthouse at Emmanuel Head in place of the day marker?' Olaf raised his eyebrows but did not reply. Their host smiled good- naturedly as he turned to the silent Kitty.

'As always, Olaf plays his cards close to his chest. My dear young lady, I do declare you are on opposite sides, he strives to light up the coast to save innocent sailors, whilst you seek the dark for your smuggling!'

His wife exclaimed in disbelief and Kitty said laughing, 'Then I will have to change my ways if I wish to gain his good opinion.'

Sir Walter looked sceptical, 'that will be a hard task... this young man will face any physical danger, but emotionally he will take few risks.'

'You are creating a fictional character again, Walter,' his wife warned.

'Oh, no, I can read Olaf like the back of my hand.'

Lady Scott reached out to their young friend and there was a mother's concern, 'Remember dear Olaf that someone who thinks too deeply, finds it hard to find happiness.'

The table was long and Olaf had been placed out of Kitty's reach. He was seated between Lady Scott and Louise. Kitty's cheeks burned pink when placed beside Sir Walter; her hostess had rouged cheeks, but the girl was stunned at how her world had changed. However, Olaf wasn't interested, too engrossed in conversation with Louise; Kitty felt stabs of jealousy.

The young man at her elbow, with curled hair and sideburns, had shoulders broadened at the sleeve head by extravagant puffs. He kept brushing against *her* full-puffed sleeves- so close and attentive was he! This was no taciturn Orkney lad!

Malcolm Mortimer liked to talk, and solely about himself. Introductions completed, he was off, and imparting his most important personal fact- *I am as yet unwed*. Every other sentence uttered, ended with the unbelievable truth, no lucky girl had come along to snap him up. And he had reached the age of thirty. Kitty tutted her surprise at the earnest man, though it was soon obvious why. Age and an already expanding waistline headed the obvious list- plump stomach rested on the table, as deft hands fielded his knife and fork with consummate skill; his success was to be weighed with the victuals rather than with the ladies.

Kitty studied her companion attentively, observing his ease with the complicated place setting; the one fork of Barraburn was a distant memory. To her left along the table, Armstrong was watching her. She tossed her head in annoyance and turned her large brown eyes back to Mortimer who was keen to impress his beautiful companion. Mortimer had no time to note her etiquette shortcomings, and besides, her time in the Smythe household had not been wasted.

His voice was educated Scots, with faint southern inflexion- enough to displease both sides of the border. In a monotone, he spoke of his education, his travels in Europe, the names of his favourite dogs and all interspersed with the pressing fact, 'I am unwed'. His favourite paintings, 'I am unwed', he had just acquired a Turner watercolour, 'I am unwed'. By the jugged hare, he had come to the end of his fascination with himself and only then did he pause for breath. He peered at Kitty,

'Tell me Miss Macnab are you enjoying your visit to my home city?' but before she could answer, 'Have you been to the Highlands where I am equally at home?'

'No, I have not ventured north of the Forth Estuary.' She achieved a reply.

'Oh, then that must be rectified. It would indeed be a delight to take you to see my northern estates.'

She smiled encouragingly.

'Regretfully I do not get to Perthshire often. I am unwed and a Scot exiled in London, but there again, London *is* the place to be. Have you been there recently?'

'I have not been south of Newcastle.'

'Gracious... surely not!' Mortimer's sister Francis, sitting opposite Kitty, gasped her disdain before turning again to give Sir Walter her undivided attention. *She* was a Mortimer who listened!

Her brother was still talking, 'Then, I must be the one to rectify your lack of travel, Miss Macnab.'

Kitty looked thoughtful. 'Do I go north, do I go south? I swear sir you would have me do the splits!'

Her escort did not notice the tease, 'Then it must be south, the Season in town is not to be missed. I am unwed and enjoy the dancing. The social events about Court keep me entertained during the winter months.'

Kitty said admiringly,

'So sir, you are acquainted with His Majesty,' she sighed, 'my only chance of seeing King George would be if he came to Edinburgh.'

Francis Mortimer said, 'So Miss Macnab the rumours have even reached you?' Mortimer's sister could not conceal her surprise.

'What rumours?' Kitty frowned at the woman who was as tall and angular as her brother was short and plump, but totally lacking his rather vulnerable charm; Mortimer needed mothering, his sister definitely did not.

The sister peered down at Kitty, who had been beneath her notice until now, and her heavily powdered face clearly showed that she had momentous news to impart.

'I have it on the best authority that King George comes shortly to Scotland.' Her words fell onto a silent table. 'What say you Sir Walter?' The woman turned to her host, eyebrows raised, and triumphantly awaiting confirmation.

'Oh, I never listen to rumours, they become Chinese whispers and therefore never to be believed.' Sir Walter glanced quickly down the table towards Lady Scott who wore an anxious wifely expression on her face. Her concern was obvious, for the eminent man was red faced whilst his fingers tapped loudly on the table.

'Fie, Sir Walter, we all sense your excitement.' Francis Mortimer was smiling from ear to ear.

Her host sighed deeply, 'So Miss Mortimer, I make a poor poker player.'

'Indeed you do, in *deed* you do…'

Sir Walter elaborately raised his hands in defeat,

'Rumour of a Royal visit is indeed to become reality-if you can call such an auspicious event by a word as mundane as *reality*!'

There was a murmur of excitement the length of the table, everyone waiting on the storyteller to embroider the details.

'Some months ago, when I was invited to dine at Calton House I persuaded His Majesty that he was a true Jacobite Highlander. And if he cared to come to Scotland he could wear plaid and tartan hose, a velvet jacket and bonnet with eagle feathers and carry a broad sword and dirk.'

There was a ripple of good natured laughter but Olaf voiced something more than amusement, 'It sounds like a theatrical costume that would better suit the Theatre Royal stage than the Palace of Holyrood!'

Sir Walter looked startled at his favourite's contempt; the proud Scot was almost childlike in his enthusiasm.

Frances Mortimer said dismissively, 'So I do wonder what His Majesty will find to entertain him here. Edinburgh society is not London.'

Sir Walter scratched his face, a spreading rash covering his swollen cheeks as he retorted, 'Young lady, now His Majesty has decided to come north it is up to everyone to show him that we Scots can put on a good show.'

'I-it is truly exciting news, Sir Walter.' Kitty was moved to side with her host, her voice steadied, 'People will be talking about it in a hundred years from now.'

'Yes, let us hope so,' the novelist still looked abstracted. 'King George has changed his mind a number of times; only a few weeks ago he was planning to go to Vienna. That was to sign the Peace Treaty ending the war that has dominated Europe for most of your young lives... thanks to Napoleon.'

He puckered his brows trying to disguise his look of satisfaction. 'Now, Edinburgh appears to have defeated Vienna; the King has chosen to come north instead. It is a great honour and I repeat we must *all* do our bit to make it a triumph.'

An elderly guest who'd been silent up to this point opened his eyes, 'Well sir I for one shall keep a low profile. I have no interest in such a spectacle.'

Sir Walter strove to smile, though his voice was edged with a hint of warning, 'George Crabbe, we have put you in our best room to enable you to see all that is going on, I trust you will pen appropriate verses to record the visit for posterity.'

The old man grinned wickedly, 'Well perhaps I should earn my keep and get a few pence for rhymes concerning King George. The question is should they be humorous or tragic? What think you Sir Walter?'

Kitty could not look at their host; his obvious desire was for the visit to be memorable not a subject for ridicule. He sat toying with his food as did Kitty, aware of her tightening waistline. In contrast Malcolm Mortimer had done full justice to the beef, hare, game, jellies and custards. Kitty had renewed fear for his jacket buttons.

Sir Walter banged his knife on the table in exasperation, 'The King's Jaunt to Edinburgh will overshadow the Congress of Vienna make no mistake. I shall personally see to that.' Scott's pronouncement filled the silence, 'Miss Macnab you will be able to regale your children and your grandchildren with the never-to-be-forgotten celebrations.'

Kitty inclined her head wanting only to please her host, whilst all about her showed very differing reactions- incredulity, amusement, fervour. She caught sight of Armstrong, his face looked as though he had just received an unexpected cargo of contraband. Suddenly she clutched at the table edge- she realised at last why John Armstrong had brought her to Edinburgh; beautiful Kitty was intended for the Court of King George the Fourth, maybe not to trap unwed Malcolm Mortimer -but someone even grander? Sweat moistened her hands, if that was the case baby Katharine could play no part in such a scheme. Had she seen her daughter for the very last time?

Olaf had been but a shadowy figure, hardly to be noticed all evening. And it was others who dominated Kitty's thoughts on the way home in Sir Walter's carriage. She pondered on George Augustus Hanover and the unwed Malcolm Mortimer, who would introduce her into court circles. Armstrong had been pure pragmatist-a forged friendship with Sir Walter Scott, on the back of the non-existent library at Barraburn farmhouse. But Sir Walter was an honourable man, what other lies would her so-called guardian use to raise them both ever higher up the social ladder?

Back at their lodgings and round the fire, Louise, Kitty and Armstrong wondered at the evening's entertainment.

'We've come to Edinburgh just at the right time. Cousin John, how clever you are. Oh Kitty, we'll make the next weeks the daftest days to remember for the rest of our lives! Oh, poor old Marion, she'll never speak to me again.'

Louise was bubbling like a glass of champagne and a weary Kitty, sinking down onto a chair, said in forced jollity,

'Louise I do believe you've set your eyes on King George himself, he is a widower is he not?'

Louise screamed with laughter. 'He is fifty four or is it fifty three? Whatever it is, he is far too old.'

'It would be expedient! You would never have to return to Holy Island.' Kitty raised her eyes and saw that she had hit the right mark as the girl sighed deeply.

'If only.' But then Louise grinned, 'Not even that would make him desirable I can assure you. Do you know he weighs nearly twenty stone and wears whalebone corsets?'

'Oh.' Kitty shuddered.

'His buttocks split his breeches and his belly is like a balloon.'

Kitty laughed out loud, 'Louise, say no more you've utterly convinced me.'

But Louise wasn't done, 'He's the most unpopular man in the land. They say the police have to pay men to cheer him.'

By this time, Kitty was almost helpless with laughter, as tears streamed down her face,

'Then why is there all the excitement about the King's visit?' Kitty looked perplexed as Armstrong came back into to the room having removed his tight frock coat for a more comfortable smoking jacket.

He said emphatically. 'He is the king and therefore the most important man in the land. It would be expedient to remember that.' He settled into his chair, lit his pipe, and the smell of expensive tobacco filled the room. Armstrong looked a contented man. He could not have heard his cousin's traitorous descriptions of their monarch.

But Louise hadn't finished and, seizing Kitty, she waltzed her around the room earning a loud complaint from her cousin as they nearly collided into his chair. Unrepentant she began to sing,

'Humpty Dumpty sat on a wall
Humpty Dumpty had a great fall
All the King's horses and
All the King's men couldn't
Put Humpty together again.

Kitty gasped for breath but Louise began the nursery rhyme again '*Humpty Dumpty...*'

'Louise!' Armstrong thundered his anger. The girl stopped in her tracks but still did not look contrite,

'Don't worry I'll be the soul of discretion in other company, but cousin you have to agree with everything I've said. It's hard for a mere mortal like me to see quite why everyone is so overcome about such a man visiting Edinburgh.'

Kitty said wonderingly, 'Yes, even Sir Walter...'

'...*even Sir Walter!*' Louise flung her arms in despair.

'He is such a dear man,' Kitty looked thoughtful, 'but an inveterate romancer.' She smiled, remembering he'd cast Olaf in the role of good lighthouse builder whilst she was the baddie smuggler- even Scott's wife had been exasperated!

'Oh well, perhaps it doesn't really matter what the King is like, though from the sound of it, Sir Walter himself couldn't have created a larger than life character!' Kitty was still smiling at Louise's wicked portrayal of George of Hanover.

She mused, 'I think Sir Walter believes his beloved Scotland is at a moment of destiny and the King's visit is symbolic. It doesn't matter that the man is ludicrous- it's his title that Sir Walter honours.'

'And we would all do well to remember that.' Armstrong paused emphatically in the enjoyment of his cigar, 'The city will benefit from the royal patronage, but so will the whole country. Sir Walter is a staunch Unionist, sensibly seeing the advantages of a joined England and Scotland.'

Smoke coiled from his pipe and there was a spurt of flame from the backed-up fire. Both girls knew to be silent. The Magistrate breathed in heavily, savouring the rich odour of tobacco. And Kitty, looking about her at the fading gentility of their lodging, the coal-singed hearth rug and the worn damask on chair arms, thought, *already Armstrong is seeing a gilded future.*

He said, 'Sir Walter is an astute man. It befits us all to follow his example!'

Kitty said, choosing to ignore Armstrong's oily tones and his barely hidden suggestion of the merits of self-advancement,

'Sir Walter is a pet and I fear it'll be too much for him. He was not himself tonight and will not be until the King's visit is over and done. It can't come soon enough.'

Kitty slept fitfully, a rhyme going over and over in her brain-the scurrilous nursery song that Louise had fitted so aptly to the royal visitor. She dreamed she was singing baby Katharine to sleep with it, *Humpty Dumpty, Humpty Dumpty,* over and over again; but the child wouldn't lie down, shrieking and clapping her hands in time to the tune. It was only when Pleasance came and began to sing the words that the child cooed and slept. Her mother was pleasing to the eye, but it was the homely maid who calmed her to sleep.

'Twice every day the waves efface
Of staves and sandelled feet the trace.'

Sir Walter's description of the sacred isle of Lindisfarne filtered into her now sleepless state; there, in that magic place, she had found momentary happiness with a man called Olaf. There Louise had tempted her with a pair of scissors. If only she had ... if *only* she had cut away her beauty then. Now it was too late.

Twenty Four

Morning and Kitty was back to reality. A heavy shower of rain overnight had freshened the streets, laid the dust, laundered away the night-soil, softened the sound of metal wheels; Edinburgh sparkled in a bright northern light, as if by royal decree.

Twenty one days, that was all, time for her child to cut another tooth, to learn another nursery rhyme, perhaps there would be one about the King's visit, and by then she would have worked her plan. The night hours had not just been for dreaming. In the early dawn she had resolved her course of action. It was so simple, so sensible that for the first time in many days she felt an inner calmness that brought a satisfied smile to her lips. All she had to do was play along with the plans of John Armstrong and then…but before she could make the most of what was on offer…she must become the kind of mother her child deserved…

She had always wanted to learn to paint, had drawn as long as she could remember; with broken twig in the cheviot frost and river mud, and just recently in the amber sand of Holy Island; new strokes that swirled and patterned into fantastic shapes with the aid of the sea. Now within her grasp were the luxury of paper and brush. Armstrong himself had advocated self-interest; who was she to be any different?

The smell of oil paint, heavy and cloying in the north-facing studio of Alexander Naismith was intoxicating and there was the warm smile of daughter Charlotte to calm them. Easels with an assortment of canvases and in every stage of completion, dotted the room. City castle and streets painted in all times of day sky-lined the views and Kitty thought *here's a man recording the times in paint just as Sir Walter is doing in words.* How lucky is Edinburgh and its talented citizens.

Charlotte already had a work in progress, but she stopped to welcome the girls and to furnish them with their tools. Genteel, well-brought-up Louise was relaxed and confident, this pastime was nothing new to her. Kitty could feel her hand shaking, 'I-I am very much the beginner.'

'That is how father likes it. Besides everyone can draw, little children are best though, because they are natural.'

'Then my squiggles will pass muster.'

'Of course, Kitty!'

Louise giggled. 'No prizes to predict there will soon be endless pictures of His Majesty looking larger than life.'

Charlotte smiled, 'From all that I hear, one will need a broad canvas to depict our sovereign, not to mention gallons of paint in every colour of the rainbow. Still that's better than the dull brown I hear they will paint the Picture Gallery in Holyrood Palace so as not to eclipse the King.'

'Oh, is that where he is staying?' Louise was showing her apparent fascination for every little detail of the visit. Her ridicule of their monarch was for private viewing only.

'No, the Palace is not nearly good enough for King George, it has long ceased to be a royal residence; hence the paint brushes out to cover up the filth and grime accumulated from many grace and favour residents living there. They've already been turned out just for the Grand Reception that the King will be hosting.'

'So, see you there.' Louise aired her knowledge of the event and of their attendance. She, Louise knew of Armstrong's plans- Kitty pursed her lips, annoyed yet again that the two cousins hadn't included *her* in their discussions.

But at that moment a be-smocked Alexander Naismith entered and there was no more time for female chatter in the presence of the master. The time passed in a haze of enlightenment and Kitty soon relaxed, absorbing every word of instruction as though she was tidal sand at the return of the sea. She had imagined a sea of colour but this first lesson was in black and white.

'Good drawing lies behind all good portraits and all good landscapes.'

Charlotte handed out carbon. Kitty felt the pleasure of touch as her fingers clasped the slender strip and she began to draw. Everyday objects, a cup and saucer- but she struggled with the oval shape, tea in this Wedgwood cup would end up in the saucer. So was her life - shapeless and difficult to control!

'Now for your imagination… close your eyes and you will see!' The artist's assured Edinburgh voice was prophetic.

Kitty saw the rocky outcrop below Emmanuel Head in a curved shape following the line of dolerite rock. Her thick charcoal shadowed the hard surface and then she covered it with soft seal fur. Here was the unity of land and sea… and her and Olaf…though she knew-once her eyes were open again- that it could never be.

· Meanwhile, she hardly heard the hammering that had started up in the street outside and had continued through the morning, so that by the time they were back in York Place and walking towards Picardy Place, the noise was deafening. Men with hammers, piles of wood and ladders, thronged the pavement. The girls stared in disbelief as buildings disappeared behind shields of wood in front of their eyes. Every possible surface was being covered with observation stands so that no citizen would fail to see their fabled visitor.

Mrs Harriet Siddons lived in Picardy Place, chaos outside, serenity within. It was another world. The drawing room was draped with white muslin and mahogany tables, crowded with delicate china ornaments, filled every space. Huge vases of flowers garlanded the grand piano-forte in and around the window. Kitty eyed the beautiful room and was immediately glad of her small feet in their delicate slippers.

Louise noted the obstacles with obvious concern, her feet were large!

Mrs Siddons cast a sweeping glance over the new arrivals and, without formality, began her tuition as if there was no time to waste. Acknowledging the girls with a perfect deep low curtsy, she indicated they should do likewise. Louise shuffled her feet in agonised indecision, almost colliding with one of the sofa tables. She giggled nervously. Kitty bit her lip so as not to show her disdain for all this ridiculous gesturing, but her movement was perfect- as agile as a feral goat. Side tables were nothing worse than giant boulders jutting out on hillside paths!

Kitty began to enjoy herself, whilst poor Louise floundered.

Mrs Siddons said crisply, 'Practise makes perfect, it is important to make a good impression upon entrance. Now we will retreat.' She made it sound as though it was of military significance. 'Hold out your dresses as if they are ball gowns and turn with a wide sweep of the skirt as low to the floor as you can.'

The girls did as instructed and their hostess raised her eyebrows. 'Be graceful, ladies, be graceful. It is always very necessary when you have the great honour of being presented to the King.'

Louise collapsed onto the floor and Kitty giggled, 'You should see yourself!'

Back in the privacy of their lodging, the Smythe girl was rehearsing both the curtsy and retreat as though her very life depended on it, whilst Kitty had subsided into a chair and, by the look on her face, intended to stay there. She'd had enough prancing about for one day.

Louise stopped in front of her with hands on hips and scowled at her companion, saying coldly. 'Come on Kitty, its important not to let Cousin John down. I know you're better than me, but that's not saying much.'

Concentration written large on her face, Louise curtseyed low and this time there was a satisfied smile on her face. But as she strove to stand she tripped, and lying flat on the floor she withered Kitty not to laugh.

'Louise, you've lost your sense of humour with all this nonsense. How can you take it seriously?'

'Take what seriously?' Armstrong had returned, tavern visits heavy on his breath. Seeing his face, it would seem humour had not been his tipple.

Kitty observed his cheeks were drink-reddened, his thinning hair wind-blown, his cravat was askance; he looked the essence of countryman corrupted by city life! Her inner loathing for the man filled her throat. She said provocatively, 'So Cousin John, it is to be seen you have not been learning etiquette from Mrs Siddons.'

Louise looked horrified. Armstrong peered down at Kitty with a mixture of emotions on his face, and she rose to her feet to be equal at eye level. She stood now, relishing the feel of the solid floor rather than the slithering and sliding of some grotesque etiquette movements that had made her look and feel ridiculous.

There they both faced each other in a long silence. It was Farmer Armstrong who spoke first, his words issued cold and crisp.

'Sometimes a young dog is whipped into learning, sometimes it is given treats. Whatever the course of training chosen, the result, is always the same. Perhaps I mistook what method *you* would prefer my dear?'

Kitty shrugged her shoulders, 'so then the obvious alternative is to find another master and to run away to a better patch.' Her face was inscrutable.

Armstrong belched his fury in the stench of stale beer. 'That's one solution, but what happens when the cur...or bitch returns tail between its legs, to howl at its master's locked gate?' Armstrong answered his own question. 'It will not gain entry. Its warm bed with litter will be the wrong side of the door.'

She had let her loathing take control. Unemotional Olaf would not have spoken as she had done, *he* would have bided his time.

As silly Louise had said, twenty one daft days and then the party would be over. Whatever Armstrong's reasons for bringing them to the Celebrations, at the end they could all, like the King, go home. And when that time came all she needed was an open door to Barraburn and enough time to gather up what was hers.

Twenty Five

She had shown her hand- and no winning card-player ever did! How foolish to continue the losing streak begun on Holy Island. She needed a poker face and quiet tongue.

So when Armstrong presented himself early evening, groomed and smelling of perfume, offering an arm to either girl she accepted it happily enough. He had been very drunk earlier -did he even *remember* her indiscretion?

Either way, his girl cousin remembered every word. Louise was coolly watchful and Kitty knew she could become like Marion in their relationship.

Kitty had left her new shawl lying carelessly on the bed, Louise tut- tutted as she scooped it up and thrust it round Kitty's shoulders without ceremony, shepherding her towards the door.

'Show or necessity, our Paisleys *are to be worn*, Cousin's one hundred pounds must be shown to effect.' Her tone and words sought to make Kitty feel guilty.

Kitty made no reply, instead, she clutched the shawl close about her shoulders with an exaggerated sweep, as though she could not step over the doorstep without it. Both girls were making a point, for the evening was balmy, and citizens taking the evening air were making the most of it, out to show off more than expensive shawls. Ladies in light dresses, men in extravagant puffed sleeves, tight waisted frock coats - sky blue, grass green - one had no need to seek Calton Hill for the colours of nature. Summer had come to the capital!

They turned in the opposite direction from the one Kitty had taken the previous evening to find the hill. Was Olaf this very moment climbing up there for his evening walk? However much she desired it there would be no hope of a chance encounter, theirs was a different destination.

But at the top of Leith Walk they turned east and there before them was the green space that dominated this end of town. Armstrong was going with the stream of folk out for their post-dinner entertainment, to see and be seen. They filed across a high arched bridge to the fashionable side of the hill. The new Town lay below them, whilst Arthur's seat cast shadows on Holyrood Palace away to their right.

Late evening sunshine spotlighted the skyline. Armstrong pointed to a tower. 'That was built to commemorate Nelson's victory over the French and Spanish at Trafalgar.' And when they reached it they stopped to admire the crenellated building; at the entrance a plaque affirmed Armstrong's words. *Built by the grateful citizens of Edinburgh- to teach their sons, when duty requires them, to die for their country.* Armstrong turned to Kitty.

'Your father must have regaled you with tales of the battle.' He smiled benignly.

'Aye, Trafalgar was all he could talk about whether drunk or sober.' The rough country girl aired her displeasure and Armstrong looked about to see if they had been overheard.

Louise was aghast at the careless jibe. Kitty lowered her eyes, her words were formal, 'And I assure you I have left that all behind me. Ahead is where I look.'

Armstrong nodded and there was a satisfied smile.

'I can give a performance as well as Mrs Siddons on stage at the Theatre Royal. I'll need no prompting for my lines.' She sounded the consummate actress.

Louise said sarcastically, 'So then watch out Kitty for the building works ahead of you.' Piles of stones and sand and ladders littered the ground.

'What are they going to build here, Cousin?'

'The National Monument to mark those lost in the Napoleonic wars.' Armstrong was a mine of information. 'They say Sir Walter is to lay the foundation stone next week.'

'Is there no one else in this city who can do anything?' Kitty looked horrified, 'The poor man is horribly overworked. I do hope he survives it all.'

'He would have it no other way. You worry too much about him. Sir Walter wants to be in on the act. He would not thank you for a back seat.' Armstrong's voice was sharp.

'Perhaps you're right- a novelist always writes the *whole* story.' Kitty sought to agree. Armstrong had spoken the truth, but she worried; the unsightly facial rash had shown Sir Walter's state of health.

Armstrong muttered, 'Like many in this city we have much to thank him for already, and so it will be for the next few weeks. He opens important doors for us that would otherwise be closed.'

They loitered at the top of the hill, Armstrong looking about him, eyeing the other late evening strollers as though seeking a known face. Kitty kept her eyes lowered for she knew that the lean intelligent face that she sought would not be here however long they hovered; the unfashionable wild side of the hill was for Olaf, not this preening ostentation! The girls waited for Armstrong to move on but still he stood uncertainly by the pile of builders' materials.

Kitty said skittishly, 'Perhaps Sir Walter is going to build the National Monument himself too. Is he a stone mason as well as everything else?'

'Oh, Kitty, you are far too clever for your own good.' Louise scowled at the other girl's quip though only yesterday she would have giggled at the nonsense.

'Oh look, there's a face we recognise.' Louise dug Kitty in the ribs, 'You must have made an impression on him.' Kitty's heart jumped with expectation and then plummeted. Disappointed, she somehow managed to find a smile, for her diner partner, Malcolm Mortimer, was bowing low over her hand.

'T'is well met,' Armstrong strove to look surprised, but the young man's words made it a useless gesture.

'I have tickets to enter the Tower, or at least the ground floor building around it. I hope it is agreeable with you, Miss Macnab?' Kitty inclined her head.

'I cannot say until I know what there is to see.' She sounded as truculent as Louise and she hastened to say,

'Whatever it is, we shall find it diverting.' She smiled up at the newcomer and his anxious expression showed it must be the story of his life; how long before he bemoaned his unmarried state?

'I swear I am intrigued.' She looked at the battlemented building, 'Are we allowed to guess what it contains?'

Mortimer, dressed in soldier's uniform, clicked his high boots together in acquiescence. 'I swear if we were to stay here all night you would not guess its previous occupants.'

Armstrong spoke his impatience, 'Then good sir, you should tell us quickly.'

But Mortimer was enjoying the limelight. 'No, it's quite impossible to guess who lived here with his family and reindeer.'

'Reindeer?' The two girls shouted their surprise in unison.

'Then it must be a Laplander.' Kitty spoilt his story and she saw the disappointment.

Mortimer said, 'How did you know that?'

'Everyone knows Laplanders and Reindeer go together.' Louise not to be outdone was scornful.

Kitty said, 'But not everyone recognises reindeer droppings, we are lucky to be so educated.' She kicked at imaginary litter on the ground- her laughter bubbling just below the surface.

Mortimer looked bemused. 'Well no matter, now the building is a tearoom.' He returned thankfully to known fact, 'The room at the base of the tower I mean.'

'We would not have guessed that in a million years.' Kitty smiled encouragingly at him.

'It is just for the King's visit.'

'Then there's no time to lose, Captain Mortimer.' Kitty made for the door. Armstrong, silent during the girls' teasing of the Scotsman, peered at her suspiciously. He knew enough of Kitty to realise the hidden laughter that smirked at the corner of her mouth. But Mortimer was oblivious.

'Do you know, they have rather ugly dark complexions, are about the height of a twelve year old and they actually wear skins and furs?'

'…the reindeer, or the Laplanders?' Kitty's innocent question brought a stuttering reply from the eager soldier.

'M-Miss Macnab, I do declare you question everything.'

He pointed to the plaque above the door that they had already noted, 'How worthy is that sentiment expressed by the citizens of Edinburgh that they would expect their dutiful sons to die for their country. I do declare, Miss Macnab you fire such a resolve in my breast.'

'Fie, Captain Mortimer- nothing so drastic! All I desire is for you to find us a table for our tea.'

The speed with which he accomplished her request reflected his desire to please. In the crowded tearoom they were shown to the best table, a hum of genteel conversation following their progress. The stylish dressed girls fitted in well with the genteel scene, as did the uniformed Mortimer. But Armstrong stuck out a mile.

'I do apologise, Mr Armstrong, that there is no liquor for sale,' Mortimer aimed to be the perfect host, 'but there is coffee or tea and pastries, all served with a view.' Armstrong nodded affably enough, striving to be on his best behaviour.

They had been placed at a window table affording an extensive panorama over the city below, it looked beautiful set against the sunset backdrop. When the waitress brought their tray of tea, Kitty did not know where to fix her gaze- drop scones, rich plum cake and raspberry tarts- all good Edinburgh fare, filled the table. Kitty buttered her scone and the group was silent as the plates were cleared; Mortimer was obviously partial to Dundee cake. Throughout the room, voices rose when new plates of delicacies arrived.

'We are well served, sir, all our needs, and our safety guaranteed by *you*.' Kitty murmured her appreciation.

'So, Captain Mortimer you have volunteered to be part of the cavalry to protect his Majesty, whilst he is in Edinburgh.' Armstrong pointed at his blue and green uniform. 'That is to be lauded.'

'Indeed, we shall have many duties- guards, escorts, even spear carriers- in Sir Walter's pageant.'

'Not too dangerous then, certainly not life threatening.' Louise giggled. 'Not like these pastries. They are inordinately good.' She helped herself to another and Mortimer took the last. Their host lent back on his chair and smiled indulgently as, from nowhere, another plate appeared.

'Oh, meringues are my absolute favourite!' Louise was delighted. Kitty eyed the fluffy white balls with amazement; no hand could have fashioned such delicacy. Louise needed no second invitation. Kitty gingerly felt the smooth curve between her fingers as she lifted it to her plate and then watched in dismay as it broke into a dozen pieces. She flushed scarlet. It had been an accident waiting to happen.

'Kitty!' Louise's voice was condemning, 'you must know how delicate meringues are!'

'So, you will find it melts in your mouth,' Mortimer was eager to gloss over Kitty's clumsiness, 'but even better is the confection that awaits you in London… eclairs, newly come from France…' Mortimer beamed at Kitty, oblivious of her continued heightened colour, 'they are called so because they disappear like lightening.' He wiped his lips with his napkin, 'I cannot wait to see your pleasure when you taste them for the first time; the chocolate and choux pastry are a combination made in Heaven.'

Kitty inclined her head, 'So London is indeed ahead of Edinburgh even in confectionary. But tell us of more substantial matters, 'You say you are to be guard to his Majesty?' She looked impressed as if the new subject was of equal weight to the cakes.

'Oh, Kitty, let us dwell on the pleasures of eating the very latest French gateaux just a little longer.' Louise was in one of her moods.

Mortimer looked about him and lowered his voice; obediently, the girls leaned forward to catch what their host had to say,

'Our duty is to guard against the radicals congregating in the city. Many of the lower classes have been contaminated with talk of REBELLION.' He looked personally affronted. If he accepted Kitty's banter without question, Malcolm Mortimer was less pleased to note the levity in the other girl's voice, 'It is quite reprehensible that The Scotsman newspaper supports their ideas.'

'So, how clever of Sir Walter to think up the King's jaunt to take their minds off such things,' Kitty smiled, 'cheering crowds will surely drown out any protest. We promise to shout loudly when His Majesty passes us and of course even louder when you Captain Mortimer, ride past. They will be able to hear us back on Holy Island, won't they Louise?'

'*Holy Island*? When do you return?' Mortimer's face was a mixture of emotions. 'I trust you will be there in person to see the fine sight of the King's Yacht sail past on his homeward voyage. You will not see the like again.'

'Indeed sir, are you privy with the King's journey home?' Louise put down her cup and surveyed the eager man.

He peered round the room, all the nearby tables were noisy with chat, but he lowered his voice even more, and again his audience leaned forward,

'Let me just say I have also volunteered to be part of the guard on the King's return voyage. The Royal George will carry not just the valuable cargo of the King himself, but all the jewels and valuables used to adorn the visit to Edinburgh. Our weapons then will be other than pageant replicas, I *do* assure you.'

Louise had the grace to look impressed, 'How fortunate is His Majesty to have in his employ such as you, Captain, whilst Kitty and I can only wave our Union Jacks as his procession passes us by.'

'Young ladies, you will enhance the scene! I shall sit astride my horse with straight back, knowing that you are watching.'

'The girls will be there I do assure you.' Armstrong rose from his seat, 'Thank you, captain, for our evening entertainment.' A half hour of pleasantries and Armstrong had had enough, a High Street tavern his next immediate port of call. He was already halfway to the door.

Outside in the cool evening air, Mortimer was reluctant to say farewell. 'Our visit has been timely. Tomorrow, Calton Hill will be very different, the bell tents of the artillery men are to be pitched here, whilst twelve guns will crest the summit. Six more cannon are to be placed on Salisbury Crags astride Arthur's Seat.' He waved in the direction of the imposing extinct volcano that dominated the city skyline. 'You can already see the outline of the giant bonfire being built there.'

'Also Sir Walter's idea I believe. Hasn't he urged the citizens to carry wood and combustibles up to the summit, so that the hill will look on fire for the King's arrival?' Armstrong strove to keep a tone of enthusiasm, but he was already pacing up and down. 'So we await the King with impatience. It is said he cannot be here until Tuesday at the very earliest.'

'Indeed, but tomorrow is the first of Sir Walter's Pageants, so during the day there is plenty to keep you entertained, ladies. And in the evening may I accompany you to the Theatre? I have taken the liberty of hiring a box in the hope that it might meet with your approval.'

Mortimer bowed at their ready acceptance, his hand, lingering on Kitty's gloved fingers. He looked smug. He had not uttered the fact that he was unwed one single time, even in his reference to a combination made in Heaven!

The absence of liquor was remedied speedily when they got back to their lodgings, and both Armstrong and Louise were silent as they devoured their first glass of the burnished gold liquid that mirrored the sunset colouring the Forth. Kitty had hoped to see Armstrong disappear off to the High Street, but he stood beside the fire-place in thoughtful mood.

'You tease Captain Mortimer unmercifully!' his gaze was directed at Kitty. 'You should have the wit to see it is in your interest to remain at the very least civil.' He clenched his hands around the glass as though about to shatter it. His manner told clearly he was very annoyed and he did not need to put into words his chagrin. Hadn't he been the one who had shown lenience in his Magistrate's Court, to a lawless girl facing deportation and now, because of him, she resided, Paisley-shawled, in Scotland's capital city. And she was acquiring skills that would find her curtseying at the feet of King George the Fourth?

Louise, unaware of the background to her cousin's anger, looked amused, her tone regarding her friend was now more conciliatory. 'Why cousin, Kitty means no harm. The captain doesn't even notice.' Then a note of sarcasm crept into her voice, 'So there are no prizes to be had for guessing who will be seated beside our benefactor at the play tomorrow night.'

'Aye, and he's a young man to be encouraged,' Armstrong downed a second glass, 'A very wealthy young man with considerable assets.'

'And yet unwed, so he keeps telling us, so where are all the grasping matrons of Edinburgh and their eager daughters?' Louise sniggered.

'I think they cannot compete with the pastries! Like King, like courtier!' Kitty grinned, 'The lucky lady would be forever sewing on his waistcoat buttons-pop –pop—pop.' She pushed out her stomach as she imitated fasteners, stretched across an extended belly, flying in all directions.

Armstrong took a swig of his whisky and chose to ignore her flippancy. 'It would seem to me that he is a young man of discernment. To my mind, the ladies here are somewhat grey-coloured in their looks and personality.' He lit a cigar as he stared across at Kitty. The billowing smoke could not hide the fact that she had never looked better, gone were the gaunt years of hand-to-mouth living; and all of it thanks to Magistrate Armstrong.

She thought, 'I stand before him again awaiting sentence, only this time ...? And she knew she had moved on.

'So play your cards right, Kitty and you'll have your own house in New Town Edinburgh, not just a rented apartment at the top of Leith Walk.' Louise wagged her slender finger at Kitty. 'Is that what you appear to be saying, Cousin John?'

'...exactly that!' The man's voice was hard, 'A far cry from your Cheviot hovel.' Kitty stared into implacable eyes and irises, hard brown as impacted mud, stared back at her- no warmth of fresh ploughed furrow- but hill land etched by storm wind.

She said, 'There are plenty of fish in the sea, why Mortimer? He is just an unmarried landowner with court connections. There must be a Duke who owns a palace and is slim enough to keep his waistcoat fastened.' She tossed her head defiantly. 'I'm sure I can look higher than Mortimer.'

Louise looked from one to the other, poker-faced observer in a cat and mouse game. She said levelly, 'You always have an answer, Kitty, but I guess it is Cousin John who holds the trump card.'

'Indeed!' Armstrong towered over Kitty. 'Beggars cannot be choosers. She is lucky to have Mortimer knocking at her door.'

'But he doesn't need to be the only one,' Kitty fingered her hair, showing she knew very well that her worth lay in her dark untamed beauty.

'*Oh, no*?' Armstrong smirked down at her. 'Only desperate Mortimer will ever offer marriage. There will be no queue of suitors and *you* know the reason.' His words lanced the air and Kitty tensed; the unspoken fact, pushed out of mind but ever there; her small daughter- ever a reminder.

Not long now before she held the child in her arms; just a few more days of dallying with the captain, being part of a magnificent spectacle and then as Armstrong hinted, she would be back in her Cheviot hovel. There with little Katharine, who above anything else needed her mother's love, surely!

Kitty in her need to feel again her child, was lost in thought and Armstrong, misconstruing her silence, laughed scornfully. His next words arrived icy cold like a sudden hill storm. Slowly he emphasised each word,

'You have no choice, my dear; because you and I both know there will be no stampede for your favours.' He looked from Kitty to Louise,

'You should know cousin that hidden behind your friend's skirts is a clinging child.' His voice rose. 'And that child was born from the sin of incest! *Hers is a terrible secret that no man could possibly forgive!*'

Louise's incredulous gasp cut the silence like a dagger thrust, her eyes darting in disbelief from Kitty to Armstrong, 'I don't believe it!'

But the look on her face showed she already had, her eyes glinted. 'Marion always wondered about your past. Wait till she hears-.'

Armstrong interrupted, 'But no need to concern yourself my dear Kitty, I promise you the desperate Mortimer will be the exception; he alone will accept your little so-called 'sister' as part of the deal.'

He was beside the door and his parting words filled the silence, 'And as wife to a flexible husband with entrance to court circles you will find glittering opportunities elsewhere.'

Twenty Six

The small dark room was bitterly cold, there would be no fire until nightfall and then only after she'd roamed far for kindling; yet how could she leave the child alone, hot with fever? She looked at the flushed face against the purple cushion, it clashed jarringly but the soft damask surely gave comfort and was the only object in the room that did. Long ago she had taken it from a room that was over-cushioned and brought it back to her bare cottage. She'd always loved pretty things! Even kept her grandmother's tulip decorated cups, chipped and cracked until finally smashed in the storm-flood that had taken the whisky still and with it her sinning father. Had it been just pride that had made her want something other than just her mug, plate and spoon?

That old stark world waited their return. She could almost feel the slippery satin of the cushion that touched her memory though her hands were empty. Kitty was wide awake now, companioned by her disturbed past; she *must* put it behind her!

Imagine instead the view from the Calton Hill tearoom, their tea-party waiting for the great event; for the King, in elaborate costume, to strut in front of the city backdrop. Expectation must surely be like a dose of laudanum!

Only two days left, suspended in this unreal world and their diary was full, no time for her to brood, to worry about the uncertain future. *It lay in the lap of the gods* or in the moment when *she* chose to take charge again of her own destiny.

Tonight she would sit bejewelled in a box in the Theatre Royal. Kitty had never been to the Theatre, she stifled a laugh, she'd never been to painting classes, never sat beside the most eminent writer of his time; everything had changed in the last heady days when she'd even dared to glimpse herself behind the window of an ashlared town house instead of huddling in a meagre unfurnished room back in her homeland hills. To fulfil that dream she only had to play a part like the playhouse actors. She would enter the theatre lobby with Captain Mortimer and heads would turn wondering the identity of the unknown beauty who graced his arm!

Kitty was alone; Louise had not withdrawn to the bedroom with her. She could hear the low voices the other side of the door that no doubt droned Kitty's colourful life story. She had no desire to hear what was being said. She could guess only too well the details that would leave Louise momentarily speechless before the future impossibility of keeping such a secret. Kitty had seen the first surprise and recoil and then the gleam- the delight that the knowledge could turn Kitty into a pummelled sister Marion. Hidden innuendo and little touches of menace would follow that would give the vindictive girl hours of sport. Kitty gazed at her mirror reflection, she imagined Louise behind her… friend or enemy?

She knew the answer only too well. Louise had been desperate to escape island confines, saving her card winnings to achieve just that and willing to pay her way if necessary with the handsome Patterson- seen as her saviour in more ways than one. Both she and Marion carrying a torch for the captain of their brother's boat, an open joke cruelly ridiculed in the Fisherman's Arms Tavern. How humiliating was that? Yet, since leaving the island, Louise had uttered no word of complaint and had not mentioned the skipper since the night he'd punished Olaf. But Louise had let the barbaric humiliation happen without lifting a finger.

Olaf! How he stirred her emotions-so like her in many ways and yet so different; Olaf imprisoned by a sea that took hostage children, who innocently played with seals but accepted, on the incoming tide, grand pianos and bloated bodies. His childhood had so nearly wrecked his life. But the herring shed punishment had liberated him from his past. How she longed to stand beside him on his windswept beach, likewise cleansed of all that had gone before. It could never be. Never again would the seals sing for them, for soon he would hear of her past.

Did Louise know Olaf lived just minutes away? Fate could not be so cruel as to allow *them* to meet. Surely Louise would see no sport in telling Mortimer the truth about her, it could not be in the girl's interests to spoil her Cousin's plans. Kitty wrung her hands; how much more would be wrung from the censorious Orcadian.

Kitty feigned sleep when Louise came to bed and also in the morning when she rose. The girl went out early as did Armstrong and only then was Kitty able to rise from her bed. The eastern sun shone through the window, clear and full of promise, the kind of day that would have had her out in the hills from daybreak.

She dressed in her blue calico that looked as if the sea had invaded the land when she trod the lonnens of Holy Island. It was faded now in the city grime. But the day was set fair, no need for Paisley Shawl. It lay at the bottom of the bed, richly patterned and ridiculously expensive. How ludicrous would it look with her simple dress? She smoothed the cotton skirt, feeling it's reassurance, she would not stand out in a crowd; no longer the well-to-do young lady who needed a chaperone wherever she went in the city.

As she neared the poorer end of town the streets were bustling, and the women sported shawls, though home-knitted. Night soil, waste and smoking chimneys cut the air like a butcher's knife, fetid and repugnant. The noise in the closes and wynds about Holyrood Palace pierced her ears, every sound that could be made resonating in the narrow alleys like hill thunder; shouting, banging, hammering as though Doomsday was tomorrow. She dodged the workmen frantically installing new lamps to light the King's way.

Whatever the smell and din, Edinburgh would shine on the great day; she pictured every candled window beaming patriotic welcome. Armstrong had already purchased theirs, a facsimile of the Castle in a showy wax effigy that would burn wastefully to nothing, but the delight whilst it lasted would replicate all the endless frippery that was the visit to end all visits.

She was not alone in her destination and she paused in a wave of frustration. Arthur's Seat, the rugged hill that dominated the city, towered high and wild, a craggy animal that crouched as though about to leap. A 'sleeping lion' they called it, for it hid a dormant volcano that had fired the skies millennia ago. A wild place, where Kitty had seen its green steep slopes as her salvation, an upland tramp that would help to clear her brain.

But half the population seemed to be in need of its restorative powers and her feet fell in beside a laughing, happy crowd that told immediately why they were there. Every man, woman and child was lugging wood up the steep hillside; impossible shapes that needed both ingenuity and stamina. Every possible source had been robbed for the beacon; old rabbit hutches, chicken coops, broken beds all invaded the slopes on heads and shoulders hiding the carrier. It looked as though the rubbish had acquired legs. Old and young puffed and heaved, stopped for breath then carried on upward. Some more affluent citizens climbed empty-handed-their servants the uncomplaining pack horses!

'Let me help you,' Kitty took pity on an elderly woman who strove to keep bundle and shawl in place, staggering beneath a fireside rocker. Had it really outdone its use?

'I'll take it.' Kitty feeling conspicuous with her hands empty, repeated her offer.

'Thank you, hen!' The woman dropped her load to the ground in obvious relief, salvaged a few manageable strips of wood so she was not left empty handed and continued upward. Kitty was left with most of the unwieldy bundle to manhandle up the final sharp climb to the summit. She merged into the procession, mutterings and oaths all about her as the slope got steeper. She stopped for breath and stared back down at the city below, it lay covered by a haze of yellow smoke dotted by a thin line of bright lights where the Edinburgh Gas Company were testing their lamps along Dalkeith Road. Above it all on the hillside, a flash of sunlight burned golden. The drab northern capital was changing colour.

A man grinned at her as he shuffled his load from one shoulder to the other, 'you mind, I'd only do it for him, trust Sir Walter to think up something like this.'

Kitty giggled, 'Only he could persuade half the population into doing such a thing.'

'Fine by me, though he'd no get me to read one of his books- come to think of it, they'd make a good blaze!'

'Oh, no!' Kitty looked horrified, 'They're the last things that should go up in flames.'

'You could be right, lassie. Anyway this is a good way to get rid of our rubbish... you'll not be missing that chair.' He pointed at the worn seat that had once graced the old woman's home, 'from the look of it, no one is going to scavenge that from the bonfire.'

Kitty fell behind as she stopped to gather her breath, she no longer walked long miles and it showed. She wiped a circle of perspiration from her brow and from around her neck, her smell was a day's border foray. Malcolm Mortimer should see her now! Yet already she could feel her pressure headache dispelled. And once free of her load, she would walk on leaving all the crowds behind.

The gathered pile was already enormous, staves -no part of an architect's plan – had built a wooden cathedral that arched haphazardly to the heavens. Someone seized her load.

'Here, let me have it that must have been heavy.'

'Only at the end,' Kitty laughed, happy the unexpected task had made her feel useful and included.

'There's a place round here that will take it.' Strong hands grappled with the unwieldy shape and the carrier set off for the other side of the beacon and she followed. His clothes were grimy his shirt hung out of his breeches. And from his smell, he and his clothes would need to see soap and water at the end of the day. 'Thanks, it all helps'. The grimy faced custodian of the celebratory bonfire looked down at her- a shared smile of achievement on both their faces. They gasped together.

'Olaf!'

'Kit!'

Kitty laughed, 'I didn't recognise you in your old clothes.'

'Nor I you.' They stared at each other and it was Kitty who recovered her voice first.

'Well it's no surprise you're here. Clever Sir Walter to see a lighthouse builder would be just the right architect for his light-tower.'

They laughed together, Olaf's face like that of a small boy that has just built his first sandcastle.

'I'm not really needed.' The expression of doubt she had learned to recognise stilled his smile, 'It's really just a question of piling on the rubbish, the more the merrier.'

'Come on, lads put it here.' He guided two boys to a space in the burgeoning beacon and a few minutes were spent adjusting the rubbish as carefully as if he was constructing an elegant building.

'I'm sure designer Robert Adam didn't take any more care than you are taking when he built the Regent Bridge on Calton Hill.' Kitty smiled encouragingly as Olaf came back to stand beside her. 'Perhaps they'll call this tower after you?' She said flippantly, glad to see him re-emerge.

'I would hope not,' he assumed a mock expression of horror; 'I wouldn't want to think that what I build would be so short-lived.'

'Perhaps not, but your bonfire helps to make people feel part of the King's visit. This morning's work is the best thing I've done in days.' Kitty grabbed at a piece of wood that jutted out and pushed it into place. It smelt of tar and she smoothed her grubby hands down her shirt, a tell-tale dirty mark patterned the blue. Olaf looked perturbed and then as Kitty giggled he said,

'It suits you.'

'What does?'

'Untidy hair, dirty face, grubby clothes.'

She stared up at him, a smile spreading across her face. He bent down and lightly brushed a smudge from her cheek.

He was unsmiling. 'In Edinburgh you are a beached seal adrift on rocks with the tide going out. Why don't you go back to where you belong, Kit?'

She frowned, 'So where would you say I belong?'

He stood just inches from her and she could feel his agitation. But there was no forthcoming answer.

'Alright Olaf, if you don't know about *me*, where do you think *you* belong, do you really know?'

Pale blue eyes blinked his displeasure and Kitty placed a comforting hand on his arm. She felt him tense as he stepped away from her. Sir Walter's words rang in her ears, Olaf cannot cope with emotion. Her hand fell to her side, her fingers bereft. They were inches apart, yet a chasm separated them, too deep, too sheer to step across.

'I saw your escort at the tearoom; his uniform is eye-catching.' Olaf's tone was measured. So he had been on the hill that evening!

Kitty sniggered, 'Then wait till he sits astride his horse, he tries to convince himself I am ready to swoon at the sight.'

Olaf looked contemptuous, 'Then make sure you don't do it near the hooves, front or back.'

'You're full of good advice today, we should all be very attentive, *'put it here, don't put it there'.* She mimicked him as he took another load of wood from a young lad.

But she waited impatiently for him to return to her. He said, 'I've seen someone else who doesn't fit into city life.' His mouth closed in a firm line of disapproval. 'I cannot imagine why he is here.'

Kitty looked puzzled, 'Someone I know?'

'Yes.'

'Who then?'

'Dougal Patterson.'

'P-Patterson- here?' The girl stared in disbelief. 'What does he here-*his bandy legs are best suited to a ship's deck?*'

Olaf laughed, 'Indeed- a fish out of water. Yet he seemed very at home when I followed him to a High Street Tavern- he was flashing his money about or rather her money.'

'Her money...?' Kitty was only capable of repeating his words.

'Louise's...!'

'Louise... Louise Smythe, but that's not possible.'

'No, not in the alehouse, no respectable woman would set foot in such a place, but beforehand in the narrow wynd. I cursed I was not near enough to overhear their conversation.'

Kitty stood silent, suddenly fearful. She said, 'you must be careful, Olaf, perhaps he means further trouble for you.'

'What do you mean? He has no quarrel with me' Olaf was guarded in his quick denial.

'Once he did.' She stared back into Olaf's incomprehension. 'I was witness to the herring shed scene.'

'Oh.' Olaf looked startled, and then a strange expression flitted across his face. 'You saw my just punishment?'

'Yes.'

'So now you know why I could never live up to your exacting expectations.'

'Oh, Olaf...'

'You said you could never forgive a wrecker.'

She stammered, 'B-but, Olaf you were a *young lad*. You've atoned for it, and like a man taken your punishment.'

She said, 'Let it be, Olaf. You know it is time to put it behind you.'

'Aye.'

'So what is Patterson's business here?' Surely he hasn't come to cheer George of Hanover.'

Olaf echoed her disbelief, 'No, never that!'

'Then it must be because of Louise, perhaps he regrets his treatment of her and has come to make amends.'

'I wonder...' Olaf sounded less than convinced.

Kitty sighed, 'Up until now Louise has been a limpet, but now I think we're no longer friends. Olaf....' a surge of climbers brought more offerings to the pyre and Olaf was engulfed, their conversation forcefully interrupted.

Kitty left him in a flux of wooden offerings climbing ever higher on the celebration bonfire. She thought of the mountain of tasks heaped on the willing workhorse that was Sir Walter. Hopefully he was surrounded by folk like Olaf.

Her feet trod the downward path and reluctantly her thoughts came back to Louise and Patterson. The girl had shown no interest in any beau in town, only Mortimer for Kitty. So she knew that Cousin Armstrong had come to Edinburgh to find Kitty a wealthy husband. She had come along as chaperone. Louise had bargained that absence would make Patterson's heart grow fonder. It looked as though it had worked.

So many unanswered questions, surely Armstrong had known Kitty's devotion to her daughter would preclude her compliance in a marriage; and yet he was hell-bent on pursuing the captain. He'd been furious when Kitty had said there were other fish in the sea. Why Mortimer?

The busy back streets of the Old town crowded in on her. She emerged from the dark passage of West Bow, the overhanging third floors of the tenements acting as unwanted sunshades. Smoke rose from every chimney, washing on poles thrust from windows hung limp, gathering the soot. A strident choir of barking dogs and boys loud with iron hoops drowned out the raucous call of the fishwife. But the fish stall did brisk business; people sat leaning against the shop fronts with plates of oysters balanced on their knees. A man handing over his penny to the white capped fishwife expertly opened the shell with his other hand and slipped the seafood greedily down his throat. Kitty heard the satisfied gulp. The stall provided cheap food for the poor. Some said it was an aphrodisiac; well, there were plenty of poor around! Kitty quickened her pace, her eyes fixed on the ground avoiding the shells scattered by the human tide. You didn't need to be by the sea for a pungent smell of fish.

    She turned a corner and almost fell over an urchin, nose and eyes streaming in a noisy despair. 'Hush, child,' she looked about for the mother but the little girl was alone. She bent to the child's level hastily seeking in her pocket for a piece of tablet, the sweet candy made in every other kitchen of the city, rich and poor. The snivelling stopped, the grin was instant and Kitty found herself wiping the streaming eyes with her linen handkerchief. With a rush of pity she hugged the child to her and the frail little body felt soft and needy. She thrust the linen into the little girl's hand and the look of astonishment showed that the new owner could not believe her luck. Shakily, Kitty got to her feet, and watched the child skip away with her prize. Her poor home would not have seen the like.

    Kitty gulped down her concern and caught sight of a sign swinging above her head.

The Edinburgh Emporium for Hair.

    The loud creak of the board spelt out a message, shorn of her enticing locks she would become the mother that her own little daughter hungrily awaited. It swung backwards and forwards, repeating the unwanted truth. She muttered, 'I'll not go down that road it leads only to poverty and a hovel, where my own child will end up crying in the gutter for a piece of candy.'

    That was reason enough to keep her from crossing the threshold of the emporium; her black curls her chance for a very different life. And if she played her cards right they would include little Katharine. Behind the grill of the shop's small display window a wig enticed those less endowed... in contrast to her locks it looked thin and mousy.

Beside the Emporium a narrow stair curled upward linking ground floor with fourth floor casement. A woman adorned in a wig, sat at a window staring down into the street as a man started up the steps, his feet taking them two at a time.

Twenty Seven

It was a riot, as loud and fraught as any rebellion. Crowds of people in Shakespeare Square streaming out of the Oyster House and Red Lion Tavern into the seething mass of humanity around the Theatre Royal. Hundreds jostled shoulder to shoulder thrust against the railings that kept them away from the Pit and Gallery entrances of the Playhouse. A stampede threatened as those trying to get in, came up against those gate crashers being evicted.

Mortimer and his party were onlookers, kept aloof high above the mob within his carriage.

He frowned in annoyance, 'Recently theatre attendance has fallen, but because of the King's visit every lesser person wants to be part of the scene.' And he raised his voice as shouts from the mob threatened to engulf them. 'Do not fear, ladies, you will not come to any harm,' Mortimer comforted as their carriage came to a halt in front of the main entrance to the building. The seething mass retreated behind the arms of two official looking crowd controllers. The new noise was iron on stone and the harmony of hooves from two obedient bay horses.

'We feel quite safe with you, dear Malcolm, after all, you've been given the task to protect His Majesty!' Kitty looked at the flush of concern on their escort's face,

'Besides, look at that couple of worthies.' she indicated the two men at the main doors of the Theatre dressed in flaxen wigs, light blue coats over red vests and carrying stout sticks.

Mortimer looked smug. 'They are Bow Street Runners brought up especially from London. Not just here to control the

Edinburgh Theatre goers but to keep an eye on the knuckles and sneaks also drawn to our city by the King's visit.' He was the informed man of the world.

'Knuckles and sneaks...?' Kitty liked showing her ignorance.

'Pickpockets and burglars, my dear Kitty, how refreshingly innocent you are.' He took her arm protectively. They had alighted at the portico amidst a sedate throng of gentry all kept apart from the masses in carriages that had forced their way through the seething crowds. Above the Theatre Pediment, Scotland's Shield of red and gold with the Lion Rampant newly hung was surrounded by scarlet festoons and drapery.

Kitty accepted Mortimer's arm as they entered the foyer which was cool and quiet, as though words from the stage could reach thus far. She sparkled in a feeling of abandon that took her by surprise. Why not? Tonight Cinderella... what lay beyond midnight was another day! Louise also glowed in an undercurrent of anticipation and Kitty thought, *we are like two understudies playing our scripted parts.*

New dresses had been delivered yet again, and Kitty in pale lilac felt many eyes turned to rest on her as the privileged evening audience briefly assembled under the portico and then disappeared inside the inner sanctum. There was a comforting hum of expectation and she was acceptably part of it. Sophisticated entertainment awaited, no longer did she belong in the raucous gutter outside!

Even in that select audience they had the best seats. The box lifted them above the throng so that they could see and *be* seen. And it was not just any old box. Mortimer had acquired the Royal enclosure itself awaiting its future more illustrious occupant. The red damask seats cushioned the play in a haze of luxury. Their box was too near the stage to give the best view, but that was of small concern as necks craned from the Pit and Gallery, all eyes on the Royal Box to see the substitute royal party. Kitty returned the stares, giddy in the audience spotlight.

Mortimer sat close, her every need his only concern. He handed her opera glasses to see on stage Mrs Harriet Siddons, the actress and etiquette teacher who was playing Scott's heroine Jeannie Deans. In this special production of 'Heart of Midlothian,' she was become larger than life; her every move accentuated in rehearsed elegance. Kitty felt a thrill of satisfaction that this woman was also teaching *her* to fill the role of superior lady!

The interval came in a flash and Kitty had heard little of the play, her eyes and mind having been fixed on the audience. The heavily made-up and costumed actors paled to insignificance beside the ladies of Scotland and their husbands who all looked to her as though she was royalty. Gossip had never sounded so loud in a constant murmur of chatter throughout the first two acts!

Their escort, swelling with pride, led them out of the Royal Box by its newly constructed entrance, testimony to the size of the next occupant, the ageing Monarch. Champagne, made possible by the peace with France, awaited them in the foyer. They sipped it as though it was their regular refreshment; small price that Mortimer hovered at Kitty's elbow. He looked flustered, puffed in his puffed-sleeve coat, his hair curling about a face that held a permanent self-satisfied smile moistened by rivulets of sweat. He bowed from left to right at each enquiring glance so that his newly acquired air of possession also threatened to burst his buttons.

The King's visit intruded everywhere, but no more so than in the Theatre Royal. Outer appearance was everything and the past days had been frantic to get it right. The crumbling plaster was in the final throes of redecoration, expensive re-gilding and rich crimson drapes seeking to hide the obvious decay of the old building; though the newly installed gas lights showed the improvements were but surface deep. Kitty thought of Sir Walter, the pageantry and pomp he was providing to shore-up the King's visit to the city was doing its very best to conceal the mundane reality of every-day life.

Gentry were all about her, moving as though they had all been to Harriet Siddons' Etiquette Classes. Kitty straightened her back, held her head high. She fingered her sophisticated hairstyle, but there was no need, it crowned her head as though she were a Queen. She brought her arm to rest lightly on that of Mortimer and he sought her hand in ardent attention.

'The interval is as entertaining as the play,' Kitty showed her pleasure, 'such elegance!' she exclaimed.

'There is no one as beautiful as you, dear Kitty,' Mortimer was breathless in his eagerness, 'and though this is a glittering occasion it is nothing in comparison with the King's Ball to be held in the Assembly Rooms.' He squeezed her arm. 'I hope you will give me the honour of being my partner. It would make me the happiest man alive.'

Kitty inclined her head, 'If his Majesty is to be there and you are on guard, surely I would only get in the way?'

'No never that, even his Majesty would envy me if you were on my arm.'

Farmer Armstrong took a noisy swig of his champagne looking and obviously feeling out of place. 'My dear young sir, it is the young ladies who are honoured to be in your company.' The silver words rolled off the lips of a man more at home on smuggler routes than in gilded city theatre.

'And may I say, Sir-the King is ably served by the brave young men of Scotland.' Armstrong spluttered his flattery, and Mortimer, never averse to compliments, pondered the words, then frowned.

'Brave you say? I am sure King George is in no danger. His subjects north of the border are equally as loyal as those in the south. The Scots are not as volatile as the English and we do not expect any misadventure during the King's visit here.'

'Then what of his return journey to London?' Louise giggled, 'You say the English are volatile? Do you have cause for such a belief? Does danger wait for him south of the border?'

Mortimer laughed nervously, 'Of course not, I fear only because I am no sailor.'

'Sailor…? What is this Mortimer, are you taking to the high seas?' A passing army officer interrupted his words and the next few minutes were taken up with introductions as the newcomer gazed openly in admiration of Kitty. The girl could feel her escort basking in the reflected glory. She hadn't heard him complain about his unmarried state for several hours. She felt a stab of sympathy for the hapless man.

Louise was bored and her usually quiet voice rose a pitch. 'So, the amateur soldier is about to become an amateur mariner.'

Mortimer said stiffly, noting her emphasis on amateur, 'I return south with His Majesty on the Royal Yacht as part of his Scottish body-guard. All I hope is that it will be a calm sailing.'

'I have heard one is eager to die if one is stricken with sea-sickness.' Kitty looked deadly serious as she sympathised and Mortimer's friend, Captain Grant, raised his eyebrows in mock horror.

Mortimer sighed heavily, but said, 'There are two reasons for my reluctance to embark on the journey,' he looked about him, lowering his voice as though he feared Hanover spies, 'not just poor sailing legs but a fervent desire to remain in Edinburgh. Believe me, Miss K-Kitty if it were not for my allegiance to King George….'

Louise snapped, 'But how gratifying, dear Mortimer, to know you are prepared to suffer physical discomfort in the service of his Majesty.'

He gave a quick nod of self-satisfaction. 'Yes the protection of King George is paramount whatever the dangers.' In his new found bravado, stormy seas drained away from the safe confines of the theatre.

Kitty said lightly, 'A sea voyage is always to be feared, even on a summer day. I've been in a nor'easter that blew for three days. Even on land I could not keep my feet.'

Mortimer stuttered, 'I-I only have to look at the sea to turn green.'

Louise said, now fully enjoying the banter, 'How unfortunate is that? It will clash with your uniform. But I have to admit- it's a treacherous coast twixt Scotland and England for even the hardiest sailor.'

'Enough.' Armstrong exploded in annoyance, and Kitty, acknowledging that they'd tormented their plaything enough, turned to her dejected companion.

'The voyage will be plain sailing, after all it would not be right to have a sea-sick King.'

'No, indeed... my cousin is Captain of the Royal Yacht and it would not reflect well on him. Besides we guard not only the valuable *person* of His Majesty, but all the *irreplaceable* Royal plate. Also, the household valuables that King George brings with him on such a grand state occasion...they'll be on board too!'

'Oh,' Kitty gasped in horror, 'how terrible it would be for all that to end up floating in the sea.' The vision of glittering state treasure beaded between the bobbing heads of grey seals was almost too realistic.

Louise laughed flippantly, 'Don't worry I'm sure King George wouldn't drown, and he's got more than enough blubber to keep *him* afloat. But...' she sniggered, 'if the worst did happen, old Janet might very well end up wearing the Royal Crown!'

Twenty Eight

Just a few days to go, and the streets of Edinburgh, Old Town and New, seethed with visitors and residents alike, all desperate to be part of the pantomime gripping the city. Depending on age and class they strolled, or skipped from spectacle to spectacle. They admired the gunners drilling in Holyrood Park, the spectator stands that were gradually covering Castle Hill, and the Piper and tartan clad Highlanders guarding the entrance to Sir Walter's residence. Haughty ladies graced gentlemen's arms in an invasion of nobility from country estates willing for once to suffer the city summer dust. The pavements were crowded and many risked life and limb as they took to the roads trying to avoid the carriages carrying the elderly to their next point of interest.

Kitty blessed the confusion as she stalked Louise along Princess Street. Her morning headache was as noisy and muddled as the scene about her, where was the Smythe girl going and why? Louise, clearly animated, strode with purpose, and Kitty guessed that the island girl must have a prearranged meeting with Patterson. Olaf still figured large in her fears, was he the reason for the unpredictable Patterson to be here and yet...?

Dodging folk going in the opposite direction towards the soldiers' parade ground, Louise was like a hound trailing a known scent. Kitty, close behind, calmed her unease inhaling deeply the early morning air. Back in the Cheviots, she had thrived on intrigue!

Louise reached the carriage rank beside the Theatre Royal. The evening audience had gone, and Kitty, stopping beside a raised tail and foaming animal excretion, almost choked. But of greater concern to her was if horses were involved in her quarry's morning foray. Thankfully, the girl ignored the cries for custom, and only glanced at the waiting queue before continuing westward on her own two feet.

Suddenly, Louise swung right on to the slopes of Castle Hill and into a forest of wood grown up over night with staves and planks. That would give seats to the King's trusty subjects like roosting birds on branches. The feathered variety must have long since flown for the din was a thousand bird-scarers, shattering the warm, soft day of early August. Shouting, banging, solid thuds as planks joined with uprights providing yet more seats.

Kitty scoured the labyrinth where Louise had disappeared a few feet ahead of her. Where had she gone? She stood hesitant. A workman leered at her and another, spitting out a mouthful of nails on to the churned up grass, winked at her,

'Are ya looking for a roost, hen?'

Kitty shook her head and quipped, 'Why, does the early bird get the best view?'

'Ma cock starts to crow at dawn, but it works at any hour.' The workman laughed and took a menacing step towards her.

'So you've had time to fall off yer perch and into yer ain shit then!'

Furious, Kitty evaded his outstretched hand by plunging under the planking seats into a cellar of black that for a second, blinded her. How dare the man see her as easy game? She was trembling with anger. She stood stock still, waiting for her heart to return to normal and for her eyes to get accustomed to the gloom. But it was a certain sound that transfixed, above Kitty's head was no crowing bird but the well-known Holy Island burr of Patterson and, listening more intently, she heard the muffled voice of Louise- was she embracing the fisherman, her words lost in his gansey?

'You're late.' Kitty pictured Patterson extricating himself from Louise. She'd seen no evidence that the self-contained man returned the girl's feelings, yet this assignation had been fixed and she hoped she was about to discover the reason. She blessed the makeshift edifice that gave her a sort of foxhole cover.

'What kept yer?' The man was less than gracious and it wasn't just the eavesdropper who picked up his dubious temper. Kitty could imagine the permanent frown of the hard-done-by fisherman and the placatory reaction of the girl- more usually the one who needled, but now herself, desperate to please. The unseen eavesdropper knew Patterson was handsome even with a scowl on his face.

'You'll be glad you came when you hear this.' The girl strove to sound non-committal but there was scarcely hidden glee and Kitty stiffened, was it the bomb-shell of Kitty's bastard child that had made Louise so sure of Patterson's interest? Surely, that belonged more to ladies teatime-tattle than to a secret rendezvous.

Patterson's next words went some way to calm her fears, 'so, have yer discovered where Armstrong will be the morrow?'

'Yes, our stand is opposite the quay in Leith Dock. As promised, Mortimer has acquired the best seats. He has his uses! We'll be seated with the cream of Edinburgh Society.' She laughed. 'I do wish you would tell me why Armstrong's where-a-bouts are so important to you…' Louise had on her teasing voice, the one she used to annoy sister Marion, but it carried less weight with the hardened sea captain.

'You'll larn soon enough.' Patterson snapped, then his voice changed, 'So he'll be amongst the bigwigs!'

Kitty could hear his steps move closer to his companion, and peering up through the slats she could see the dark shapes of his boots, 'It's no business of yours what I have with

Armstrong…but I niver forget a wrong. The time has come to larn him a lesson, he'll not forget it in a hurry.'

'He was wrong to dismiss you from the Sea Plunder.' Louise was anxious to agree and Kitty saw the shadow of her arm as she moved closer to him.

'You're reet there, and yer brother isn't too chuffed either. He's left the island… he's had enough.' Patterson laughed bitterly and Louise said, devoid of sisterly concern.

'Where will you get new work?'

'Ah've got that covered. Yer'll find out soon enough.' He was dismissive. 'Well, ah'm off.'

'Don't go, Dougal…' Kitty could hear desperation in the girl's voice. 'Th-the Royal Yacht will be a fine sight off Emmanuel Head on its journey back from Edinburgh.'

'Aye!' Patterson sounded disinterested.

Louise sniggered, 'August storms …surely await?'

'Can't wait. Once am the new owner of Sea Plunder ah'll be out in rough and calm seas alike.'

'Owner of the Sea Plunder?' Louise whispered her surprise, then, 'So how about bigger fish? The Royal George arrives in the port of Leith tomorrow and what goes up must go down, if you get my meaning?' Louise laughed heartlessly.

'What are yer getting at?' She had got his interest.

'King's ships are no more immune from wrecking than any other.'

Patterson laughed. 'Oh, aye?'

'Oh, yes.' Louise was gabbling in her excitement now she had Patterson's full attention. 'Kitty's new beau will be on board with the King.'

'So, how does that help?'

'He's besotted with Kitty.'

'And so..?'

'She will tell him she is returning to Holy Island.' Louise's ideas were only one jump ahead of her voice as she answered Patterson's doubts.

'And..?'

'She'll beg him to get the ship to sail close to the shore for a lover's glimpse.'

'And how can Kitty's admirer achieve that little manoeuvre? Is he captain of the ship as well as being soldier and lovesick beau?' Patterson was disbelieving.

'The Captain of the Royal Yacht is Mortimer's impecunious cousin, dependant on *him* for supporting his growing family.'

'So how will the goody Miss Macnab cooperate? Is she equally smitten with the soldier?'

'No, of course she isn't...but there are ways and means of forcing her hand.'

'Meaning..?'

'Our friend has a dark secret,' Louise's voice had risen in her desire to impress her companion, tapping feet told that Patterson was growing ever impatient, lighter steps moved above Kitty's head and she ducked involuntarily, her life was being trampled into the dust.

'Oh, yes our lovely Kitty, would you believe, has a child?'

'So!' Patterson exhaled his surprise, 'how did yer discover that?' His voice was nò longer monotone.

'My dear cousin let it out in a fit of rage.'

'So-o-o- where is the bairn?'

'At Barraburn. I think John Armstrong, in his dotage, sees her as his own little foundling to spoil at will and in return…'

'He's no the father is he?' Patterson was warming to the girl's story and Kitty almost cried out in revulsion.'

'Oh no… something much more regretful!' Winner Louise was about to play her trump card.

But Patterson, not interested in tittle-tattle interrupted, 'So, wouldn't news of illegitimate child upset the boyfriend?'

'Armstrong thinks not, he believes the man is desperate.'

Patterson laughed. 'He's not the only one who'd be eager to get Miss Kitty into bed.'

Louise ignored the remark. 'Well the dark secret is out and because of it she could secure us a *canny cargo*.'

'It soonds a bit far-fetched.'

Louise giggled, 'Mortimer's face was green just thinking about the sea voyage. He won't need any persuasion to move nearer to the coast.'

'Miss Macnab would be harder to persuade. Not a lady to be easily influenced.'

'You haven't heard her talking in her sleep about the child; then I didn't understand, now I do.'

'So you see her as devoted mother?' The man's voice was hard.

'Oh Kitty's changed, she's seen the city lights and what wealth can offer her. Dining at the table of Sir Walter Scott has affected the judgement of our young country girl. I watched her preening beside the great man, she's mesmerised by him, she'd do anything just to stay in her new sophisticated world. She's already thinking Mortimer can offer her a better life.'

Kitty heard Patterson's snort of disbelief.

'Then she'll hardly agree to entice her beau on to the rocks.'

'No, that could be a problem.' Louise sounded her first doubt. 'Come on Dougal, you can think of a plan.'

'Umm,' the noise was ominous and then there was a murmur of triumph, 'leave it to me.' Patterson's voice had changed pitch.

Louise was admiring, 'So it doesn't need a scholar to come up with a good storyline. I'm sure you can outdo our revered novelist in a twist at the end. Dougal...'

Bang, a crescendo of hammer on nail into wood drowned any further words. Hammer... hammer... hammer, the blood pounded in Kitty's ears. Bang, bang, thud and a heartfelt oath as one of the workmen obviously hit his thumb. Just as suddenly the racket ceased, and Patterson was still holding forth,

'So, as you say wu've got two weeks for all the festivities.' He was pondering the information. 'Time for Miss Macnab to enjoy the new world she covets before she is snatched from it!' Kitty cowered from the feet directly above her. 'Then I'll go to Barraburn for the child. When the mother knows I have her little dear in my keeping she will be only too pleased to lure the King's yacht on to the rocks; no choice when it's either the King or the daughter in danger.' For the first time Patterson sounded involved. 'But first, I'm going to get even with Armstrong!'

Twenty Nine

The mid-day light of Princes Street blinded Kitty as she staggered out into a scene of confusion. People, horses, and carriages were heading in the direction of tomorrow when King George the Fourth would land in their capital city. Today did not matter, but it did to her.

For the second time that morning she was trembling, first the foul workman and his uncouth attention and now her child threatened in a plot that used the innocent as bait. Her past even now dominated her present and future. Somehow she had to stop the inevitable.

Who could she turn to? Olaf! Her desperation furnished just one name. She needed his sense, his lighthouse dependability. But even as the reassurance came to her she knew she could never involve him in her plight. Lighthouses flashed a warning, stay away, do not come any nearer. No, she could never reveal her shame to Olaf; he would rebuff the muddied waters that churned about the wreck that was Kitty Macnab.

If not Olaf, then Sir Walter, the one man in the city who solved everything for everyone; pacified the warring Highlanders in their fancy dress costume, started the building of the National Monument on Calton Hill and found the hidden Scottish Royal jewels. He had also organised a welcoming giant bonfire on Arthur's Seat and instructed the citizens in pamphlets on their code of dress and behaviour so that nothing could possibly go wrong to mar the visit. He'd almost come to the fruition of his latest, *story*, and there was no room in it for a shipwreck subplot. How could she involve him in an ending that would not only kill the King but, surely, the ageing puppet master as well? The world-renowned novelist, already very close to nervous exhaustion, would never get over such a *tragedy!*

The tall buildings either side of the street cut out the summer sky focusing on the pandemonium of street life and it whiplashed her to her senses; she could almost feel the cut of the leather thong against her cheek as she descended into Castle Street; the mournful sound of the highland pipes at the door of Sir Walter wailing their dirge.

She stopped before she reached number thirty nine; she alone was the one to alter the ending that Louise and Patterson wanted to write. In the unreality of the city streets her country realism struggled, but she knew what she *had* to do. Her future path held no desperate Malcolm Mortimer, no scheming John Armstrong, no wrecking Louise and Patterson. When all were caught up in the excitement of the King's Procession, she would escape; return to collect her daughter and together they would disappear. It meant walking away from Olaf, but then she had always *known* that was the inevitable ending.

Olaf, had already intuitively imagined her shorn of the whore locks that kept her on the old path. The time had come for her to change her life. She imagined the waves that even now washed clean the shores of Holy Island. How she longed to be so cleansed.

She turned away from the Georgian splendour of Castle Street, climbing resolutely back into the muddle of the Old Town; Edinburgh was no place for her and never had been. Her dream of pale green walled salon with dark green drapes and carpet with a hint of mauve, had *always* been beyond her reach. The natural green of country was where she belonged. Childish feet did not belong on thick piled carpet.

Her mission in the poor part of town complete, she walked back to their genteel lodgings. Now there were no children in gutters, no raucous cries, and no smell of fish. A hand fell on to her shoulder and she jumped as though it was the excise man's dread touch. Louise, a vision of fair curls and sparkling eyes, stood grinning at her, as though meeting her friend was something that happened every day on the fashionable Edinburgh street.

'Kitty, are you on your way back to Picardy Street? Hope you haven't forgotten that our gowns for the King's Ball are to be delivered this fore noon?'

'No I had not forgotten!' Kitty sighed, yet more frippery to fashion their charade!

Next day, Kitty woke with a feeling of excitement that she had not felt in weeks, the looked-for-day had arrived at last. She was about to take charge of her own destiny. Louise was already dressed in her best city gear, as Kitty opened her eyes. She closed them again, suddenly wanting to delay the day, but an impatient Louise banged the shutters back onto the bedroom wall with a thud of wood that no one could ignore,

'Come on Kitty, how can you lie in bed?'

'From the gloom outside it would appear we have unroyal weather for the very royal day.'

'Don't bother to look at it. I'm not going to.'

'But it's blowing half a gale; and the rain is horizontal.'

'Shipwreck weather! Drowned bodies always appear by the ninth day,' Island Louise voiced her truism.

'What are you talking about?' Kitty sat up with a jolt.

'I thought that comment would get you out of bed.'

Kitty lay down again and pulled the bedclothes over her head, but Louise said, tugging them back with an almighty heave,

'Don't you remember we teased Mortimer about King George floating amongst the Holy Island rocks? On such a day it's quite possible. I can just picture his bloated body even more bloated than it already is, can't you?'

Kitty stretched wearily, 'you talk nonsense, the King, is already safe in Leith Harbour amongst the waiting flotilla of masts and sails.' She frowned at the girl's traitorous words.

'Yes, but he has a return voyage to make.'

'Haven't you forgotten he has Mortimer to protect him?' and both girls dissolved in helpless laughter. Why had she said it? She certainly felt no fellow feeling with Louise, but there must be no hint of the change. And she felt a twinge of liking for the less than perfect captain.

Louise shrugged her shoulders, 'Well, even the King cannot control nature.' Louise gesticulated to the window, 'By rights it should be hot and sunny on a day like today but then life isn't like that, is it Kitty?'

'Isn't it?'

'No, you know quite well it isn't,' Louise sighed melodramatically, 'but your friends want the best for you Kitty, and that means Malcolm Mortimer if you've any sense.'

Kitty inclined her head as though in agreement.

'£1,000 a year commission- that's what your Malcolm gets and it would be enough for you to live on in some style, don't you think?'

'Indeed.'

'You don't sound convinced. Do you crave more?' Louise sounded disapproving, 'I look for less, so I hope *you'll* help me get the man I want.' Her voice reflected the moral high ground and she looked smug.

'Who's that?'

'Dougal Patterson.'

'Oh?' Kitty tried to look surprised. 'Well he's handsome,' she smiled at Louise's flushed cheeks, 'and you're certainly not gold-digging there.'

'No, but I know he'll make something of himself,' Louise tossed her head, 'city life isn't for him, he's here in Edinburgh but returns to Holy Island before the celebrations. He says the islanders have plans to greet the Royal George on its return voyage. Dougal plans to build a giant welcoming bonfire.'

'That must always attract the King towards his cheering subjects.'

'Yes, hopefully the yacht will sail as close to the island as possible for the villagers to see His Majesty.'

'So do you think I should suggest to Mortimer that he tries to persuade the ship's captain to do just that?'

Louise gasped her surprise. 'Gracious Kitty, you must be a thought reader; what a *wonderful* idea!'

As Louise had said, you couldn't guarantee anything in this life. Wednesday August 14th came and went, King George and Kitty Macnab both trapped by the Edinburgh weather. The Royal Person was storm-bound in the Port of Leith. Many bedraggled watchers waited in vain until they heard the unwelcome news broadcast through the dripping streets, that the King would not emerge that day. The caged Kitty, captive with her limpet friend, was kept up to date by Mortimer's message boy. She paced abstractedly, wondering at the state of Sir Walter, the ring master, just waiting to crack his whip. Lady Scott would need all her diplomacy to calm the increasingly impatient man in his intense frustration. Kitty strove to hide her impatience but minutes seemed like hours.

Night gloom followed the non-event day and engulfed the chimney-tops, but suddenly it was flared by a huge tower of light ablaze on Arthur's Seat. The giant bonfire, built by the King's loyal subjects, lit the night sky, firing a brilliant salvo of welcome that could not be missed by anyone in the city, let alone the becalmed King. Its message shone out- *the Capital's welcome will be worth the wait.*

On her last day in Edinburgh, Kitty sat idly before the mirror brushing her hair; even though there was no sun to catch the highlights, it shone. Beautiful locks were needed to greet the King. Tomorrow the King would come and the locks would go.

Thirty

Dawn, Thursday the 15th of August, and the bonfire still blazed for the start of the long, bedlam day. The rain stopped, an early sun glimmered and the rain-washed streets shimmered in the fresh start. The King's visit to Scotland come at last! And Kitty Macnab would be going in the opposite direction, her place already booked on the south-bound coach. No treason hers! She would cheer the royal visitor as heartily as all the rest, then wipe the city dirt from her fashionable slippers. Her clarty boots, Cinderella-like, would return her to the kitchen.

Her Hair Emporium appointment was midday. In the poor part of the town far removed from royal pomp, the heavy weight of her beauty would be cut from her. Today heralded a new beginning, the blame of her past life left behind.

But, still to live through, was the Royal arrival, the spectacle, the pomp and the ceremony come to a city that, until now, had felt side-lined! So much excited anticipation that no-one could ignore it; least of all Kitty throughout her final hours in Edinburgh.

The best place in town was on the Waterside of Leith. Mortimer had been as good as his stuttering word, his inbred confidence promising ringside seats and effortlessly achieving them. Surely all this would earn the reward he desired most- the resolution of his unmarried state. Would he have gone along with the reckless suggestion that could endanger the Royal Yacht just because he was infatuated with her? She would never know. *Wrecker* would never be a name associated with Kitty Macnab.

Silk stockings, satin slips, scarlet under the virginal white, Mrs Hamilton had found her humour in clothing the girls for the great day. Kitty's expensively gloved hands smoothed her skirt in an effort to calm the nerves. Armstrong was in light trousers tapered to the ankles and fastened by straps under his square-toed shoes: he looked both elegant and flustered. His broad face was like some cartoon sun flaring high above his paisley cravat. *What a sham he is,* thought Kitty, *looking and feeling so out of his depth; the magistrate would be far better off seated atop his reliable farm horse than on the insubstantial seats built skyward.*

Still, Kitty felt that Armstrong was an enigma... magistrate and smuggler; could he plot against the King- was *he* one of the radicals hunted by soldiers like the ones who had stopped them on their journey northward? How unlikely was his friendship with Sir Walter- pillar of the Tory Establishment. Had it been nothing but a callous subterfuge to gain acceptance in to the elite Edinburgh society? Again she would never know, today he was the figure of respectability seated in the very best seats in town, amongst the highest citizens of Scotland.

The wooden stands, built for the spectators, surrounded the Waterside and had been stacked against every possible surface. The platforms would house twenty times more people than mere windows and they rose from pavement to second floor, even to the roof slates. A few dare-devil boys clung to chimneys- a risky but uninterrupted grandstand view. Slender poles and ropes held these viewpoints in place against buildings half hidden by streamers and bunting. But, all decorations looked sadly bedraggled from yesterday's downpour. The city's welcome was tired even before it started!

Seated early, they watched as their fellow spectators negotiated the makeshift stand, elegant ladies in every coloured gown, gentlemen in their best attire. Here was the cream of Edinburgh society. Kitty did not recognise a single face, but then they were newly come to such a gathering. But there was some good-natured banter, bad tempers left behind in the disappointment of yesterday. Friend greeted friend and stranger alike, it was one of those days! Armstrong was going out of his way to acknowledge their neighbours, the lady beside him smiled graciously and a few pleasantries were exchanged, though Kitty could not hear what was being said.

The stand swayed giddily as seats were taken and Kitty grasped the nearest pole at each new arrival; the pavement was a long way down. She looked skyward, envying the seagulls that swooped freely above with a grandstand view and no gravity- defying seats to cling to. Their raucous calls screamed their derision and in return she felt a twinge of her old bravado. They were not the only ones close to freedom!

Not much longer! She peered across to the harbour, it was a sea of boats and more boats, bobbing like eager ducks about the Royal George which waited for the King to spread his largesse to a vast and hungry horde. Rainbow colours smothered ships, buildings and lamp posts; red, white and blue Union Jacks proudly fluttering in the gentle breeze proclaiming the union of Saltire and Flag of St George. The noise was at fever-pitch, excitement, impatience, ribald good humour waiting to erupt in a cascade of hysteria. Pungent smells of perspiring bodies, their toilet long thrown out with the morning slops, combined to make her head swim. Now all she wanted was for it to be over!

This red-letter day! To be described repeatedly in the future to her enthralled daughter around some cottage fire. But for now it was all happening, a breath-taking chaos! The swirl of pipes, the cavalry trumpets and the infantry drums ended dramatically by a single gun on the Royal Yacht. 'Boom…boom!'

Pandemonium again as the cannon of the fleet and batteries on Calton Hill took up the welcome. Not to be outdone the people began to cheer, a sedate ripple turning to a giant wave as it spread relentlessly from stand to stand and street to street -flooding now every quarter of Leith and beyond, up to the capital city. Kitty joined in, it hardly mattered what they were cheering, it was what your neighbour was doing; restraint was no part of this day.

To a man the spectators stretched forward- desperate not to miss a single minute of the show, though there was no imposing King! A short five-foot figure, as round as he was high that could only *be* the King stood outlined by courtiers. He was here on Scottish soil. But in his drab blue uniform he was disappointingly unimpressive. Another salvo of guns, another spectator surge and Kitty felt their crow's nest quiver as though some giant bird had landed on its delicate framework. She lurched with the rest and caught another fleeting glimpse of His Majesty in Admiral's uniform. The National Anthem swelled above the tumult, drowning the cheers. In a few minutes, the excitement would have come and gone.

The Procession was ready to move off. Again the improvised stand lurched forward as the watchers sought a last glimpse of thistle and sprig of heather in the King's cocked hat. Kitty the sea-sick sailor, grabbed at the flimsy framework as a late-comer climbed aboard their vantage point. There were cries of protest from the seated watchers, as the intruder obscured their view. How dare he? The important citizens of Edinburgh were affronted. The elegantly attired ladies clutched at their skirts as the high-booted intruder began to push his way along the line of seats. Anger followed him, and genteel hands pushed him from their line of vision and away from their wives.

The interloper started to shout. 'Where are yer, Armstrong…hiding behind women's petticoats yer bastard? Let the world see yer for what you really are!' The accent was unmistakeable! With a shock of surprise Kitty saw that it was Dougal Patterson. She had forgotten all about him in the excitement, but now she remembered his promise of retaliation against his former employer. Fear grabbed her and she clutched Louise at her side. The other girl's face was impassive- she continued to stare straight in front of her! Not so the other watchers, heads turned, surprise, annoyance, and then reluctant interest at the promise of a close-up fisticuffs.

'Let's see what yer fine friends will think of yer after I've shown them yer real character.'

Patterson's face was contorted with loathing, his eyes wild. The Holy Islander was no part of this celebration. Kitty thought *what a time and place to settle scores*. It could not have been more public. But swaggering Patterson flourished on an audience, and he had a captive one here.

'Come on, Armstrong time to confess to all these folk what yer really like? Not quite the gentleman you make yourself out to be. *Ye're* nee the law-abiding citizen! Here you see, ladies and gentlemen, a *master* of deception. He's an out and out *crook*!' The woman beside Kitty gasped and her eyes narrowed; there were murmurs of 'Shame, shame-.' Already the worthy citizens had taken sides and the closest to Armstrong were gently edging away. Patterson had worked his audience even before he reached his quarry.

As Patterson arrived just inches from him, the Magistrate, crimson faced, leapt to his feet and grabbed hold of his assailant.

Immediately all about them disintegrated into *mayhem*. Tearing wood, splitting poles, snaking ropes and upending planks. The ineffectual streamers cruelly exposed the flimsy perch that had held their trust. Slowly… it tumbled like a pack of Louise's cards into the route behind the retreating King… bodies hurtled through the air like cards shuffled in over-eager hands. Screams of fear and cries for help mingled with the music of the retreating band. Kitty saw Armstrong plunge past her without a sound as she clung on to the pole inches from her chest. Her hands tightened around the slippery stave and then she too was FALLING.

Thirty One

'Kit...' She could hear him calling her, his voice urgent, but she could not answer. She lay helpless at the foot of the lighthouse on rocks jagged and sharp. When she moved, the pain was intense. 'Kit.' Why couldn't he see her? She could see him, framed in the harsh scouring of the warning light, flashing, flashing every half minute exposing her danger and his indecision. Why didn't Olaf come down from his secure perch? She was holding out her hand to him. But already she knew the answer, had known it from the first time she'd met him. He did not see her in the role she craved. To him Kitty Macnab was no heroine and there would be no happy ending. 'Kit-Kit,' the voice ebbed with the tide so that when it retreated all her bruised body wanted to do was to crawl back to the safety of the land she loved and the solace of grass on earth.

 The sounds had changed, no longer could she hear the constant swell of waves and with them the smell of rotting vegetation and fish; the air was heavy with scrubbing and disinfectant. Her hands no longer caught desperately at jutting rocks; in their place was smooth skin. She could hear singing.

 'I am a man upon the land
I am a selkie in the sea
And when I'm far frae every strand,
My home it is in Skule Skerry.'

 She was floating with the selkies; their skin was smooth and cool in the gentle swish, swish of morning waves. She had never felt so happy.

 'I am a man upon the land

I am a selkie in the sea-'

So why had Olaf retreated to the land, cravenly forsaken those trusty, animal friends of his childhood? The singing stopped; had the moon ceased to move the tides? She mouthed her protest. Silence... nothing but a breath on her cheek, an onshore breeze refreshing her fever. She opened her eyes and just inches away was the intense blue-eyed concern of Olaf, searching her face in the apparent fear that he would miss her waking.

'Kitty... at last!' His soft voice was filled with relief. The hand that had been smoothing her palm clasped her fingers in a tight heartfelt grip and then, with an embarrassed grin, he let go.

'Olaf?' Her hand sought his retreating fingers and their reunited hands rested on a brown coarse material that was neither sand nor earth. She peered at the blanket. Ripples of sunlight from an open window cast a pattern of waves. But this was no seaside. The hospital smells invaded her nostrils.

Activity and odour united in sterility, white towels, white coats, white screens, and white walls that shell-wrapped them from the outside world.

'Olaf, where am I...? She struggled to raise her head but it swam in a blur of pain, and he reached out to steady her.

'...and you were singing—it was beautiful,' tears stung her eyes.

'You are in safe hands, Kit. Now you will get better.'

'Better? Where am I?'

'In the Royal Infirmary! There was an accident.'

'Accident?'

Screams, falling, thunderous noise, pain that pierced like a knife through her body and then intense darkness. She struggled to remember. Olaf bent close and whispered into her ear. 'I have to go, I have an urgent meeting, but I will come back. Just get back your strength, dear Kit.'

She squeezed his fingers and then he was gone. He had called her 'Kit?' Her fingers sought her head and she felt the short spikes of hair that plastered her sweating brow. Her mop of hair was no more: had it been cut away by hospital scissors?

The next time she woke there were the same noises, the same overpowering smells, but a new face at her bedside. She studied it through veiled eyes. It was not Olaf, but a young man about his age with a jolly face and plump cheeks; his smile was instant as he caught her gaze.

'Welcome back to the land of the living.'

She smiled weakly, 'I'm glad to be back, thank you.'

'Somewhat extreme of you, if you don't mind me saying, just to get out of all that nonsense of the king's visit,' the young man in the white coat laughed, 'But I should be thanking you- the accident meant I had a good excuse when my young lady wanted me to stand with her on Calton Hill to openly cheer the charade.'

'Cheer?'

'Yes would you believe? I don't want her to know I'm no Royalist. Not yet anyway.'

'The King's visit!' Kitty exclaimed, 'Now I remember- the stand-Patterson-Arm-.'

'It was an accident waiting to happen. It's a wonder there weren't more deaths.'

'Deaths?'

'Aye, it was mostly fractured hips and thighs, broken ribs and arms, but one man died.'

'One man died?'

'A chap by the name of Armstrong. A visiting Englishman.'

She wanted to scream her relief, but all she managed was a deep sigh.

'Your head was a mess! But it's in the past now. You'll soon be home.'

'Thank you, doctor.'

'No doctor yet, just a student learning the ropes.' He waved some papers in his hand, 'You're a special case you know and I've been allotted to keep a journal on you.'

'Special case, that sounds bad!'

'Not at all, but you're lucky to be in this smaller ward, the main ones are over two hundred feet long. Imagine the cries of pain, and annoyance, magnified ten times over! Two lesser rooms are set aside for the more interesting patients, one for females the other for men. But, it's not every day we get injured folk falling from the sky. Perhaps His Majesty brought his wildfowlers with him. Anyway you were sitting targets!'

His good natured laugh went out with him through the wide glass door. She lay back in her bed and closed her eyes, the other special cases moaned, coughed, cried out. Feebly she raised her head to see if Louise lay beside her, but it was an elderly lady with bandaged head.

Louise could be *anywhere*, even in one of the main wards. After the accident it must have been total confusion, the girls would not have fallen neatly side by side to be carried and placed together in the next beds.

White coated figures scurried between beds, there were muffled cries of discomfort, clanking of bed pans, someone was screaming. Kitty lay back on the pillow, aware that her head throbbed in harmony.

She had been lucky. She stretched gingerly, no broken bones, just a bad headache. She thought of the medical student's words. One man dead! She'd had no need to question his name. The sight of Patterson's face minutes before the accident-shouting the truth about Armstrong. The sea captain had planned assassination of character by words. And the Gods had been on his side, he could not have seen that his adversary would be removed by an act of God.

Armstrong was dead, and her only feeling insistent relief. He had gone from her life, the man who had rescued her and her child. For whatever reason she knew now it had *not* been altruistic. There was no Armstrong! She was free from all obligations; at last she could stand on a windswept hillside and no kestrel would hover menacingly.

She frowned; somewhere at the back of her mind there was still fear. What was it? She sighed, whatever it was she knew there was no more Jock Macnab, and no more John Armstrong and- with *their* demise came the realisation that the old Kitty no longer existed! Her hand shot to her head, and she felt spiky hair sticking out in all directions. So now, she was plain, no nonsense Kit.

She nestled down into the prickly blanket, so much to take in and digest!

He was back with his notebook; the student doctor lifting her arm to take her pulse. She smiled. 'Thank you.'

'No need to thank me, its Olaf you need to be grateful to.'

'Olaf?'

'Aye, a friend of mine as well as yours.' He grinned knowingly. 'I also come from Orkney but from Kirkwall, so we had to come all the way to Edinburgh to get to know each other. And one thing I've learned about him is he's persistent; like a ferret. A few days after the accident, friend Olaf came pestering, wanting to know if we had a girl here unclaimed by family or friends.'

'So I asked him if she was beautiful and he said *yes*.'

Kitty blushed.

'Well, under the bruising and the blood. After that he came back the next day and the next... ...got a bit fed up with him singing that song all the time. But it did the trick, eventually you responded.'

'It's a lovely song reminds me of...'

'Olaf?' the young man grinned, 'He'll be back, I can tell you. Here in High School Yards we are minutes from the College. He's worn the steps away leading up to this ward.'

'Gracious, how long have I been in the hospital?'

'A fortnight!'

'Two weeks!' Kitty tried to sit bolt upright but her head swam again. Helpfully, he pushed her back onto the mattress.

'Yes, you missed it all. The King has been and is about to be gone. Not that I'm sorry. It will be good to have the old city back to normality,' he leant closer lowering his voice,

'Like Olaf, I'm sick of all this royal hysteria, Mary, my sweetheart can think of nothing else. And all of it for an obese old man; heaven help us we wouldn't have a bed big enough for him if someone had taken a pot shot.' He grinned as he pencilled a comment about his real patient into her notes.

Fourteen days, his words rang in her head. She had lain there all that time, senseless whilst the event of the century had come and gone and she had missed it! Her laugh mingled with a moan of pain.

But then she remembered she'd already made up her mind to escape as the King arrived. That should have been days ago. Why then did the news upset her? She closed her eyes, the better to concentrate.

When she opened them Olaf was standing at the foot of the bed, his brown face set in concentration. She smiled and held out her hand but he stayed where he was.

'Jimmy says you are on the mend. You'll be allowed out either tomorrow or the next day, that is if you do not have a relapse.' His frown reflected his concern.

'Oh no, I feel so much better and according to your medic Jimmy, it is thanks to you.' A look of annoyance flashed across her visitor's face and Kitty could have kicked herself.

'He talks too much.'

'Unlike the Orcadian I know.'

Olaf shrugged his shoulders, 'So you know that what I do say, I mean.'

'Oh yes. I know exactly!' She laughed. 'You once said you are the sea and you were right, in with the tide and out with the tide. It's almost as though the light of the moon controls your every movement. No deviation, no ability to change.' She strove to make her voice light.

Olaf looked perplexed. 'But you're wrong, the sea changes. The bang on your head makes you speak nonsense.

Have you forgotten the nor'easterly and the scale of the waves that day?'

'Of course not, it was threatening but you found the lea of the island for us.'

'And you'd the sense to dress in sensible clothing, trousers and sou'wester. Your satin frock and kid gloves had to be cut from you in the wreck of the stand.'

'Oh.'

'And you've lost your hair, I'm sorry.'

'No you're not.' Kitty's hands went to her head. Short spikes and thick tufts were caught up in cotton gauze. 'I'd planned to go to the Hair Emporium anyway, but doctor's scissors got in first.' She strove to flatten her unruly locks,

'...so does my new hair style suit me?'

'Suit you?' Surprise registered, 'Does it matter?'

'No matter!' The silence hung heavy. *She wanted to say please will you sing the selkie's song again- it is the most beautiful sound I have ever heard,* but she lay and picked at the blanket in a soundless rhythm of disquiet.

'Sir Walter says you are to go to Castle Street to recuperate.'

'Oh.' Kitty smiled her gratitude and relief.

'George Crabbe has departed, so you will have the best room.'

Kitty raised her eyebrows 'Did he write his poems?' Her memory was returning, the guest poet, just another of Sir Walter's endless kindnesses.

'Aye.' Olaf grinned. 'A very unromantic poet compared to Sir Walter. How about this for a first verse? -

'Of old when a monarch of England appeared
In Scotland he came as a foe;
There was war in the land, and around it were heard
Lamentation, and mourning and woe.'

They laughed together and Olaf said, 'Whatever you think of its poetic merit, most Scots would agree with the *lamentation and woe* bit as far as England is concerned. We are old enemies.'

'So, Humpty Dumpty has put us together again.' Kitty grinned back at him and Olaf raised his eyebrows in an elaborate question mark. Kitty sighed happily, her feeling of well-being was the greater with Olaf beside her, relaxed and friendly.

'And you say tomorrow I am to go to Castle Street? The Scotts are too kind.'

'Indeed.' Olaf frowned. 'As usual, he does too much. It is plain to all, that Sir Walter is chronically sick, his recurring depression only distanced by opium.'

Oh dear, niggles of worry throbbed her still bandaged head... cotton wool inside and out.

'I shall return tomorrow. Sir Walter is to send his carriage for your conveyance. He sends his apologies that he will not be at home to receive you. Thursday August the twenty ninth is the day he bids the King adieu. His Majesty sails on the afternoon tide.'

'Oh, what about Louise?' The question that had been bothering her, came to the surface in a sudden insight, but it was too late for the retreating figure. It was the Orcadian Jimmy who heard the anxiety in Kitty's voice.

'What about her? Was that the fair girl?'

'Yes.' Kitty raised herself on her elbow, desperate to hear news of the girl who had been beside her just minutes before the crash.

The doctor winked. 'I didn't tell you, Olaf asked after her as well. But don't worry it was only after he had found you. He didn't sing her a lullaby.'

'Was she here in the hospital?'

'Yes, but only over-night, in the ground floor main ward. She wasn't one of the serious casualties of the accident. She came to seek you before she left, but you were dead to the world.'

He had moved on to the next bed, the old woman had gone; there was an immobile figure in her place. Kitty closed her eyes, another special case for the students to study; the cries from along the ward echoed round the high ceiling like sea gulls wheeling and screeching about a stormy sky. Her head spun with the discordant sound.

'Sorry,' medic Jimmy had returned to stand at the bottom of her bed. 'Sorry,' his face was as serious as that of his Orcadian friend. 'I shouldn't have used the word lullaby, it is totally wrong. Olaf didn't want you to sleep, he wanted you to *live*. That's why he came every day for hours on end. He did our job for us. T'was he who brought you back to the land of the living!'

Thirty Two

Questions and unwanted answers raged through her brain mingling with deep gratitude. Olaf had coaxed her back to life in a devoted vigil. Only now, she had to face a lonely future; one she owed to both him and Edinburgh Royal Infirmary.

During the long night hours she tossed and turned in recurring pain; submerged by her overpowering feelings for Olaf and by her growing horror that she had lain so long in hospital. What if Olaf hadn't sung his song to her? Where was Louise? Why hadn't *she* come to visit? And where was Patterson? Fourteen days Kitty had lain helpless, oblivious of the world and its happenings. All troublesome questions, but always she returned to Olaf; matter of fact, remote and very dear.

Where had Louise gone? Was Armstrong really dead? Yes! Was Louise still in Edinburgh? No! Already she knew the answers. The girl would be back on Holy Island, back in the bosom of her family, back with Patterson? Everyone going home, even the King and there to watch his progress south would be the Smythe family and the other islanders waiting to catch a glimpse of the Royal Yacht. She struggled to focus on why the image disturbed her so much.

Suddenly, the enormity of the threat that she had overheard Patterson and Louise planning-hit her like a lightening-bolt... she *had* to act.

The luxury of a hot bath and then outside clothes! Kitty dressed quickly in her panic to be gone. The coarse wool skirt and blouse from the hospital poor-fund had seen better days, thin and darned and now her only possessions in the world. The dark navy paled her cheeks and hung loose about her slight frame. She stood up and then sat down again on the bed. Weakness made her dizzy, not helped by the fetid smell of boiled cabbage. She needed the fresh air that blew, beyond the infirmary door, in the town meadows and out beyond, to a sea shore.

Olaf was a diffident figure in the waiting room, still tall and gangly, though the Stevenson family fare had filled out his frame. He shot to his feet when he saw her, eager, yet embarrassed at his mission and impatient to be gone. She could only marvel that he'd sat immobile at her side for so long, his sole activity to sing the beautiful selkie song in a voice hushed with caring.

Stiffly, he offered her his arm and they made for the exit just as Olaf's friend Jimmy appeared for his rounds. They made an awkward group on the staircase. Beyond the bright well-ventilated ward the building looked shabby, though scrubbing brushes and carbolic soap sought to hide its age.

Jimmy indicated the broad stairwell, 'Built for the use of sedan chairs would you believe?'

Kitty laughed, 'Then not for the likes of folk like me.' She indicated her second-hand clothes. 'But thanks to you I can walk away on my own two feet.'

'You'll be taking Kitty to the sea, Olaf. She needs plenty of fresh air and sea breezes. They will clear her head!'

Olaf made no reply but he seized his friend's hand, shook it warmly and Kitty did likewise. She was mute! If only it were possible in real life for the prayers she'd uttered lying prone in a hospital bed to be answered.

Only when they were seated in Sir Walter's coach did she address her escort.

'Where is Louise?'

'Louise Smythe? Haven't you seen her?'

'No, not since we were on the stand watching the King's Procession.'

'You needn't worry, she came to no harm. I have seen her several times since. Yes, with that fellow you were with on Calton Hill, the fop in the soldier's uniform. They seemed remarkably friendly. No accounting for taste!' Kitty smiled at Olaf's tone of voice but made no comment.

'I asked her about you, but she said you'd gone back to your home in the Cheviots.'

Kitty sat stunned, a variety of expressions crossing her face.

'She said that?'

'Yes, she was emphatic.'

'Olaf, please, please will you take me to Holy Island?' Then as there was no response, 'Doctor's orders, remember.'

Her companion frowned dismissively, 'Jimmy is like all Orcadians, he thinks the sea is some miracle balm. Unfortunately it isn't.' He shook his head, 'He's forgotten that it's often said that life is like the Orkney climate, one of the vilest on earth.' He sounded bitter.

Kitty looked at him, Olaf was in a strange mood. 'Gusters blow most days, calm intervals are few and far between.'

'Here isn't that much better. Look at the weather today.'

They peered out at the threatening sky, the wind had risen and Kitty thought of her lost paisley shawl; it would have been a blessing on such a day. Did it now lie torn and filthy under a pile of splintered wood?

Impulsively she seized Olaf's hands, they were warm and she remembered her waking dreams when he had soothed her back to life with his own fingers. Now they lay unresponsive to her clasp; already he was clamming up into his old reserve.

'Since when did you let the weather bother you Olaf? We *must* go to Holy Island.'

He looked at her and worry puckered his brow. 'Kitty, you need rest and care and where better than in Castle Street? Your room is already prepared, the fire lit. Lady Scott is dying to tell you about the gold coloured dress she wore to the King's Drawing Room Reception.'

'How can you think I am interested in such things?'

'Perhaps not, but enjoy the Scott's hospitality. It need only be for a week or so and then you can escape from such triviality.' Olaf laughed apologetically. 'After that if you want to go to Holy Island you will be ready to take such a journey. I'm sure Sir Walter would put his coach at your disposal.' His words distanced him from the enterprise.

Cries from the street interrupted his platitudes. The carriage had come to a halt, the horses' hooves impatient on the cobbles in the chaotic traffic of the last day of the King's visit. George Hanover still controlled the capital even in the final hours of his presence.

Olaf said, 'Tomorrow the city will return to normal.' He frowned down at her, 'It will be difficult to readjust to the status quo whatever that is, I can hardly remember life without…'

'Please listen to me, Olaf. Unless we go to Holy Island there will be no normality anywhere in the land and…and…' She could not voice her greatest fear, was little Katherine even now in the clutches of Patterson? Surely the child no longer figured in his schemes now that her mother was not involved, but…?

Olaf could hear the desperation in her voice and now he took hold of her hand, and she clung on to him, as though she feared he might open the door and escape from her out into the teeming city.

She stuttered, 'There is a plot against the life of His Majesty King George. Holy Island will see the biggest wreck in its history if we *don't* do something about it.'

Thirty Three

Squalls of rain carried low in an easterly wind obscured the island. It lay out there somewhere tantalisingly close but beyond their reach. Stuck on the mainland, they waited Canute-like, willing the tide to ebb. Huddled together at the water's edge in a make-shift shelter built for such times, they braved the rain. It sprinkled through the gaps in the roof like a salt cellar heaping continuous brine. Kitty bit her lip, hardly able to contain her impatience whilst Olaf stood aloof and reserved. The familiar salt taste told her she was back where the sea dominated all life and she felt a strange exhilaration. She could smell its tang on the warm wet cloth of Olaf's jerkin and she moved closer. He was tense, his broad shoulders offered refuge over and above the flimsy hut but he made no move to hold her.

    She moved away. What had she expected, enough that he had agreed to come. This was not quite what Doctor Jimmy had ordered then how could he possibly understand? To know how desperate was her need to find that her child was miles away from here, safe and-?

    She whispered, looking up at the silent man beside her, 'We had to come, we owe it to Sir Walter, a sick man- he'd never have got over seeing his dreams for Scotland lost on the treacherous coast of Northumberland!'

    'Aye, it would finish him and that would be regrettable.' His scarcely concealed impatience hung heavy, Olaf was more withdrawn than ever since Sir Walter's coachman had turned his face homewards in the direction of Edinburgh. She could see in the Orcadian's pale blue eyes the struggle to believe in her certainty that treason was on the incoming tide. But, in contrast, Kitty had felt a mounting excitement since the last city tenement had been lost to view; her old recklessness sweating her palms and making her fragile head pulse. She knew Olaf had learned the salutary lessons of life, he would never dive off rocks without testing the water first. Yet he'd been prepared to follow her madcap suggestion.

She peered into the haze-shrouded waves, Orcadian Jimmy had been right, the sea in all its changing moods called both her and Olaf and she'd no need to look at her companion to know that he too, below his unease, was changed. It was as though the water reflected a light in their eyes that could not be seen in shaded city streets. Excitedly Kitty seized hold of his cold fingers as a shadow of land out beyond the bay was suddenly reality. A rock-cradled island focused their world into a simmering volcano -waiting to erupt.

Olaf followed her gaze, 'He's clearan up.' And he laughed. 'The weather is always known as 'he' in Orkney. It will be starnlit tonight.'

'Aye, I think it will.' Kitty couldn't smile at his use of local Orkney words; a deep sickness ate away at her-*my child...my bairn...where is she now...?* And out in the mist, a small, insignificant drop in the ocean floated, unaware that history could be about to be made there. At risk- the life of a King ...yes...and Sir Walter too but she was only a coiled spring ready to go anywhere, do anything to find her bairn before it was too late. By starnlight they would know. She shuddered, a flippant Louise had laughed at the bulbous image of King George floating with the seals.

Forward, back, forward, back, the waves hit the shore in a belligerent surge before retreating slowly and deliberately as though already the wreckers' accomplice. Over on the island Louise and Patterson waited for their prey knowing that with just a little help from them, nature could reap her reward.

'Can't we risk it?' Kitty peered across the flats.

'Another hour and it will be safe to cross.' Olaf, eyes fixed like a telescope on the obscured horizon, shook his head, 'Patience, we'll reach the island with time enough to spare as long as we wait for the right state of the tide.' He was terse but as he caught sight of her face, 'No need to risk *your* life, you're of more value than the King.' Once again he was the caring watcher at her hospital bed.

'Do you really think that?' she asked. If *only* she'd been able to tell him about the danger to her baby, her child.

He laughed abruptly. 'What am I supposed to think? How do I know you haven't led me here on a wild goose chase?'

'Oh no.' Kitty stiffened. 'The threat is real, I know it.'

'But I've followed you blindly.'

She shook her head, 'You've come without question but I don't believe it was just to please me.'

'No.' Again he was abrupt and she sensed below his calm exterior that he simmered. She shivered as the chill wind invaded the gaping walls,

'Are we mad Olaf, to be here on such a day? I wager the king is tucked up below deck, certainly not looking for any welcoming bonfires. I can almost hear him vowing he'll never journey north again and as for Mortimer,' she let out an exclamation of sympathy, 'I can just imagine the colour of *his* skin.'

She moved to the edge of the shelter and the rain splattered her face. 'If the weather continues like this, Mortimer won't even be in a state to remember that his new girlfriend, Louise awaits on shore. The Royal George will sail by out of reach of the island's hidden rocks and Mortimer and all the entourage will never know of their lucky escape. And then as you say all our effort will have been in vain.'

Olaf didn't reply and an agitated Kitty shook his arm.

'You must believe what I told you about Louise. You can't start having doubts now.'

Olaf's face darkened and he said, 'I watched her expression as she informed me you had left Edinburgh.'
'But Louise is a poker player, you know that.'
'Yes, and I have played many winners.' He shrugged his shoulders, 'Sometimes when they sense victory- they let down their guard. I saw she was lying. It was *then* I went to The Infirmary!'

Pilgrim House looked just as it had done the first time she had seen it, solid and substantial, set in the middle of the island and sheltered from the worst vagaries of the weather. Then she had been astride Henry Smythe's mount, and she had crossed the sea in a state of shock mingled with enchantment, straight into the arms of two pretty fair-haired girls belonging to an eminent island family. They had seemed the fairy-tale sisters she had never had, but sisters quarrel don't they?

It was easy to forget she had gone there to spy for Armstrong. She waited, her breath suspended, the noise resounded across the hall flags and then footsteps; one set only and no childish cries. A valuable silver boat had brought her to this! Was her child in danger because of it?

The look on Louise's face was a study. A full pontoon held by an opponent's hand could not have caused greater disbelief, but hers was no novice game and the smile of welcome was speedy.

'Kitty! Oh my goodness, how wonderful!' The girl expertly masked her surprise.

'Yes, I've come back. There's nowhere better to convalesce than at the seaside.' Kitty hugged Louise to her, relief flooding her like a high tide. The girl had no crying child at her skirts...unless she was asleep deep within the house' thick walls...

'Kitty I thought you'd disappeared off the face of the earth, or then perhaps just gone back to Barraburn.' Louise laughed at the extreme alternatives. 'After all you would have good reason for the latter surely, a caring mother's place is *there*.' Already, she was speaking her disapproval.

Kitty could find no reply.

'A-are you alone?' Louise peered beyond her visitor.

'Of course!'

'Well not any more, dear Kitty, you have the Smythes to care for you now. Wait till Marion sees you!' Louise pursed her lips, 'She wouldn't believe all our city adventures, but she'll listen to you.'

Still they stood on the step. Louise was dressed and ready to go out. And her clothes told that she was dressed for the elements.

'Yes, the King's Jaunt north is something we'll remember long after he has returned to London.' Kitty agreed.

'Aye, and even now he travels home so all is not lost for poor Marion, she'll get a glimpse of him today, though a poor second best, as she well knows. You've just missed her. The whole village is gathering on the castle slopes, there isn't a better view on the whole island.' Louise was keeping Kitty on the step and was looking impatient. 'Mother has provided free beer for the men, cordial for the ladies, and cakes and sweeties for the children.'

'Why have they all gone there?' Kitty tried to look surprised.

'This very evening, His Majesty sails within sight of the island and all his loyal subjects will be out to cheer.' Louise smiled. How plausible she was!

Kitty frowned... but it was too late to fear she had over-reacted; when eavesdropping on Louise and Patterson- had she believed too readily the plot against King George? And all because of that terrible storm she'd witnessed causing the ship wreck on Plough Rock.

That was something she would never forget. Wreckers were an abomination! Her whisky smuggling had been a harmless cat and mouse game depriving the government of revenue. In stark contrast was the luring of innocents to a watery grave to the intonation of prayers. Now once again Louise was smiling her innocence; Kitty's common sense might tell her the previous ship's loss off Holy Island had been inevitable; that no prayers had sent it to its doom but only cruel nature. Yet Kitty had learnt that the unholy combination of islanders and sea could be an evil force.

'The whole village plans to wave King George on his way. It will be a fitting end.' Louise waved her hand in the direction of the sea and a large diamond on her right hand flashed its presence. Hurriedly she clasped one hand over the other but not before Kitty had seen the tell-tale sign. It could mean one thing only, the scheming girl had promised herself to the desperate Mortimer and he, in return? In that give-away gesture the expensive jewel confirmed the threat; Kitty knew she had *not* been wrong.

'Aren't you going to invite me in? Kitty pushed past the girl, over the threshold into the spacious hall. Pilgrim House, its very name a welcome for travellers; beeswax polish and roses made it feel like home. A Westminster clock chimed four o'clock, time for afternoon tea. But today this was no homely refuge. Louise was no demure lady waiting for callers -if her dress was anything to go by. Neither was she a lady in white muslin, ready to wave a flag for His Majesty. A heap of oilskins piled beside the hall table empty of visiting cards awaited their wearer. Kitty pulled her hospital shawl about her shoulders, the spacious entrance felt threatening.

Louise eyed Kitty's second-hand clothes with hardly concealed distaste and hurriedly led her straight to the back kitchen. She glanced over her shoulder to see she was being followed and said. 'I am in haste- all the staff have gone already.'

Kitty said quickly, 'Of course, don't let me delay you. Excuse my appearance, as you can see I've borrowed these from the hospital poor box. If my belongings are still here I should go upstairs and change?'

Louise shook her head dismissively, 'They've been put down in the cellar, but are easily retrieved, if we hurry.' Then, 'Do you plan to stay with us? Where will you go now that Cousin John is no more? His woman Pleasance will be wondering what has happened to you.' A flood of questions, but before Kitty could answer, Louise posed another,

'Is the woman still looking after your daughter?' Did that question mean Kitty could cease doubting that little Katharine was safe? Not with Louise's talent for deceit.

Louise was fidgety, 'Are you sure you're alone?' she peered at Kitty, 'You almost look the radical in that outfit.' The about-to-be-dressed-in-oilskins lady was disparaging.

Kitty laughed, 'Don't worry, shabby garments will never turn me into a revolutionary,' coquettishly, she lifted her darned skirt, 'Look, underneath I still have my expensive red satin petticoat, though a bit the worse for wear since the accident.'

'So... red for radical!' Louise smirked, 'But I'll believe you, dear Kitty. Now our mutual friend is a different matter.'

'Who is..?'

'Olaf!'

'Olaf?' Kitty repeated the name in astonishment.

'Don't look so surprised, the Orkney Islands and their inhabitants feel more allegiance to Norway than they ever do to Great Britain. I warned already that you didn't know the real reason for him being in England!'

Thirty Four

The white beacon at Emmanuel Head gleamed in the evening sun. The rain had gone as on a whim and the August evening was calm. Olaf had been right about 'clearan up', but, yet again, she felt those stabs of chilling doubt about him after Louise's words.

Kitty took the north path away from the village and its inhabitants. The Castle mound was not where Louise had planned to go, nor Patterson. She walked quickly across the grass on the thin, sandy soil, inch-cropped by the island sheep. No hill bluff obscured the horizon, ahead; she could see the solid marker positioned to warn all ships off the island's northeast shore. Perhaps one day there would be a lighthouse? For now, it was just a giant bonfire that lit the evening sky.

Flames danced high. Bonfires welcomed. They had beaconed the length of the coast on the King's outward journey. She doubted that Holy Island had dutifully built one then, but now here was a glorious blaze acknowledging the King's triumphal return. Fires of greeting so why not here? Kitty felt a deep unease.

Who had lit it? Was it Patterson or *Olaf* or both? The question was nonsense and yet-the primeval red of fire was also the radical red… Orkney radical? Why had Olaf agreed to her wild, madcap plan to come to the treacherous island, when sense led directly to Castle Street? And Olaf was eminently sensible. Even his benefactor, Sir Walter, lauded his maturity as he noted regretfully the Orcadian's lack of emotion and human involvement. No passion except for his beloved lighthouses; but perhaps even they were just a screen to mask a rebel's devotion to his high northern roots? He'd openly acknowledged the old animosity between England and Scotland... what possible allegiance did the Orcadian owe to Hanoverian George?

Doubts bombarded like the squealing gulls above her head, Louise's sinister suggestion that Olaf was a radical was a stitch nagging her ribs. Fear caught in her throat. She stopped to catch her breath and spotted an advancing figure. It was not Olaf.

Old Janet, stick-straight, stumbled along the track on collision course. It seemed a lifetime since the islander had blocked Kitty's path on her first day on the Island, raising a scrawny finger to emphasize her words, 'Do not go to Emmanuel Head.' Her warning then had baffled Kitty. Would the strange old woman repeat the caution?

'Haste girl, to the Head before its too late,' the old crone drew alongside but did not stop. The words were as stinging as sea salt and Kitty groaned, already, the old woman foresaw the maritime disaster that was timed for sunset, the one to beat all other island wrecks.

'Olaf, Olaf.' Where *was* he? It had been his idea for her to go to Pilgrim House to find out anything that might reveal Louise's plans, and to wait for him there. He would find Patterson. And she'd gone without question, desperate to ensure that her daughter was not in the clutches of Louise and Patterson.

She had found an edgy Louise, her pale cheeks flushed. Could it really be that the King's yacht was destined to go no further? That the Royal George, like many vessels plying the dangerous coastline, would end its journey on the deadly island rocks? This end would be aided by a disaffected Patterson and the smitten girl. Louise had foreseen the lighting of a bonfire. But surely Olaf was not to be included in their schemes?

Here on the north coast, the island was deserted, the crowds behind her on the slopes of Lindisfarne Castle-fishermen, their wives, their children- the same voyeurs as before but now no blasphemous prayer- *Dear Lord send her to us*, that was treason beyond their thinking; their only need on this gala day was to glimpse the King and the State ship- the likes they had never seen before. Wrecking for them was *no* part of this epic day... but Patterson and Louise...?

She must find Olaf. Where was he? Where was Patterson? At least she knew that Louise was out of harm's way. Kitty had locked her deep in the Pilgrim House cellar. She'd turned the key on her, knowing that the girl's cries would go unheeded in the emptied house. There was only one place for servants and masters alike this evening, the grandstand view from Bebloe Crag where earlier castle builders had seen the value of the site.

She would continue on towards the fire-it was all she could do... but what, and who, would she find there...but for the enormous blaze, Emmanuel Head was deserted. The setting sun flashed in rebound from the marker at the island tip, blinding her in its streak of fire and then there she saw a black dot invading the colour. It was the unmistakeable figure of Olaf, dwarfed by the giant bonfire.

Louise had talked jokingly of the decoy to lure the King on to the island rocks! The tufted grass was like rock-strewn sea and she zigzagged in and out of the hazardous clumps, her feet slipping and slithering in her panic... for there were two figures now- highlighted by the flames- and they were fighting. Patterson sturdier, used to hauling ship-ropes and heavy cargoes, Olaf lighter but more agile. The two were locked in combat, inches from the flames and as Kitty reached them she saw a flash of steel; but billowing smoke blocked her view and made her choke. Burning kelp and rotten wood polluted the air as did the fisherman's furious oaths. Kitty screamed her fear as loud as the watching, wheeling whitemaas.

Two against one, then an almighty crack of skull on stone, an exclamation of rage and a figure crumpled in a slow descent like a boat upending. Patterson lay still.

'Kit!' The Orcadian wiped his sweating face; blood seeped into his right eye and his lips were bloated.

'Kitty, what the hell are you doing? I told you to stay with Louise...' he turned his back on her and began to beat at the fire, a scrap of rusting corrugated-iron gripped in his bare hands; the flames shot into the sky, vertical streaks of anger from a giant heap of beach-combed timber.

Was he trying to put the fire out or fanning the flames?

Kitty shouted, 'You're good at building fires, Olaf Magson, Arthur's Seat, now Emmanuel Head. A signal fit for a King... or the deadly weapon of a *radical*.'

'What... what...?'

'Aren't all Orcadians radicals?'

'Of course!'

She spluttered, 'A radical *and* a pyromaniac?'

'Me?' Olaf looked momentarily perplexed, then pointing at the stirring figure at his feet, 'We must get rid of him.'

'Get *rid* of him?'

Frantically Olaf looked about him and then he was down on the rubbish-strewn beach, returning with a thick coil of rope. In a few deft moves, the ship's captain was tied to the stile at the field edge. Loud groans told he was returning to the land of the living.

'We must douse the fire. Damn!' High shooting flames shouted defiantly a King's welcome.

'Look, there isn't time!' Kitty pointed at the three tall masts of the Royal Yacht with the Royal Ensign in the middle moving purposefully toward the island.

'The King is coming...!' Kitty gasped her dismay. The silence about them, showing starkly their isolation. Only Olaf and she stood between the yacht and disaster.

'We've *got* to warn them.'

She could hear only the sound of sea on rocks and the rebounding waves on the Sea Plunder that lay off shore, waiting for Patterson and his accomplice Louise. Drawn up at the water's edge was Patterson's small boat ready to transport them over to the larger vessel.

'Come on!' Kitty was already running, Olaf close on her heels.

The boat's oars lay in a shallow pool of water. Kitty's hands grasped the dripping wood as Olaf pushed the vessel out into the tide. Quickly Olaf fell into a rhythm but Kitty struggled. Her present weakened state making it hard for her to even hold on to the blades

'Kit, just watch me. We need to move as one, as one day it will surely be.' His words skimmed the water in a surge of promise.

Her sweating hands fumbled as she fixed her eyes, trustingly, on his back; backwards, forwards, backwards, forwards-his rhythm was hypnotic compulsion.

The yacht kept coming, the King seemingly determined that his triumphant jaunt would end only when he was finally returned to his London palace.

They were minnows menaced by a sea monster. Olaf stood up, waving his arms. He began to shout, 'ALTER COURSE-UNSEEN ROCKS!'

Kitty wobbled to her feet beside him and joined in the warning. Someone on board answered with a wave of their hand, and then another.

'It's useless.' Kitty yelled, 'They think we're the welcoming party.' A rounded figure appeared at the rail and a regal salute acknowledged their frantic display.

Olaf shouted, 'Steady the boat, I've got to try and get on board the yacht!' Already he was tearing at his jerkin and shirt. Swallowing her dismay, Kitty seized the oars, the boat lurched sideways then righted itself, another minute and Olaf would be in the heaving sea. Fear gripped her -and then she remembered her petticoat!

The next minute it was in her hand, the red satin streaking the sky like a fiery comet. 'DANGER- ALTER COURSE!' She waved the scarlet flag of warning in a wide arch, lifted it again in arms that ached and then Olaf had seized it.

'Good, lass, good lass!' His hand raised the fiery-coloured clothing again and again high above his head and then once more for a final, exultant sweep of the darkening sky for, slowly, the Royal George was altering course.

Thirty Five

Sunset flared the sea to red satin as they floated on the incoming tide, their discarded jerkin and petticoat drifting about the rocks where Kitty had dreaded the royal treasure would float.

Kitty breathed deeply, she wanted this moment to last forever. Olaf had tight hold of her hand she could smell and feel the buffeting water, its persistent murmur like a remembered melody. And then in lazy recall, a descant lifted above the bay; haunting, mystical, it brought welling tears to her eyes. Feet away, the escort seals swam, soft grey heads amongst rounded rock caps.

With a yelp of joy, Olaf shouted, 'Time to unite sea with land.'

They swam to the shore and their footsteps showed their path before the tide swept in to cover tracks. They stood shy now, just inches apart. Olaf smiled down at her and gently wiped her eyes; the sting of salt from his finger-tips made her blink. 'I am the sea,' he had said.

'Look, the selkies are following us…they're inquisitive.' A young seal had swum after them to the water's edge. 'Do they really take off their pelts and dance like humans?'

'You don't believe me?' Olaf shook his head in disappointment. 'I thought you knew me well enough by now.'

'Oh I do!'

'I hope so!' he stared down at her, 'You know Kit, I didn't expect you to take off your petticoat, but you did.' He laughed and his hands were on her waist and tracing her sodden skirt. The borrowed garment sank onto the sand in a deflated circle and Kitty stepped out of it, her long legs glistening in the last rays of the sun. Olaf murmured, 'Now, Kit you're free to dance with me as wildly as any seal.'

They danced, their feet barely touching the sand frantic steps that needed no music, at arm's length then closer and closer as their rhythm slowed until Olaf's arms were about her and they moved as one. He began to sing,

I am a man upon the land
I am a selkie in the sea
And when I'm far from every strand
My home it is in Skule Skerry

His lips were close, 'these words are as old as time, and they come from a man of the sea with thoughts now only of home.'

'It is very beautiful, but does a sailor ever come home?' She moved away from him, 'Isn't he like this sand, neither land nor sea but a bit of both.' Forcefully, she dug her toes into the ochre particles and they parted momentarily but as she moved her foot they slipped back into place.

Kitty bent and picked up a handful of the sand and deliberately sprinkled it into Olaf's palm, a gentle cascade that became a splayed heap. 'It's like an egg-timer measuring our time here. And it would seem to say it's nearly over.'

'*No*, why do you say that?' He stared down at her, troubled now by her strange mood. 'Egg-timers are like the tide, they repeat and repeat.' He seized her hand, and she laughed to lessen the power of his grip. His face showed his hurt.

'Besides I'm no sailor. My feet are firmly on the ground. Remember lighthouses always have rock solid foundations.'

'That's the difference between us, Olaf, my feet keep walking.'

'Then it is time for you to stop.'

Oh how she wanted him, wanted to lie with him here on the darkening beach.

'Kit-Kitty,' roughly, he pulled her to him and his passionate kiss took her breath away, but she stood limp in his arms. Then he turned away from her and strode up into the dunes.

The tide had retreated; her dress lay drying upon an isolated clump of Marram grass. Time to retrieve it! Her fingers felt like thumbs as she tried to do up the buttons, feeling the chill of the early morning. Dressed, she carried her boots until she was some distance away from the sleeping figure. She had stolen one last long look at the man she loved.

And it was dawn! No more looking back. She turned westward, away from the sun appearing above the horizon for the start of a beautiful day. The curlews called lazily over the flats, somewhere the seals would be singing.

Olaf! Her life's journey had led to him, to the man she knew she wanted above all other; she had found him at the sea edge only to lose him on the rocky shore.

'Olaf loves you, Olaf loves you,' the curlews cried their knowledge. Yes, she knew that too. But he loved the new Kit. Not the girl with bastard child. The early gulls swooped low above her head in a tirade of abuse.

'I know, I know, don't worry I'm going,' she cried her certainty, 'and you'll not follow me, you, like he, belong to the sea.'

'But *I* shall follow you, Kitty wherever you go, surely you know that now?'

Olaf was standing in front of her, his breath agitated.

She stared up at him, 'Please, Olaf, I have to go.' And as he seized her hands she said desperately, 'I return to another.'

He took a step back. 'Another?'

'Aye, someone waits for me at Barraburn. I have been too long gone. Please, Olaf, do not try to stop me.'

He said, 'You return to your child?'

'Child?' She stared at him, the breath taken from her...
'...so you know?' His pale blue eyes flickered and she smiled.
'Yes, I have a small child and it is to her I go.' A wave of relief flooded over her, she had sickened of secrets. 'Katharine is my own flesh and blood and now openly to be acknowledged.'

She added, 'I suppose Louise told you.'

'Yes, after the accident! She thought it would be reason enough to stop me searching for you.'

'But it wasn't.' Kitty's voice was a whisper.

'Kit, you should have stayed long enough to hear the last verse of the selkie song.'

He began to sing,

It shall come to pass on a summer's day
When the sun shines hot on every stone
That I shall take my little young child
And teach her to swim the foam.

He smiled down at her, 'Every child needs both mother and father. I cannot wait to meet Katharine, I know she will be as lovely as her mother.'

Kitty began to walk; the mainland hovered on the skyline; the tide was out, no need to wait for a boat. There was nothing to stop them. He was beside her, her hand in his,

'So, Olaf now you know my shore was rocky, as was yours...'

'Then together, we will build a lighthouse.'

Made in the USA
Charleston, SC
14 May 2014